INVISI ☁ W9-BEB-227

"The time has surely come, gentlemen, for us to dally no longer, but to concentrate our efforts on what must be the only viable line of reasoning open to us:

"I state, quite categorically, that the race of beings we have come to refer to as the *Lunarians* originated here on Earth, as did the rest of us. Forget all your fantasies of visitors from other worlds, interstellar travellers and the like. The Lunarians were simply products of a civilization which developed here on our own planet and then died out for reasons which we have yet to determine.

But to vanish without a trace? Without a single trace? Hunt couldn't accept that. There had to be another answer... and he was going to find it!

A COMPELLING SPECULATION THAT ALTERS THE REALITIES OF THE PAST AND THE POSSIBILITIES OF THE FUTURE . . .

Inherit
the
Stars

James P. Hogan

A Del Rey Book

BALLANTINE BOOKS • NEW YORK

A Del Rey Book
Published by Ballantine Books

Library of Congress Catalog Card Number: 76-56444

ISBN 0-345-30107-2

Manufactured in the United States of America

First Edition: May 1977
Eighth Printing: November 1982

Cover art by Darrell Sweet

To the memory of my Father

prologue

He became aware of consciousness returning.

Instinctively his mind recoiled, as if by some effort of will he could arrest the relentless flow of seconds that separated nonawareness from awareness and return again to the timeless oblivion in which the agony of total exhaustion was unknown and unknowable.

The hammer that had threatened to burst from his chest was now quiet. The rivers of sweat that had drained with his strength from every hollow of his body were now turned cold. His limbs had turned to lead. The gasping of his lungs had returned once more to a slow and even rhythm. It sounded loud in the close confines of his helmet.

He tried to remember how many had died. Their release was final; for him there was no release. How much longer could he go on? What was the point? Would there be anyone left alive at Gorda anyway?

"Gorda . . . ? Gorda . . . ?"

His mental defenses could shield him from reality no longer.

"Must get to Gorda!"

He opened his eyes. A billion unblinking stars stared back without interest. When he tried to move, his body refused to respond, as if trying to prolong to the utmost its last precious moments of rest. He took a deep breath and, clenching his teeth at the pain that instantly racked again through every fiber of his body, forced himself away from the rock and into a sitting position. A wave of nausea swept over him. His head sagged forward and struck the inside of his visor. The nausea passed.

He groaned aloud.

"Feeling better, then, soldier?" The voice came clearly through the speaker inside his helmet. "Sun's getting low. We gotta be moving."

He lifted his head and slowly scanned the nightmare wilderness of scorched rock and ash-gray dust that confronted him.

"Whe—" The sound choked in his throat. He swallowed, licked his lips, and tried again. "Where are you?"

"To your right, up on the rise just past that small cliff that juts out—the one with the big boulders underneath."

He turned his head and after some seconds detected a bright blue patch against the ink-black sky. It seemed blurred and far away. He blinked and strained his eyes again, forcing his brain to coordinate with his vision. The blue patch resolved itself into the figure of the tireless Koriel, clad in a heavy-duty combat suit.

"I see you." After a pause: "Anything?"

"It's fairly flat on the other side of the rise—should be easier going for a while. Gets rockier farther on. Come have a look."

He inched his arms upward to find purchase on the rock behind, then braced them to thrust his weight forward over his legs. His knees trembled. His face contorted as he fought to concentrate his remaining strength into his protesting thighs. Already his heart was pumping again, his lungs heaving. The effort evaporated and he fell back against the rock. His labored breathing rasped over Koriel's radio.

"Finished . . . Can't move . . ."

The blue figure on the skyline turned.

"Aw, what kinda talk's that? This is the last stretch. We're there, buddy—we're there."

"No—no good . . . Had it . . ."

Koriel waited a few seconds.

"I'm coming back down."

"No—you go on. Someone's got to make it."

No response.

"Koriel . . . ?"

He looked back at where the figure had stood, but already it had disappeared below the intervening rocks and was out of the line of transmission. A minute or two later the figure emerged from behind the nearby boulders, covering the ground in long, effortless bounds. The bounds broke into a walk as Koriel approached the hunched form clad in red.

"C'mon, soldier, on your feet now. There's people back there depending on us."

He felt himself gripped below his arm and raised irresistibly, as if some of Koriel's limitless reserves of strength were pouring into him. For a while his head swam and he leaned with the top of his visor resting on the giant's shoulder insignia.

"Okay," he managed at last. "Let's go."

Hour after hour the thin snake of footprints, two pinpoints of color at its head, wound its way westward across the wilderness amid steadily lengthening shadows. He marched as if in a trance, beyond feeling pain, beyond feeling exhaustion—beyond feeling anything. The skyline never seemed to change; soon he could no longer look at it. Instead, he began picking out the next prominent boulder or crag, and counting off the paces until they reached it. "Two hundred and thirteen less to go." And then he repeated it over again . . . and again . . . and again. The rocks marched by in slow, endless, indifferent procession. Every step became a separate triumph of will—a deliberate, conscious effort to drive one foot yet one more pace beyond the last. When he faltered, Koriel was there to catch his arm; when he fell, Koriel was always there to haul him up. Koriel never tired.

At last they stopped. They were standing in a gorge perhaps a quarter mile wide, below one of the lines of low, broken cliffs that flanked it on either side. He collapsed on the nearest boulder. Koriel stood a few paces ahead surveying the landscape. The line of crags immediately above them was interrupted by a notch, which marked the point where a steep and narrow cleft tumbled down to break into the wall of the main gorge.

From the bottom of the cleft, a mound of accumulated rubble and rock debris led down about fifty feet to blend with the floor of the gorge not far from where they stood. Koriel stretched out an arm to point up beyond the cleft.

"Gorda will be roughly that way," he said without turning. "Our best way would be up and onto that ridge. If we stay on the flat and go around the long way, it'll be too far. What d'you say?"

The other stared up in mute despair. The rockfall, funneling up toward the mouth of the cleft, looked like a mountain. In the distance beyond towered the ridge, jagged and white in the glare of the sun. It was impossible.

Koriel allowed his doubts no time to take root. Somehow—slipping, sliding, stumbling, and falling—they reached the entrance to the cleft. Beyond it, the walls narrowed and curved around to the left, cutting off the view of the gorge below from where they had come. They climbed higher. Around them, sheets of raw reflected sunlight and bottomless pits of shadow met in knife-edges across rocks shattered at a thousand crazy angles. His brain ceased to extract the concepts of shape and form from the insane geometry of white and black that kaleidoscoped across his retina. The patterns grew and shrank and merged and whirled in a frenzy of visual cacophony.

His face crashed against his visor as his helmet thudded into the dust. Koriel hoisted him to his feet.

"You can do it. We'll see Gorda from the ridge. It'll be all downhill from there. . . ."

But the figure in red sank slowly to its knees and folded over. The head inside the helmet shook weakly from side to side. As Koriel watched, the conscious part of his mind at last accepted the inescapable logic that the parts beneath consciousness already knew. He took a deep breath and looked about him.

Not far below, they had passed a hole, about five feet across, cut into the base of one of the rock walls. It looked like the remnant of some forgotten excavation—

maybe a preliminary digging left by a mining survey. The giant stooped, and grasping the harness that secured the backpack to the now insensible figure at his feet, dragged the body back down the slope to the hole. It was about ten feet deep inside. Working quickly, Koriel arranged a lamp to reflect a low light off the walls and roof. Then he removed the rations from his companion's pack, laid the figure back against the rear wall as comfortably as he could, and placed the food containers within easy reach. Just as he was finishing, the eyes behind the visor flickered open.

"You'll be fine here for a while." The usual gruffness was gone from Koriel's voice. "I'll have the rescue boys back from Gorda before you know it."

The figure in red raised a feeble arm. Just a whisper came through.

"You—you tried. . . . Nobody could have . . ."

Koriel clasped the gauntlet with both hands.

"Mustn't give up. That's no good. You just have to hang on a while." Inside his helmet the granite cheeks were wet. He backed to the entrance and made a final salute. "So long, soldier." And then he was gone.

Outside he built a small cairn of stones to mark the position of the hole. He would mark the trail to Gorda with such cairns. At last he straightened up and turned defiantly to face the desolation surrounding him. The rocks seemed to scream down in soundless laughing mockery. The stars above remained unmoved. Koriel glowered up at the cleft, rising up toward the tiers of crags and terraces that guarded the ridge, still soaring in the distance. His lips curled back to show his teeth.

"So—it's just you and me now, is it?" he snarled at the Universe. "Okay, you bastard—let's see you take this round!"

With his legs driving like slow pistons, he attacked the ever-steepening slope.

chapter one

Accompanied by a mild but powerful whine, a gigantic silver torpedo rose slowly upward to hang two thousand feet above the sugar-cube huddle of central London. Over three hundred yards long, it spread at the tail into a slim delta topped by two sharply swept fins. For a while the ship hovered, as if savoring the air of its newfound freedom, its nose swinging smoothly around to seek the north. At last, with the sound growing, imperceptibly at first but with steadily increasing speed, it began to slide forward and upward. At ten thousand feet its engines erupted into full power, hurling the sub-orbital skyliner eagerly toward the fringes of space.

Sitting in row thirty-one of C deck was Dr. Victor Hunt, head of Theoretical Studies at the Metadyne Nucleonic Instrument Company of Reading, Berkshire—itself a subsidiary of the mammoth Intercontinental Data and Control Corporation, headquartered at Portland, Oregon, USA. He absently surveyed the diminishing view of Hendon that crawled across the cabin wall-display screen and tried again to fit some kind of explanation to the events of the last few days.

His experiments with matter–antimatter particle extinctions had been progressing well. Forsyth-Scott had followed Hunt's reports with evident interest and therefore knew that the tests were progressing well. That made it all the more strange for him to call Hunt to his office one morning to ask him simply to drop everything and get over to IDCC Portland as quickly as could be arranged. From the managing director's tone and manner it had been obvious that the request was couched as such mainly for reasons of politeness; in reality this was one of the few occasions on which Hunt had no say in the matter.

To Hunt's questions, Forsyth-Scott had stated quite frankly that he didn't know what it was that made Hunt's immediate presence at IDCC so imperative. The previous evening he had received a videocall from Felix Borlan, the president of IDCC, who had told him that as a matter of priority he required the only working prototype of the scope prepared for immediate shipment to the USA and an installation team ready to go with it. Also, he had insisted that Hunt personally come over for an indefinite period to take charge of some project involving the scope, which could not wait. For Hunt's benefit, Forsyth-Scott had replayed Borlan's call on his desk display and allowed him to verify for himself that Forsyth-Scott in turn was acting under a thinly disguised directive. Even stranger, Borlan too had seemed unable to say precisely what it was that the instrument and its inventor were needed for.

The Trimagniscope, developed as a consequence of a two-year investigation by Hunt into certain aspects of neutrino physics, promised to be perhaps the most successful venture ever undertaken by the company. Hunt had established that a neutrino beam that passed through a solid object underwent certain interactions in the close vicinity of atomic nuclei, which produced measurable changes in the transmitted output. By raster scanning an object with a trio of synchronized, intersecting beams, he had devised a method of extracting enough information to generate a 3-D color hologram, visually indistinguishable from the original solid. Moreover, since the beams scanned right through, it was almost as easy to conjure up views of the inside as of the out. These capabilities, combined with that of high-power magnification that was also inherent in the method, yielded possibilities not even remotely approached by anything else on the market. From quantitative cell metabolism and bionics, through neurosurgery, metallurgy, crystallography, and molecular electronics, to engineering inspection and quality control, the applications were endless. Inquiries were pouring in and shares were soaring. Removing the prototype and its originator to the USA—totally disrupting carefully planned production and marketing schedules—bordered on the catastrophic. Borlan knew this as well as anybody. The more Hunt turned these things over in his mind, the less plausible the various possible explanations that had at first occurred to him seemed, and the more convinced he became that whatever the answer turned out to be, it would be found to lie far beyond even Felix Borlan and IDCC.

His thoughts were interrupted by a voice issuing from somewhere in the general direction of the cabin roof.

"Good afternoon, ladies and gentlemen. This is Captain Mason speaking. I would like to welcome you aboard this Boeing 1017 on behalf of British Airways. We are now in level flight at our cruising altitude of fifty-two miles, speed 3,160 knots. Our course is thirty-five degrees west of true north, and the coast is now below with Liverpool five miles to starboard. Passengers are free to leave their seats. The bars are open and drinks and snacks are being served. We are due to arrive in San Francisco at ten thirty-eight hours local time; that's one hour and fifty mintues from now. I would like to remind you that it is necessary to be seated when we begin our descent in one hour and thirty-five minutes time. A warning will sound ten minutes before descent commences and again at five minutes. We trust you will enjoy your journey. Thank you."

The captain signed himself off with a click, which was drowned out as the regulars made their customary scramble for the vi-phone booths.

In the seat next to Hunt, Rob Gray, Metadyne's chief of Experimental Engineering, sat with an open briefcase resting on his knees. He studied the information being displayed on the screen built into its lid.

"A regular flight to Portland takes off fifteen minutes after we get in," he announced. "That's a bit tight. Next one's not for over four hours. What d'you reckon?" He punctuated the question with a sideways look and raised eyebrows.

Hunt pulled a face. "I'm not arsing about in Frisco for four hours. Book us an Avis jet—we'll fly ourselves up."

"That's what I thought."

Gray played the mini keyboard below the screen to summon an index, consulted it briefly, then touched another key to display a directory. Selecting a number from one of the columns, he mouthed it silently to himself as he tapped it in. A copy of the number appeared near the bottom of the screen with a request for him to confirm. He pressed the Y button. The screen went blank for a few seconds and then exploded into a whirlpool of color, which stabilized almost at once into the features of a platinum-blonde, who radiated the kind of smile normally reserved for toothpaste commercials.

"Good morning. Avis San Francisco, City Terminal. This is Sue Parker. Can I help you?"

Gray addressed the grille, located next to the tiny camera lens just above the screen.

"Hi, Sue. Name's Gray—R. J. Gray, airbound for SF, due to arrive about two hours from now. Could I reserve an aircar, please?"

"Sure thing. Range?"

"Oh—about five hundred . . ." He glanced at Hunt.

"Better make it seven," Hunt advised.

"Make that seven hundred miles minimum."

"That'll be no problem, Mr. Gray. We have Skyrovers, Mercury Threes, Honeybees, or Yellow Birds. Any preference?"

"No—any'll do."

"I'll make it a Mercury, then. Any idea how long?"

"No—er—indefinite."

"Okay. Full computer nav and flight control? Automatic VTOL?"

"Preferably and, ah, yes."

"You have a full manual license?" The blonde operated unseen keys as she spoke.

"Yes."

"Could I have personal data and account-checking data, please?"

Gray had extracted the card from his wallet while the exchange was taking place. He inserted it into a slot set to one side of the screen, and touched a key.

The blonde consulted other invisible oracles. "Okay," she pronounced. "Any other pilots?"

"One. A Dr. V. Hunt."

"His personal data?"

Gray took Hunt's already proffered card and substituted it for his own. The ritual was repeated. The face then vanished to be replaced by a screen of formatted text with entries completed in the boxes provided.

"Would you verify and authorize, please?" said the disembodied voice from the grille. "Charges are shown on the right."

Gray cast his eye rapidly down the screen, grunted, and keyed in a memorized sequence of digits that was not echoed on the display. The word *POSITIVE* appeared in the box marked "Authorization." Then the clerk reappeared, still smiling.

"When would you want to collect, Mr. Gray?" she asked.

Gray turned toward Hunt.

"Do we want lunch at the airport first?"

Hunt grimaced. "Not after that party last night. Couldn't face anything." His face took on an expression of acute distaste as he moistened the inside of the equine rectum he had once called a mouth. "Let's eat tonight somewhere."

"Make it round about eleven thirty hours," Gray advised.

"It'll be ready."

"Thanks, Sue."

"Thank you. Good-bye."

"Bye now."

Gray flipped a switch, unplugged the briefcase from the socket built into the armrest of his seat, and coiled the connecting cord back into the space provided in the lid. He closed the case and stowed it behind his feet.

"Done," he announced.

The scope was the latest in a long line of technological triumphs in the Metadyne product range to be conceived and nurtured to maturity by the Hunt-Gray partnership. Hunt was the ideas man, leading something of a free-lance existence within the organization, left to pursue whatever line of study or experiment his personal whims or the demands of his researches dictated. His title was somewhat misleading; in fact he *was* Theoretical Studies. The position was one which he had contrived, quite deliberately, to fall into no obvious place in the managerial hierarchy of Metadyne. He acknowledged no superior, apart from the managing director, Sir Francis Forsyth-Scott, and boasted no subordinates. On the company's organization charts, the box captioned "Theoretical Studies" stood alone and disconnected near the inverted tree head *R & D*, as if added as an afterthought. Inside it there appeared the single entry *Dr. Victor Hunt*. This was the way he liked it—a symbiotic relationship in which Metadyne provided him with the equipment, facilities, services, and funds he needed for his work, while he provided Metadyne with first, the prestige of retaining on its payroll a world-acknowledged authority on nuclear infrastructure theory, and second—but by no means least—a steady supply of fallout.

Gray was the engineer. He was the sieve that the fallout fell on. He had a genius for spotting the gems of raw ideas that had application potential and transforming them into developed, tested, marketable products and product enhancements. Like Hunt, he had survived the mine field of the age of unreason and emerged safe and single into his midthirties. With Hunt, he shared a passion for work, a healthy partiality for most of the deadly sins to counterbalance it, and his address book. All things considered, they were a good team.

Gray bit his lower lip and rubbed his left earlobe. He always bit his lower lip and rubbed his left earlobe when he was about to talk shop.

"Figured it out yet?" he asked.

"This Borlan business?"

"Uh-huh."

Hunt shook his head before lighting a cigarette. "Beats me."

"I was thinking . . . Suppose Felix has dug up some hot sales prospect for scopes—maybe one of his big Yank customers. He could be setting up some super demo or something."

Hunt shook his head again. "No. Felix wouldn't go and screw up Metadyne's schedules for anything like that. Anyhow, it wouldn't make sense—the obvious thing to do would be to fly the people to where the scope is, not the other way round."

"Mmmm . . . I suppose the same thing applies to the other thought that occurred to me—some kind of crash teach-in for IDCC people."

"Right—same thing goes."

"Mmmm . . ." When Gray spoke again, they had covered another six miles. "How about a takeover? The whole scope thing is big—Felix wants it handled stateside."

Hunt reflected on the proposition. "Not for my money. He's got too much respect for Francis, to pull a stunt like that. He knows Francis can handle it okay. Besides, that's not his way of doing things—too underhanded." Hunt paused to exhale a cloud of smoke. "Anyhow, I think there's a lot more to it than meets the eye. From what I saw, even Felix didn't seem too sure what it's all about."

"Mmmm . . ." Gray thought for a while longer before abandoning further excursions into the realms of deductive logic. He contemplated the growing tide of humanity flowing in the general direction of C-deck bar. "My guts are a bit churned up, too," he confessed. "Feels like a crate of Guinness on top of a vindaloo curry. Come on —let's go get a coffee."

In the star-strewn black velvet one thousand miles farther up, the *Sirius Fourteen* communications-link satellite followed, with cold and omniscient electronic eyes, the progress of the skyliner streaking across the mottled sphere below. Among the ceaseless stream of binary data that flowed through its antennae, it identified a call from the Boeing's Gamma Nine master computer, requesting details of the latest weather forecast for northern California. *Sirius Fourteen* flashed the message to *Sirius Twelve*, hanging high over the Canadian Rockies, and *Twelve* in turn beamed it down to the tracking station at Edmonton. From here the message was relayed by optical cable to Vancouver Control and from there by microwave repeaters to the Weather Bureau station at Seattle. A few thousandths of a second later, the answers poured back up the chain in the opposite direction. Gamma Nine digested the information, made one or two minor alterations to its course and flight plan, and sent a record of the dialogue down to Ground Control, Prestwick.

chapter two

It had rained for over two days.

The Engineering Materials Research Department of the Ministry of Space Sciences huddled wetly in a fold of the Ural Mountains, an occasional ray of sunlight glinting from a laboratory window or from one of the aluminum domes of the reactor building.

Seated in her office in the analysis section, Valereya Petrokhov turned to the pile of reports left on her desk for routine approval. The first two dealt with run-of-the-mill high-temperature corrosion tests. She flicked casually through the pages, glanced at the appended graphs and tables, scrawled her initials on the line provided, and tossed them across into the tray marked

"Out." Automatically she began scanning down the first page of number three. Suddenly she stopped, a puzzled frown forming on her face. Leaning forward in her chair, she began again, this time reading carefully and studying every sentence. She finally went back to the beginning once more and worked methodically through the whole document, stopping in places to verify the calculations by means of the keyboard display standing on one side of the desk.

"This is unheard of!" she exclaimed.

For a long time she remained motionless, her eyes absorbed by the raindrops slipping down the window but her mind so focused elsewhere that the sight failed to register. At last she shook herself into movement and, turning again to the keyboard, rapidly tapped in a code. The strings of tensor equations vanished, to be replaced by a profile view of her assistant, hunched over a console in the control room downstairs. The profile transformed itself into a full face as he turned.

"Ready to run in about twenty minutes," he said, anticipating the question. "The plasma's stabilizing now."

"No—this has nothing to do with that," she replied, speaking a little more quickly than usual. "It's about your report 2906. I've just been through my copy."

"Oh . . . yes?" His change in expression betrayed mild apprehension.

"So—a niobium-zirconium alloy," she went on, stating the fact rather than asking a question, "with an unprecedented resistance to high-temperature oxidation and a melting point that, quite frankly, I won't believe until I've done the tests myself."

"Makes our plasma-cans look like butter," Josef agreed.

"Yet despite the presence of niobium, it exhibits a lower neutron-absorption cross section than pure zirconium?"

"Macroscopic, yes—under a millibarn per square centimeter."

"Interesting . . ." she mused, then resumed more briskly: "On top of that we have alpha-phase zirconium with silicon, carbon, and nitrogen impurities, yet still with a superb corrosion resistance."

· "Hot carbon dioxide, fluorides, organic acids, hypochlorites—we've been through the list. Generally an initial reaction sets in, but it's rapidly arrested by the formation of inert barrier layers. You could probably break it down in stages by devising a cycle of reagents in just the right sequence, but that would take a complete processing plant specially designed for the job!"

"And the microstructure," Valereya said, gesturing toward the papers on her desk. "You've used the description *fibrous*."

"Yes. That's about as near as you can get. The main alloy seems to be formed around a—well, a sort of microcrystalline lattice. It's mainly silicon and carbon, but with local concentrations of some titanium-magnesium compound that we haven't been able to quantify yet. I've never come across anything like it. Any ideas?"

The woman's face held a faraway look for some seconds.

"I honestly don't know what to think at the moment," she confessed. "But I feel this information should be passed higher without delay; it might be more important than it looks. But first I must be sure of my facts. Nikolai can take over down there for a while. Come up to my office and let's go through the whole thing in detail."

chapter three

The Portland headquarters of the Intercontinental Data and Control Corporation lay some forty miles east of the city, guarding the pass between Mount Adams to the north and Mount Hood to the south. It was here that at some time in the remote past a small inland sea had penetrated the Cascade Mountains and carved itself a channel to the Pacific, to become in time the mighty Columbia River.

Fifteen years previously it had been the site of the government-owned Bonneville Nucleonic Weapons Research Laboratory. Here, American scientists, working in collaboration with the United States of Europe Federal Research Institute at Geneva, had developed the theory of meson dynamics that led to the nucleonic bomb. The theory predicted a "clean" reaction with a yield orders of magnitude greater than that produced by thermonuclear fusion. The holes they had blown in the Sahara had proved it.

During that period of history, the ideological and racial tensions inherited from the twentieth century were being swept away by the tide of universal affluence and falling birth rates that came with the spread of high-technology living. Traditional rocks of strife and suspicion were being eroded as races, nations, sects, and creeds became inextricably mingled into one huge, homogeneous global society. As the territorial irrationalities of long-dead politicians resolved themselves and the adolescent nation-states matured, the defense budgets of the superpowers were progessively reduced year by year. The advent of the nucleonic bomb served only

16

to accelerate what would have happened anyway. By universal assent, world demilitarization became fact.

One sphere of activity that benefited enormously from the surplus funds and resources that became available after demilitarization was the rapidly expanding United Nations Solar System Exploration Program. Already the list of responsibilities held by this organization was long; it included the operation of all artificial satellites in terrestrial, Lunar, Martian, Venusian, and Solar orbits; the building and operation of all manned bases on Luna and Mars, plus the orbiting laboratories over Venus; the launching of deep-space robot probes and the planning and control of manned missions to the outer planets. UNSSEP was thus expanding at just the right rate and the right time to absorb the supply of technological talent being released as the world's major armaments programs were run down. Also, as nationalism declined and most of the regular armed forces were demobilized, the restless youth of the new generation found outlets for their adventure-lust in the uniformed branches of the UN Space Arm. It was an age that buzzed with excitement and anticipation as the new pioneering frontier began planet-hopping out across the Solar System.

And so NWRL Bonneville had been left with no purpose to serve. This situation did not go unnoticed by the directors of IDCC. Seeing that most of the equipment and permanent installations owned by NWRL could be used in much of the corporation's own research projects, they propositioned the government with an offer to buy the place outright. The offer was accepted and the deal went through. Over the years IDCC had further expanded the site, improved its aesthetics, and eventually established it as their nucleonics research center and world headquarters.

The mathematical theory that had grown out of meson dynamics involved the existence of three hitherto unknown transuranic elements. Although these were purely hypothetical, they were christened hyperium, bonnevillium, and genevium. Theory also predicted that, due to a "glitch" in the transuranic mass-*versus*-binding-energy curve, these elements, once formed, would be stable. They were unlikely to be found occurring naturally, however—not on Earth, anyway. According to the mathematics, only two known situations could give the right conditions for their formation: the core of the detonation of a nucleonic bomb or the collapse of a supernova to a neutron star.

Sure enough, analysis of the dust clouds after the Sahara tests yielded minute traces of hyperium and bonnevillium; genevium was not detected. Nevertheless, the first prediction of the theory was accepted as amply supported. Whether, one day, future generations of scientists would ever verify the second prediction, was another matter entirely.

Hunt and Gray touched down on the rooftop landing pad of the IDCC administration building shortly after fifteen hundred hours. By fifteen thirty they were sitting in leather armchairs facing the desk in Borlan's luxurious office on the tenth floor, while he poured three large measures of scotch at the teak bar built into the left wall. He walked back to the center, passed a glass to each of the Englishmen, went back around the desk, and sat down.

"Cheers, then, guys," he offered. They returned the gesture. "Well," he began, "it's good to see you two again. Trip okay? How'd you make it up so soon—rent a jet?" He opened his cigar box as he spoke and pushed it across the desk toward them. "Smoke?"

"Yes, good trip. Thanks, Felix," Hunt replied. "Avis." He inclined his head toward the window behind Borlan, which presented a panoramic view of pine-covered hills tumbling down to the distant Columbia. "Some scenery."

"Like it?"

"Makes Berkshire look a bit like Siberia."

Borlan looked at Gray. "How are you keeping, Rob?"

The corners of Gray's mouth twitched downwards. "Gutrot."

"Party last night at some bird's," Hunt explained. "Too little blood in his alcohol stream."

"Good time, huh?" Borlan grinned. "Take Francis along?"

"You've got to be joking!"

"Jollificating with the peasantry?" Gray mimicked in the impeccable tones of the English aristocracy. "Good God! Whatever next!"

They laughed. Hunt settled himself more comfortably amid a haze of blue smoke. "How about yourself, Felix?" he asked. "Life still being kind to you?"

Borlan spread his arms wide. "Life's great."

"Angie still as beautiful as the last time I saw her? Kids okay?"

"They're all fine. Tommy's at college now—majoring in physics and astronautical engineering. Johnny goes hiking most weekends with his club, and Susie's added a pair of gerbils and a bear cub to the family zoo."

"So you're still as happy as ever. The responsibilities of power aren't wearing you down yet."

Borlan shrugged and showed a row of pearly teeth. "Do I look like an ulcerated nut midway between heart attacks?"

Hunt regarded the blue-eyed, deep-tanned figure with close-cropped fair hair as Borlan sprawled relaxedly on the other side of the broad mahogany desk. He looked at least ten years younger than the president of any intercontinental corporation had a right to.

For a while the small talk revolved around internal affairs at Metadyne. At last a natural pause presented itself. Hunt sat forward, his elbows resting on his knees, and contemplated the last drop of amber liquid in his glass as he swirled it around first from right to left and then back again. Finally he looked up.

"About the scope, Felix. What's going on, then?"

Borlan had been expecting the question. He straightened slowly in his chair and appeared to think for a moment. At last he said:

"Did you see the call I made to Francis?"

"Yep."

"Then . . ." Borlan didn't seem sure of how to put it. ". . . I don't know an awful lot more than you do." He placed his hands palms-down on the desk in an attitude of candor, but his sigh was that of one not really expecting to be believed. He was right.

"Come on, Felix. Give." Hunt's expression said the rest.

"You must know," Gray insisted. "You fixed it all up."

"Straight." Borlan looked from one to the other. "Look, taking things worldwide, who would you say our biggest customer is? It's no secret—UN Space Arm. We do everything for them from Lunar data links to—to laser terminal clusters and robot probes. Do you know how much revenue I've got forecast from UNSA next fiscal? Two hundred million bucks . . . two hundred million!"

"So?"

"So . . . well—when a customer like that says he needs help, he gets help. I'll tell you what happened. It was like this: UNSA is a big potential user of scopes, so we fed them all the information we've got on what the scope can do and how development is progressing in Francis's neck of the woods. One day—the day before I called Francis—this guy comes to see me all the way from Houston, where one of the big UNSA outfits has its HQ. He's an old buddy of mine—their top man, no less. He wants to know can the scope do this and can it do that, and I tell him sure it can. Then he gives me some examples of the things he's got in mind and he asks if we've got a working model yet. I tell him not yet, but that you've got a working prototype in England; we can arrange for him to go see it if he wants. But that's not what he wants. He wants the prototype down there in Houston, and he wants people who can operate it. He'll pay, he says—we can name our own figure—but he wants that instrument—something to do with a top-priority project down there that's got the whole of

UNSA in a flap. When I ask him what it is, he clams up and says it's 'security restricted' for the moment."

"Sounds a funny business," Hunt commented with a frown. "It'll cause some bloody awful problems back at Metadyne."

"I told him all that." Borlan turned his palms upward in a gesture of helplessness. "I told him the score regarding the production schedules and availability forecasts, but he said this thing was big and he wouldn't go causing this kind of trouble if he didn't have a good reason. He wouldn't, either," Borlan added with obvious sincerity. "I've known him for years. He said UNSA would pay compensation for whatever we figure the delays will cost us." Borlan resumed his helpless attitude. "So what was I supposed to do? Was I supposed to tell an old buddy who happens to be my best customer to go take a jump?"

Hunt rubbed his chin, threw back his last drop of scotch, and took a long, pensive draw on his cigar.

"And that's it?" he asked at last.

"That's it. Now you know as much as I do—except that since you left England we've received instructions from UNSA to start shipping the prototype to a place near Houston—a biological institute. The bits should start arriving day after tomorrow; the installation crew is already on its way over to begin work preparing the site."

"Houston . . . Does that mean we're going there?" Gray asked.

"That's right, Rob." Borlan paused and scratched the side of his nose. His face screwed itself into a crooked frown. "I, ah—I was wondering . . . The installation crew will need a bit of time, so you two won't be able to do very much there for a while. Maybe you could spend a few days here first, huh? Like, ah . . . meet some of our technical people and clue them in a little on how the scope works—sorta like a teach-in. What d'you say—huh?"

Hunt laughed silently inside. Borlan had been complaining to Forsyth-Scott for months that while the largest potential markets for the scope lay in the USA, practically all of the know-how was confined to Metadyne; the American side of the organization needed more in the way of backup and information than it had been getting.

"You never miss a trick, Felix," he conceded. "Okay, you bum, I'll buy it."

Borlan's face split into a wide grin.

"This UNSA character you were talking about," Gray said, switching the subject back again. "What were the examples?"

"Examples?"

"You said he gave some examples of the kind of thing he was interested in knowing if the scope could do."

"Oh, yeah. Well, lemme see, now . . . He seemed interested in looking at the insides of bodies—bones, tissues, arteries—stuff like that. Maybe he wanted to do an autopsy or something. He also wanted to know if you could get images of what's on the pages of a book, but without the book being opened."

This was too much. Hunt looked from Borlan to Gray and back again, mystified.

"You don't need anything like a scope to perform an autopsy," he said, his voice strained with disbelief.

"Why can't he open a book if he wants to know what's inside?" Gray demanded in a similar tone.

Borlan showed his empty palms. "Yeah. I know. Search me—sounds screwy!"

"And UNSA is paying thousands for this?"

"Hundreds of thousands."

Hunt covered his brow and shook his head in exasperation. "Pour me another scotch, Felix," he sighed.

chapter four

A week later the Mercury Three stood ready for takeoff on the rooftop of IDCC Headquarters. In reply to the queries that appeared on the pilot's console display screen, Hunt specified the Ocean Hotel in the center of Houston as their destination. The DEC minicomputer in the nose made contact with its IBM big brother that lived underground somewhere beneath the Portland Area Traffic Control Center and, after a brief consultation, announced a flight plan that would take them via Salt Lake City, Santa Fe, and Fort Worth. Hunt keyed in his approval, and within minutes the aircar was humming southeast and climbing to take on the challenge of the Blue Mountains looming ahead.

Hunt spent the first part of the journey accessing his office files held on the computers back at Metadyne, to tidy up some of the unfinished business he had left behind. As the waters of the Great Salt Lake came glistening into view, he had just completed the calculations that went with his last experimental report and was adding his conclusions. An hour later, twenty thousand feet up over the Colorado River, he was hooked into MIT and reviewing some of their current publications. After refueling at Santa Fe they spent some time cruising around the city on manual control before finding somewhere suitable for lunch. Later on in the day, airborne over New Mexico, they took an incoming call from IDCC and spent the next two hours in conference with some of Borlan's engineers discussing technicalities of the scope. By the time Fort Worth was behind and the sun well to the west, Hunt was relaxing, watching a murder movie, while Gray slept soundly in the seat beside him.

Hunt looked on with detached interest as the villain was unmasked, the hero claimed the admiring heroine he had just saved from a fate worse than death, and the rolling captions delivered today's moral message for mankind. Stiffling a yawn, he flipped the mode switch to MONITOR/CONTROL to blank out the screen and kill the theme music in midbar. He stretched, stubbed out his cigarette, and hauled himself upright in his seat to see how the rest of the universe was getting along.

Far to their right was the Brazos River, snaking south toward the Gulf, embroidered in gold thread on the light blue-gray of the distant haze. Ahead, he could already see the rainbow towers of Houston, standing at attention on the skyline in a tight defensive platoon. Houses were becoming noticeably more numerous in the foreground below. At intervals between them, unidentifiable sprawling constructions began to make their appearance—random collections of buildings, domes, girder lattices, and storage tanks, tied loosely together by tangles of roadways and pipelines. Farther away to the left, a line of perhaps half a dozen slim spires of silver reared up from a shantytown of steel and concrete. He identified them as gigantic Vega satellite ferries standing on their launchpads. They seemed fitting sentinels to guard the approaches to what had become the Mecca of the Space Age.

As Victor Hunt gazed down upon this ultimate expression of man's eternal outward urge, spreading away in every direction below, a vague restlessness stirred somewhere deep inside him.

Hunt had been born in New Cross, the shabby end of East London, south of the river. His father had spent most of his life on strike or in the pub on the corner of the street debating grievances worth going on strike for. When he ran out of money and grievances, he worked on the docks at Deptford. Victor's mother worked in a bottle factory all day to make the money she lost playing bingo all evening. He spent his time playing football and falling in the Surrey Canal. There was a week when he stayed with an uncle in Worcester, a man who went to work dressed in a suit every day at a place that manufactured computers. And his uncle showed Victor how to wire up a binary adder.

Not long afterward, everyone was yelling at everyone more often than usual, so Victor went to live with his aunt and uncle in Worcester. There he discovered a whole new, undreamed-of world where anything one wanted could be made to happen and magic things really came true—written in strange symbols and mysterious diagrams through the pages of the books on his uncle's shelves.

At sixteen, Victor won a scholarship to Cambridge to study mathematics, physics, and physical electronics. He moved into lodgings there with a fellow student named Mike who sailed boats, climbed mountains, and whose father was a marketing director. When his uncle moved to Africa, Victor was adopted as a second son by Mike's family and spent his holidays at their home in Surrey or climbing with Mike and his friends, first in the hills of the Lake District, North Wales, and Scotland, and later in the Alps. They even tried the Eiger once, but were forced back by bad weather.

After being awarded his doctorate, he remained at the university for some years to further his researches in mathematical nucleonics, his papers on which were by that time attracting widespread attention. Eventually, however, he was forced to come to terms with the fact that a growing predilection for some of the more exciting and attractive ingredients of life could not be reconciled with an income dependent on research grants. For a while he went to work on thermonuclear fusion control for the government, but rebelled at a life made impossible by the meddlings of uninformed bureaucracy. He tried three jobs in private industry but found himself unable to muster more than a cynical indisposition toward playing the game of pretending that annual budgets, gross margins on sales, earnings per share, or discounted cash flows really meant anything that mattered. And so, when he was just turning thirty, the loner he had always been finally asserted itself; he found himself gifted with rare and acknowledged talents, lettered with degrees, credited with achievements, bestowed with awards, cited with honors —and out of a job.

For a while he paid the rent by writing articles for scientific journals. Then, one day, he was offered a free-lance assignment by the chief R and D executive of Metadyne to help out on the mathematical interpretation of some of their experimental work. This assignment led to another, and before long a steady relationship had developed between him and the company. Evenutally he agreed to join them full-time in return for use of their equipment and services for his own researches—but under his conditions. And so the Theoretical Studies "Department" came into being.

And now . . . something was missing. The something within him that had been awakened long ago in childhood would always crave new worlds to discover. And as he gazed out at the Vega ships . . .

His thought were interrupted as a stream of electromagnetic vibrations from somewhere below was transformed into the code which alerted the Mercury's flight-control processor. The stubby wing outside the cockpit dipped and the aircar turned, beginning the smooth descent that would merge its course into the eastbound traffic corridor that led to the heart of the city at two thousand feet.

chapter five

The morning sun poured in through the window and accentuated the chiseled crags of the face staring out, high over the center of Houston. The squat, stocky frame, conceivably modeled on that of a Sherman tank, threw a square slab of shadow on the carpet behind. The stubby fingers hammered a restless tattoo on the glass. Gregg Caldwell, executive director of the Navigation and Communications Division of UN Space Arm, reflected on developments so far.

Just as he'd expected, now that the initital disbelief and excitement had worn off, everyone was jostling for a slice of the action. In fact, more than a few of the big wheels in some divisions—Biosciences, Chicago, and Space Medicine, Farnborough, for instance—were mincing no words in asking just how Navcomms came to be involved at all, let alone running the show, since the project obviously had no more connection with the business of navigation than it had with communication. The down-turned corners of Caldwell's mouth shifted back slightly in something that almost approached a smile of anticipation. So, the knives were being sharpened, were they? That was okay by him; he could do with a fight. After more than twenty years of hustling his way to the top of one of the biggest divisions of the Space Arm, he was a seasoned veteran at infighting—and he hadn't lost a drop of blood yet. Maybe this was an area in which Navcomms hadn't had much involvement before; maybe the whole thing was bigger than Navcomms could handle; maybe it was bigger than UNSA could handle; but—that was the way it was. It had chosen to fall into Navcomms' lap and that was where it was going to stay. If anyone wanted to help out, that was fine—but the project was stamped as Navcomm-controlled. If they didn't like it, let them try to change it. Man—let 'em try!

His thoughts were interrupted by the chime of the console built into the desk behind him. He turned around, flipped a switch, and answered in a voice of baritone granite:

"Caldwell."

Lyn Garland, his personal assistant, greeted him from the screen. She was twenty-eight, pretty, and had long red hair and big, brown, intelligent eyes.

"Message from Reception. Your two visitors from IDCC are here—Dr. Hunt and Mr. Gray."

"Bring them straight up. Pour some coffee. You'd better sit in with us."

"Will do."

Ten minutes later formalities had been exchanged and everyone was seated. Caldwell regarded the Englishmen in silence for a few seconds, his lips pursed and his bushy brows gnarled in a knot across his forehead. He leaned forward and interlaced his fingers on the desk in front of him.

"About three weeks ago I attended a meeting at one of our Lunar survey bases—Copernicus Three," he said. "A lot of excavation and site-survey work is going on in that area, much of it in connection with new construction programs. The meeting was attended by scientists from Earth and from some of the bases up there, a few people on the engineering side and certain members of the uniformed branches of the Space Arm. It was called following some strange discoveries there—discoveries that make even less sense now than they did then."

He paused to gaze from one to the other. Hunt and Gray returned the look without speaking. Caldwell continued: "A team from one of the survey units was engaged in mapping out possible sites for clearance radars. They were operating in a remote sector, well away from the main area being leveled . . ."

As he spoke, Caldwell began operating the keyboard recessed into one side of his desk. With a nod of his head he indicated the far wall, which was made up of a battery of display screens. One of the screens came to life to show the title sheet of a file, marked obliquely with the word RESTRICTED in red. This disappeared to be replaced by a contour map of what looked like a rugged and broken stretch of terrain. A slowly pulsing point of light appeared in the center of the picture and began moving across the map as Caldwell rotated a tracker ball set into the panel that held the keyboard. The light halted at a point where the contours indicated the junction of a steep-sided cleft valley with a wider gorge. The cleft valley was narrow and seemed to branch off from the gorge in a rising curve.

"This map shows the area in question," the director resumed. "The cursor shows where a minor cleft joins the main fault running down toward the left. The survey boys left their vehicle at this point and proceeded on up to the cleft on foot, looking for a way to the top of that large rock mass—the one tagged 'five sixty.' " As Caldwell spoke, the pulsing light moved slowly along between the minor sets of contours, tracing out the path taken by the UN team. They watched it negotiate the bend above the mouth of the cleft and proceed some distance farther. The light approached the side of the cleft and touched it at a place where the contours merged into a single heavy line. There it stopped.

"Here the side was a sheer cliff about sixty feet high. That was where they came across the first thing that was unusual—a hole in the base of the rock wall. The sergeant leading the group described it as being like a cave. That strike you as odd?"

Hunt raised his eyebrows and shrugged. "Caves don't grow on moons," he said simply.

"Exactly."

The screen now showed a photo view of the area, apparently taken from the spot at which the survey vehicle had been parked. They recognized the break in the wall of the gorge where the cleft joined it. The cleft was higher up than had been obvious from the map and was approached by a ramp of loose rubble. In the background they could see a squat tower of rock flattened on top—presumably the one marked "560" on the map. Caldwell allowed them some time to reconcile the picture with the map before bringing up the second frame. It showed a view taken high up, this time looking into the mouth of the cleft. A series of shots then followed, progressing up to and beyond the bend. "These are stills from a movie record," Caldwell commented. "I won't bother with the whole set." The final frame in the sequence showed a hole in the rock about five feet across.

"Holes like this aren't unknown on the Moon," Caldwell remarked. "But they are rare enough to prompt our men into taking a closer look. The inside was a bit of a mess. There had been a rockfall—maybe several falls; not much room—just a heap of rubble and dust . . . at first sight, anyway." A new picture on the screen confirmed this statement. "But when they got to probing around a bit more, they came across something that was really unusual. Underneath they found a body—dead!"

The picture changed again to show another view of the interior, taken from the same angle as the previous one. This time, however, the subject was the top half of a human figure lying amid the rubble and debris, apparently at the stage of being half uncovered. It was clad in a spacesuit which, under the layer of gray-white dust, appeared to be bright red. The helmet seemed intact, but it was impossible to make out any details of the face behind the visor because of the reflected camera light. Caldwell allowed them plenty of time to study the picture and reflect on these facts before speaking again.

"That is the body. I'll answer some of the more obvious questions before you ask. First—no, we don't know who he is—or was—so we call him Charlie. Second—no, we don't know for sure what killed him. Third—no, we don't know where he came from." The executive director caught the puzzled look on Hunt's face and raised his eyebrows inquiringly.

"Accidents can happen, and it's not always easy to say what caused them—I'll buy that," Hunt said. "But to not know who he is . . . ? I mean, he must have carried some kind of ID card; I'd have thought he'd have to. And even if he didn't, he must be from one of the UN bases up there. Someone must have noticed he was missing."

For the first time the flicker of a smile brushed across Caldwell's face.

"Of course we checked with all the bases, Dr. Hunt. Results negative. But that was just the beginning. You see, when they got him back to the labs for a more thorough check, a number of peculiarities began to emerge which the experts couldn't explain—and, believe me, we've had enough brains in on this. Even after we brought him back here, the situation didn't get any better. In fact, the more we find out, the worse it gets."

" 'Back here'? You mean . . . ?"

"Oh, yes. Charlie's been shipped back to Earth. He's over at the Westwood Biological Institute right now—a few miles from here. We'll go and have a look at him later on today."

Silence reigned for what seemed like a long time as Hunt and Gray digested the rapid succession of new facts. At last Gray offered:

"Maybe somebody bumped him off for some reason?"

"No, Mr. Gray, you can forget anything like that." Caldwell waited a few more seconds. "Let me say that from what little we do know so far, we can state one or two things with certainty. First, Charlie did not come from any of the bases established to date on Luna. Furthermore"—Caldwell's voice slowed to an ominous rumble—"he did not originate from any nation of the world as we know it today. In fact, it is by no means certain that he originated from this planet at all!"

His eyes traveled from Hunt to Gray, then back again, taking in the incredulous stares that greeted his words. Absolute silence enveloped the room. A suspense almost audible tore at their nerves.

Caldwell's finger stabbed at the keyboard.

The face leaped out at them from the screen in grotesque close-up, skull-like, the skin shriveled and darkened like ancient parchment, and stretched back over the bones to uncover two rows of grinning teeth. Nothing remained of the eyes but a pair of empty pits, staring sightlessly out through dry, leathery lids.

Caldwell's voice, now a chilling whisper, hissed through the fragile air.

"You see, gentlemen—Charlie died over fifty thousand years ago!"

chapter six

Dr. Victor Hunt stared absently down at the bird's-eye view of the outskirts of Houston sliding by below the UNSA jet. The mind-numbing impact of Caldwell's revelations had by this time abated sufficiently for him to begin putting together in his mind something of a picture of what it all meant.

Of Charlie's age there could be no doubt. All living organisms take into their bodies known proportions of the radioactive isotopes of carbon and certain other elements. During life, an organism maintains a constant ratio of these isotopes to "normal" ones, but when it dies and intake ceases, the active isotopes are left to decay in a predictable pattern. This mechanism provides, in effect, a highly reliable clock, which begins to run at the moment of death. Analysis of the decay residues enables a reliable figure to be calculated for how long the clock has been running. Many such tests had been performed on Charlie, and all the results agreed within close limits.

Somebody had pointed out that the validity of this method rested on the assumptions that the composition of whatever Charlie ate, and the constituents of whatever atmosphere he breathed, were the same as for modern man on modern Earth. Since Charlie might not be from Earth, this assumption could not be made. It hadn't taken long, however, for this point to be settled conclusively. Although the functions of most of the devices contained in Charlie's backpack were still to be established, one assembly had been identified as an ingeniously constructed miniature nuclear power plant. The U^{235} fuel pellets were easily located and analysis of their decay products yielded a second, independent answer, although a less accurate one: The power unit in Charlie's backpack had been made some fifty thousand years previously. The further implication of this was that since the first set of test results was thus substantiated, it seemed to follow that in terms of air and food supply, there could have been little abnormal about Charlie's native environment.

Now, Charlie's kind, Hunt told himself, must have evolved to their human form somewhere. That this "somewhere" was either Earth or not Earth was fairly obvious, the rules of basic logic admitting no other possibility. He traced back over what he could recall of the conventional account of the evolution of terrestrial life forms and wondered if, despite the generations of painstaking effort and research that had been devoted to the subject, there might after all be more to the story than had up until then been so confidently supposed. Several thousands of millions of years was a long time by anybody's standards; was it so totally inconceivable that somewhere in all those gulfs of uncertainty, there could be enough room to lose an advanced line of human descent which had flourished and died out long before modern man began his own ascent?

On the other hand, the fact that Charlie was found on the Moon presupposed a civilization sufficiently ad-

vanced technically to send him there. Surely, on the way
toward developing space flight, they would have
evolved a worldwide technological society, and in doing
so would have made machines, erected structures, built
cities, used metals, and left all the other hallmarks of
progress. If such a civilization had once existed on
Earth, surely centuries of exploration and excavation
couldn't have avoided stumbling on at least some traces
of it. But not one instance of any such discovery had
ever been recorded. Although the conclusion rested
squarely on negative evidence, Hunt could not, even
with his tendency toward open-mindedness, accept that
an explanation along these lines was even remotely
probable.

The only alternative, then, was that Charlie came
from somewhere else. Clearly this could not be the
Moon itself: It was too small to have retained an atmosphere anywhere near long enough for life to have
started at all, let alone reach an advanced level—and of
course, his spacesuit showed he was just as much an alien there as was man.

That only left some other planet. The problem here
lay in Charlie's undoubted human form, which Caldwell
had stressed although he hadn't elected to go into detail.
Hunt knew that the process of natural evolution was accepted as occuring through selection, over a long period, from a purely random series of genetic mutations.
All the established rules and principles dictated that the
appearance of two identical end products from two
completely isolated families of evolution, unfolding independently in different corners of the universe, just
couldn't happen. Hence, if Charlie came from somewhere else, a whole branch of accepted scientific theory
would come crashing down in ruins. So—Charlie
couldn't possibly have come from Earth. Neither could
he possibly have come from anywhere else. Therefore,
Charlie couldn't exist. But he did.

Hunt whistled silently to himself as the full implications of the thing began to dawn on him. There was

enough here to keep the whole scientific world arguing for decades.

Inside the Westwood Biological Institute, Caldwell, Lyn Garland, Hunt, and Gray were met by a Professor Christian Danchekker. The Englishmen recognized him, since Caldwell had introduced them earlier by vi-phone. On their way to the laboratory section of the institute, Danchekker briefed them further.

In view of its age, the body was in an excellent state of preservation. This was due to the environment in which it had been found—a germ-free hard vacuum and an abnormally low temperature sustained, even at Lunar noon, by the insulating mass of the surrounding rock. These conditions had prevented any onset of bacterial decay of the soft tissues. No rupture had been found in the spacesuit. So the currently favored theory regarding cause of death was that a failure in the life-support system had resulted in a sudden fall in temperature. The body had undergone deep freezing in a short space of time with a consequent abrupt cessation of metabolic processes; ice crystals, formed from body fluids, had caused widespread laceration of cell membranes. In the course of time most of the lighter substances had sublimed, mainly from the outer layers, to leave behind a blackened, shriveled, natural kind of mummy. The most seriously affected parts were the eyes, which, composed for the most part of fluids, had collapsed completely, leaving just a few flaky remnants in their sockets.

A major problem was the extreme fragility of the remains, which made any attempt at detailed examination next to impossible. Already the body had undergone some irreparable damage in the course of being transported to Earth and in the removal of the spacesuit; only the body's being frozen solid during these operations had prevented the situation from being even worse. That was when somebody had thought of Felix Borlan at IDCC and an instrument being developed in

England that could display the insides of things. The result had been Caldwell's visit to Portland.

Inside the first laboratory it was dark. Researchers were using binocular microscopes to study sets of photographic transparencies arranged on several glass-topped tables, illuminated from below. Danchekker selected some plates from a pile and, motioning the others to follow, made his way over to the far wall. He positioned the first three of the plates on an eye-level viewing screen, snapped on the screen light, and stepped back to join the expectant semicircle. The plates were X-ray images showing the front and side views of a skull. Five faces, thrown into sharp relief against the darkness of the room behind, regarded the screen in solemn silence. At last Danchekker moved a pace forward, at the same time half turning toward them.

"I need not, I feel, tell you who this is." His manner was somewhat stiff and formal. "A skull, fully human in every detail—as far as it is possible to ascertain by X rays, anyway." Danchekker traced along the line of the jaw with a ruler he had picked up from one of the tables. "Note the formation of the teeth—on either side we see two incisors, one canine, two premolars, and three molars. This pattern was established quite early in the evolutionary line that leads to our present day anthropoids, including, of course, man. It distinguishes our common line of descent from other offshoots, such as the New World monkeys with a count of two, one, three, three."

"Hardly necessary here," Hunt commented. "There's nothing apelike or monkeylike about that picture."

"Quite so, Dr. Hunt," Danchekker returned with a nod. "The reduced canines, not interlocking with the upper set, and the particular pattern of the cusps—these are distinctly human characteristics. Note also the flatness of the lower face, the absence of any bony brow ridges . . . high forehead and sharply angled jaw . . . well-rounded braincase. These are all features of true man as we know him today, features that derive directly from his earlier ancestors. The significance of these details in this instance is that they demonstrate an example of true man, not something that merely bears a superficial resemblance to him."

The professor took down the plates and momentarily flooded the room with a blaze of light. A muttered profanity from one of the scientists at the tables made him switch off the light hastily. He picked up three more plates, set them up on the screen, and switched on the light to reveal the side view of a torso, an arm, and a foot.

"Again, the trunk shows no departure from the familiar human pattern. Same rib structure . . . broad chest with well-developed clavicles . . . normal pelvic arrangement. The foot is perhaps the most specialized item in the human skeleton and is responsible for man's uniquely powerful stride and somewhat peculiar gait. If you are familiar with human anatomy, you will find that this foot resembles ours in every respect."

"I'll take your word for it," Hunt conceded, shaking his head. "Nothing remarkable, then."

"The most significant thing, Dr. Hunt, is that nothing *is* remarkable."

Danchekker switched off the screen and returned the plates to the pile. Caldwell turned to Hunt as they began walking back toward the door.

"This kind of thing doesn't happen every day," he grunted. "An understandable reason for wanting some . . . er . . . irregular action, you would agree?"

Hunt agreed.

A passage, followed by a short flight of stairs and another passage, brought them to a set of double doors bearing the large red sign STERILE AREA. In the anteroom behind, they put on surgical masks, caps, gowns, gloves, and overshoes before passing out through another door at the opposite end.

In the first section they came to, samples of skin and other tissues were being examined. By reintroducing the substances believed to have escaped over the centuries, specimens had been restored to what were hoped to be close approximations to their original conditions. In general, the findings merely confirmed that Charlie was as human chemically as he was structurally. Some unfamiliar enzymes had, however, been discovered. Dynamic computer simulation suggested that these were designed to assist in the breakdown of proteins unlike anything found in the diet of modern man. Danchekker was inclined to dismiss this peculiarity with the rather vague assertion that "Times change," a remark which Hunt appeared to find disturbing.

The next laboratory was devoted to an investigation of the spacesuit and the various other gadgets and implements found on and around the body. The helmet was the first exhibit to be presented for inspection. Its back and crown were made of metal, coated dull black and extending forward to the forehead to leave a transparent visor extending from ear to ear. Danchekker held it up for them to see and pushed his hand up through the opening at the neck. They could see clearly the fingers of his rubber glove through the facepiece.

"Observe," he said, picking up a powerful xenon flash lamp from the bench. He directed the beam through the facepiece, and a circle of the material immediately turned dark. They could see through the area around the circle that the level of illumination inside the helmet had not changed appreciably. He moved the lamp around and the dark circle followed it across the visor.

"Built-in antiglare," Gray observed.

"The visor is fabricated from a self-polarizing crystal," Danchekker informed them. "It responds directly to incident light in a fashion that is linear up to high intensities. The visor is also effective with gamma radiation."

Hunt took the helmet to examine it more closely. The blend of curves that made up the outside contained little of interest, but on turning it over he found that a section of the inner surface of the crown had been removed to reveal a cavity, empty except for some tiny wires and a set of fixing brackets.

"That recess contained a complete miniature communications station," Danchekker supplied, noting his interest. "Those grilles at the sides concealed the speakers, and a microphone is built into the top, just above the forehead." He reached inside and drew down a small retractable binocular periscope from inside the top section of the helmet, which clicked into position immediately in front of where the eyes of the wearer would be. "Built-in video, too," he explained. "Controlled from a panel on the chest. The small hole in the front of the crown contained a camera assembly."

Hunt continued to turn the trophy over in his hands, studying it from all angles in absorbed silence. Two weeks ago he had been sitting at his desk in Metadyne doing a routine job. Never in his wildest fantasies had he imagined that he would one day come to be holding in his hands something that might well turn out to be one of the most exciting discoveries of the century, if not in the whole of history. Even his agile mind was having difficulty taking it all in.

"Can we see some of the electronics that were in here?" he asked after a while.

"Not today," Caldwell replied. "The electronics are being studied at another location—that goes for most of what was in the backpack, too. Let's just say for now that when it came to molecular circuits, these guys knew their business."

"The backpack is a masterpiece of precision engineering in miniature," Danchekker continued, leading them to another part of the laboratory. "The prime power source for all the equipment and heating has been identified, and is nuclear in nature. In addition, there was a water recirculation plant, life-support system, standby power and communications system, and oxygen liquefaction plant—all in that!" He held up the casing of the stripped-down backpack for them to see, then tossed it back on the bench. "Several other devices were also included, but their purpose is still obscure. Behind you, you will see some personal effects."

The professor moved around to indicate an array of

objects taken from the body and arranged neatly on another bench like museum exhibits.

"A pen—not dissimilar to a familiar pressurized ballpoint type; the top may be rotated to change color." He picked up a collection of metallic strips that hinged into a casing, like the blades of a pocketknife. "We suspect that these are keys of some kind because they have magnetic codes written on their surfaces."

To one side was a collection of what looked like crumpled pieces of paper, some with groups of barely discernible symbols written in places. Next to them were two pocket-size books, each about half an inch thick.

"Assorted oddments," Danchekker said, looking along the bench. "The documents are made from a kind of plasticized fiber. Fragments of print and handwriting are visible in places—quite unintelligible, of course. The material has deteriorated severely and tends to disintegrate at the slightest touch." He nodded toward Hunt. "This is another area where we hope to learn as much as we can with the Trimagniscope before we risk anything else." He pointed to the remaining articles and listed them without further elaboration. "Pen-size torch; some kind of pocket flamethrower, we think; knife; pen-size electric pocket drill with a selection of bits in the handle; food and drink containers—they connect via valves to the tubes inside the lower part of the helmet; pocket folder, like a wallet—too fragile to open; changes of underclothes; articles for personal hygiene; odd pieces of metal, purpose unknown. There were also a few electronic devices in the pockets; they have been sent elsewhere along with the rest."

The party halted on the way back to the door to gather around the scarlet spacesuit, which had been reassembled on a life-size dummy standing on a small plinth. At first sight the proportions of the figure seemed to differ subtly from those of an average man, the build being slightly on the stocky side and the limbs a little short for the height of about five feet, six inches. However, since the suit was not designed for a close fit, it was difficult to be sure. Hunt noticed the soles of the boots were surprisingly thick.

"Sprung interior," Danchekker supplied, following his gaze.

"What's that?"

"It's quite ingenious. The mechanical properties of the sole material vary with applied pressure. With the wearer walking at normal speed, the sole would remain mildly flexible. Under impact, however—for example, if he jumped—it assumes the characteristics of a stiff spring. It's an ideal device for kangarooing along in lunar gravity—untilizing conditions of reduced weight but normal inertia to advantage."

"And now, gentlemen," said Caldwell, who had been following events with evident satisfaction, "the moment I guess you've been waiting for—let's have a look at Charlie himself."

An elevator took them down to the subterranean levels of the institute. They emerged into a somber corridor of white-tiled walls and white lights, and followed it to a large metal door. Danchekker pressed his thumb against a glass plate set into the wall and the door slid silently aside on recognition of his print. At the same time, a diffuse but brilliant white glow flooded the room inside.

It was cold. Most of the walls were taken up by control panels, analytical equipment, and glass cabinets containing rows of gleaming instruments. Everything was light green, as in an operating theater, and gave the same impression of surgical cleanliness. A large table, supported by a single central pillar, stood to one side. On top of it was what looked like an oversize glass coffin. Inside that lay the body. Saying nothing, the professor led them across the room, his overshoes squeaking on the rubbery floor as he walked. The small group converged around the table and stared in silent awe at the figure before them.

It lay half covered by a sheet that stretched from its lower chest to its feet. In these clinical surroundings, the gruesome impact of the sight that had leaped at them from the screen in Caldwell's office earlier in the day was gone. All that remained was an object of scientific curiosity. Hunt found it overwhelming to stand at arm's length from the remains of a being who had lived as part of a civilization, had grown and passed away, before the dawn of history. For what seemed a long time he stared mutely, unable to frame any intelligent question or comment, while speculations tumbled through his mind on the life and times of this strange creature. When he eventually jolted himself back to the present, he realized that the professor was speaking again.

". . . Naturally, we are unable to say at this stage if it was simply a genetic accident peculiar to this individual or a general characteristic of the race to which he belonged, but measurements of the eye sockets and certain parts of the skull indicate that, relative to his size, his eyes were somewhat larger than our own. This suggests that he was not accustomed to sunlight as bright as ours. Also, note the length of the nostrils. Allowing for shrinkage with age, they are constructed to provide a longer passage for the prewarming of air. This suggests that he came from a relatively cool climate . . . the same thing can be observed in modern Eskimos."

Danchekker made a sweeping gesture that took in the whole length of the body. "Again, the rather squat and stocky build is consistent with the idea of a cool native environment. A fat, round object presents less surface area per unit volume than a long, thin one and thus loses less heat. Contrast the compact build of the Eskimo with the long limbs and lean body of the Negro. We know that at the time Charlie was alive the Earth was just entering the last cold period of the Pleistocene Ice Age. Life forms in existence at that time would have had about a million years to adapt to the cold. Also, there is strong reason to believe that ice ages are caused by a reduction in the amount of solar radiation falling on Earth, brought about by the Sun and planets passing through exceptionally dusty patches of space. For example, ice ages occur approximately every two hundred and fifty million years; this is also the period of rotation of our galaxy—surely more than mere coincidence. Thus, this being's evident adaptation to cold, the suggestion of a lower level of daylight, and his established age all correlate well."

Hunt looked at the professor quizzically. "You're pretty sure already, then, that he's from Earth?" he said in a tone of mild surprise. "I mean—it's early days yet, surely?"

Danchekker drew back his head disdainfully and screwed up his eyebrows to convey a shadow of irritation. "Surely it is quite obvious, Dr. Hunt." The tone was that of a professor reproaching an errant student. "Consider the things we have observed: the teeth, the skull, the bones, the types and layout of organs. I have deliberately drawn attention to these details to emphasize his kinship to ourselves. It is clear that his ancestry is the same as ours." He waved his hand to and fro in front of his face. "No, there can be no doubt whatsoever. Charlie evolved from the same stock as modern man and all the other terrestrial primates."

Gray looked dubious. "Well, I dunno," he said. "I think Vic's got a point. I mean, if his lot did come from Earth, you'd have expected someone to have found out about it before now, wouldn't you?"

Danchekker sighed with an overplay of indifference. "If you wish to doubt my word, you have, of course, every right to do so," he said. "However, as a biologist and an anthropologist, I for my part see more than sufficient evidence to support the conclusions I have stated."

Hunt seemed far from satisfied and started to speak again, but Caldwell intervened.

"Cool it, you guys. D'you think we haven't had enough arguments like this around here for the last few weeks?"

"I really think it's about time we had some lunch," Lyn Garland interrupted with well-timed tact.

Danchekker turned abruptly and began walking back toward the door, reciting statistics on the density of body hair and the thickness of subdermal layers of fat, apparently having dismissed the incident from his mind. Hunt paused to survey the body once more before turning to follow, and in doing so, he caught Gray's eye for an instant. The engineer's mouth twitched briefly at the corners; Hunt gave a barely perceptible shrug. Caldwell, still standing by the foot of the table, observed the brief exchange. He turned his head to look after Danchekker and then back again at the Englishmen, his eyes narrowing thoughtfully. At last he fell in a few paces behind the group, nodding slowly to himself and permitting a faint smile.

The door slid silently into place and the room was once more plunged into darkness.

chapter seven

Hunt brought his hands up to his shoulders, stretched his body back over his chair, and emitted a long yawn at the ceiling of the laboratory. He held the position for a few seconds, and then collapsed back with a sigh. Finally he rubbed his eyes with his knuckles, hauled himself upright to face the console in front of him once more, and returned his gaze to the three-foot-high wall of the cylindrical glass tank by his side.

The image on the Trimagniscope tube was an enlarged view of one of the pocket-size books found on the body, which Danchekker had shown them on their first day in Houston three weeks before. The book itself was enclosed in the scanner module of the machine, on the far side of the room. The scope was adjusted to generate a view that followed the change in density along the boundary surface of the selected page, producing an image of the lower section of the book only; it was as if the upper part had been removed, like a cut deck of cards. Because of the age and condition of the book, however, the characters on the page thus exposed tended to be of poor quality and in some places were incomplete. The next step would be to scan the image optically with TV cameras and feed the encoded pictures into the Navcomms computer complex. The raw input would then be processed by pattern recognition techniques and statistical techniques to produce a second, enhanced copy with many of the missing character fragments restored.

Hunt cast his eye over the small monitor screens on his console, each of which showed a magnified view of a selected area of the page, and tapped some instructions into his keyboard.

"There's an unresolved area on monitor five," he announced. "Cursors read X, twelve hundred to thirteen eighty; Y, nine ninety and, ah, ten seventy-five."

Rob Gray, seated at another console a few feet away and almost surrounded by screens and control panels, consulted one of the numerical arrays glowing before him.

"Z mod's linear across the field," he advised. "Try a block elevate?"

"Can do. Give it a try."

"Setting Z step two hundred through two ten . . . increment point one . . . step zero point five seconds."

"Check." Hunt watched the screen as the surface picked out through the volume of the book became distorted locally and the picture on the monitor began to change.

"Hold it there," he called.

Gray hit a key. "Okay?"

Hunt contemplated the modified view for a while.

"The middle of the element's clear now," he pronounced at last. "Fix the new plane inside forty percent. I still don't like the strip around it, though. Give me a vertical slice through the center point."

"Which screen d'you want it on?"

"Ah . . . number seven."

"Coming up."

The curve, showing a cross section of the page surface through the small area they were working on, appeared on Hunt's console. He studied it for a while, then called:

"Run an interpolation across the strip. Set thresholds of, say, minus five and thirty-five percent on Y."

"Parameters set . . . Interpolator running . . . run complete," Gray recited. "Integrating into scan program now." Again the picture altered subtly. There was a noticeable improvement.

"Still not right around the edge," Hunt said. "Try weighting the quarter and three-quarter points by plus ten. If that doesn't work, we'll have to break it down into isodepth bands."

"Plus ten on point two five zero and point seven five zero," Gray repeated as he operated the keys. "Integrated. How's it look?"

On the element of surface displayed on Hunt's monitor, the fragments of characters had magically assembled themselves into recognizable shapes. Hunt nodded with satisfaction.

"That'll do. Freeze it in. Okay—that clears that one. There's another messy patch up near the top right. Let's have a go at that next."

Life had been reduced to much this kind of pattern ever since the day the installation of the scope was completed. They had spent the first week obtaining a series of cross-sectional views of the body itself. This exercise had proved memorable on account of the mild discomfort and not so mild inconvenience of having to work in electrically heated suits, following the medical authority's insistence that Charlie be kept in a refrigerated environment. It had proved something of an anticlimax. The net results were that, inside as well as out, Charlie was surprisngly—or not so surprisingly, depending on one's point of view—human. During the second week they began examining the articles found on the body, especially the pieces of "paper" and the pocketbooks. This investigation had proved more interesting.

Of the symbols contained in the documents, numerals were the first to be identified. A team of cryptographers, assembled at Navcomms HQ, soon worked out the counting system, which turned out to be based on twelve digits rather than ten and employed a positional notation with the least significant digit to the left. Deciphering the nonnumeric symbols was proving more difficult. Linguists from institutions and universities in several countries had linked into Houston and, with the aid of batteries of computers, were attempting to make some sense of the language of the Lunarians, as Charlie's race had come to be called in commemoration of his place of discovery. So far their efforts had yielded little more than that the Lunarian alphabet comprised thirty-seven characters, was written horizontally from right to left, and contained the equivalent of upper-case characters.

Progress, however, was not considered to be bad for so short a time. Most of the people involved were aware that even this much could never have been achieved without the scope, and already the names of the two Englishmen were well-known around the division. The scope attracted a lot of interest among the UNSA technical personnel, and most evenings saw a stream of visitors arriving at the Ocean Hotel, all curious to meet the coinventors of the instrument and to learn more about its principles of operation. Before long, the Ocean became the scene of a regular debating society where anybody who cared to could give free rein to his wildest speculations concerning the Charlie mystery, free from the constraints of professional caution and skepticism that applied during business hours.

Caldwell, of course, knew everything that was said by anybody at the Ocean and what everybody else thought about it, since Lyn Garland was present on most nights and represented the next best thing to a hot line back to the HQ building. Nobody minded that much—after all, it was only part of her job. They minded even less when she began turning up with some of the other girls from Navcomms in tow, adding a refreshing party atmosphere to the whole proceedings. This development met with the full approval of the visitors from out-of-town; however, it had led to somewhat strained relationships on the domestic front for one or two of the locals.

Hunt jabbed at the keyboard for the last time and sat back to inspect the image of the completed page.

"Not bad at all," he said. "That one won't need much enhancement."

"Good," Gray agreed. He lit a cigarette and tossed the pack across to Hunt without being asked. "Optical encoding's finished," he added, glancing at a screen. "That's number sixty-seven tied up." He rose from his chair and moved across to stand beside Hunt's console to get a better view of the image in the tank. He looked at it for a while without speaking.

"Columns of numbers," he observed needlessly at last. "Looks like some kind of table."

"Looks like it . . ." Hunt's voice sounded far away.

"Mmm . . . rows and columns . . . thick lines and thin lines . . . Could be anything—mileage chart, wire gauges, some sort of timetable. Who knows?"

Hunt made no reply but continued to blow occasional clouds of smoke at the glass, cocking his head first to one side and then to the other.

"None of the numbers there are very large," he commented after a while. "Never more than two positions in any place. That gives us what in a duodecimal system? One hundred and forty-three at the most." Then as an afterthought, "I wonder what the biggest is."

"I've got a table of Lunarian–decimal equivalents somewhere. Any good?"

"No, don't bother for now. It's too near lunch. Maybe we could have a look at it over a beer tonight at the Ocean."

"I can pick out their one and two," Gray said. "And three and . . . Hey! What do you know—look at the right-hand columns of those big boxes. Those numbers are in ascending order!"

"You're right. And look—the same pattern repeats over and over in every one. It's some kind of cyclic array." Hunt thought for a moment, his face creased in a frown of concentration. "Something else, too—see those alphabetic groups down the sides? The same groups reappear at intervals all across the page . . ." He broke off again and rubbed his chin.

Gray waited perhaps ten seconds. "Any ideas?"

"Dunno . . . Sets of numbers starting at one and increasing by one every time. Cyclic . . . an alphabetic label tagged on to each repeating group. The whole pattern repeating again inside bigger groups, and the bigger groups repeat again. Suggests some sort of order. Sequence . . ."

His mumblings were interrupted as the door opened behind them. Lyn Garland walked in.

"Hi, you guys. What's showing today?" She moved over to stand between them and peered into the tank. "Say, tables! How about that? Where'd they come from, the books?"

"Hello, lovely," Gray said with a grin. "Yep." He nodded in the direction of the scanner.

"Hi," Hunt answered, at last tearing his eyes away from the image. "What can we do for you?"

She didn't reply at once, but continued staring into the tank.

"What are they? Any ideas?"

"Don't know yet. We were just talking about it when you came in."

She marched across the lab and bent over to peer into the top of the scanner. The smooth, tanned curve of her leg and the proud thrust of her behind under her thin skirt drew an exchange of approving glances from the two English scientists. She came back and studied the image once more.

"Looks like a calendar, if you ask me," she told them. Her voice left no room for dissent.

Gray laughed. "Calendar, eh? You sound pretty sure

of it. What's this—a demonstration of infallible feminine intution or something?" He was goading playfully.

She turned to confront him with out-thrust jaw and hands planted firmly on hips. "Listen, Limey—I've got a right to an opinion, okay? So, that's what I think it is. That's my opinion."

"Okay, okay." Gray held up his hands. "Let's not start the War of Independence all over again. I'll note it in the lab file: 'Lyn thinks it's a—' "

"Holy Christ!" Hunt cut him off in midsentence. He was staring wide-eyed at the tank. "Do you know, she could be right! She could just be bloody right!"

Gray turned back to face the side of the tank. "How come?"

"Well, look at it. Those larger groups could be something like months, and the labeled sets that keep repeating inside them could be weeks made up of days. After all, days and years have to be natural units in any calendar system. See what I mean?"

Gray looked dubious. "I'm not so sure," he said slowly. "It's nothing like our year, is it? I mean, there's a hell of a lot more than three hundred sixty-five numbers in that lot, and a lot more than twelve months, or whatever they are—aren't there?"

"I know. Interesting?"

"Hey. I'm still here," said a small voice behind them. They moved apart and half turned to let her in on the proceedings.

"Sorry," Hunt said. "Getting carried away." He shook his head and regarded her with an expression of disbelief.

"What on Earth made you say a calendar?"

She shrugged and pouted her lips. "Don't know, really. The book over there looks like a diary. Every diary I ever saw had calendars in it. So, it had to be a calendar."

Hunt sighed. "So much for scientific method. Anyway, let's run a shot of it. I'd like to do some sums on it later." He looked back at Lyn. "No—on second thought, you run it. This is your discovery."

She frowned at him suspiciously. "What d'you want me to do?"

"Sit down there at the master console. That's right. Now activate the control keyboard . . . Press the red button—that one."

"What do I do now?"

"Type this: FC comma DACCO seven slash PCH dot P sixty-seven slash HCU dot one. That means 'functional control mode, data access program subsystem number seven selected, access data file reference "Project Charlie, Book one," page sixty-seven, optical format, output on hard copy unit, one copy.' "

"It does? Really? Great!"

She keyed in the commands as Hunt repeated them more slowly. At once a hum started up in the hard copier, which stood next to the scanner. A few seconds later a sheet of glossy paper flopped into the tray attached to the copier's side. Gray walked over to collect it.

"Perfect," he announced.

"This makes me a scope expert, too," Lyn informed them brightly.

Hunt studied the sheet briefly, nodded, and slipped it into a folder lying on top of the console.

"Doing some homework?" she asked.

"I don't like the wallpaper in my hotel room."

"He's got the theory of relativity all around the bedroom in his flat in Wokingham," Gray confided, ". . . and wave mechanics in the kitchen."

She looked from one to the other curiously. "Do you know, you're crazy. Both of you—you're both crazy. I was always too polite to mention it before, but somebody has to say it."

Hunt gave her a solemn look. "You didn't come all the way over here to tell us we're crazy," he pronounced.

"Know something—you're right. I had to be in Westwood anyway. A piece of news just came in this morning that I thought might interest you. Gregg's been talking to the Soviets. Apparently one of their materials labs has been doing tests on some funny pieces of metal alloy they got hold of—all sorts of unusual properties nobody's ever seen before. And guess what—they dug them up on the Moon, somewhere near Mare Imbrium. And—when they ran some dating tests, they came up with a figure of about fifty thousand years! How about that! Interested?"

Gray whistled.

"It had to be just a matter of time before something else turned up," Hunt said, nodding. "Know any more details?"

She shook her head. " 'Fraid not. But some of the guys might be able to fill you in a bit more at the Ocean tonight. Try Hans if he's there; he was talking a lot to Gregg about it earlier."

Hunt looked intrigued but decided there was little point in pursuing the matter further for the time being.

"How is Gregg?" he asked. "Has he tried smiling lately?"

"Don't be mean," she reproached him. "Gregg's okay. He's busy, that's all. D'you think he didn't have enough to worry about before all this blew up?"

Hunt didn't dispute it. During the few weeks that had passed, he had seen ample evidence of the massive resources Caldwell was marshaling from all around the globe. He couldn't help but be impressed by the director's organizational ability and his ruthless efficiency when it came to annihilating opposition. There were other things, however, about which Hunt harbored mild personal doubts.

"How's it all doing, then?" he asked. His tone was neutral. It did not escape the girl's sharply tuned senses. Her eyes narrowed almost imperceptibly.

"Well, you've seen most of the action so far. How do *you* think it's going?"

He tried a sidestep to avoid her deliberate turning around of the question.

"None of my business, really, is it? We're just the machine minders in all this."

"No, really—I'm interested. What do you think?"

Hunt made a great play of stubbing out his cigarette. He frowned and scratched his forehead.

"You've got rights to opinions, too," she persisted. "Our Constitution says so. So, what's your opinion?"

There was no way off the hook, or of evading those big brown eyes.

"There's no shortage of information turning up," he conceded at last. "The infantry is doing a good job . . ." He let the rider hang.

"But what . . . ?"

Hunt sighed.

"But . . . the interpretation. There's something too dogmatic—too rigid—about the way the big names higher up are using the information. It's as if they can't think outside the ruts they've thought inside for years. Maybe they're overspecialized—won't admit any possibility that goes against what they've always believed."

"For instance?"

"Oh, I don't know . . . Well, take Danchekker, for one. He's always accepted orthodox evolutionary theory—all his life, I suppose; therefore, Charlie must be from Earth. Nothing else is possible. The accepted theory must be right, so that much is fixed; you have to work everything else to fit in with that."

"You think he's wrong? That Charlie came from somewhere else?"

"Hell, I don't know. He could be right. But it's not his conclusion that I don't like; it's his way of getting there. This problem's going to need more flexibility before it's cracked."

Lyn nodded slowly to herself, as if Hunt had confirmed something.

"I thought you might say something like that," she mused. "Gregg will be interested to hear it. He wondered the same thing, too."

Hunt had the feeling that the questions had been more than just an accidental turn of conversation. He looked at her long and hard.

"Why should Gregg be interested?"

"Oh, you'd be surprised. Gregg knows a lot about

you two. He's interested in anything anybody has to say. It's people, see—Gregg's a genius with people. He knows what makes them tick. It's the biggest part of his job."

"Well, it's a people problem he's got," Hunt said. "Why doesn't he fix it?"

Suddenly Lyn switched moods and seemed to make light of the whole subject, as if she had learned all she needed to for the time being.

"Oh, he will—when he gets the feeling that the time's right. He's very good with timing, too." She decided to finish the matter entirely. "Anyhow, it's time for lunch." She stood up and slipped a hand through an arm on either side. "How about two crazy Limeys treating a poor girl from the Colonies to a drink?"

chapter eight

The progress meeting, in the main conference room of the Navcomms Headquarters building, had been in session for just over two hours. About two dozen persons were seated or sprawled around the large table that stood in the center of the room, by now reduced to a shambles of files, papers, overflowing ashtrays, and half-empty glasses.

Nothing really exciting had emerged so far. Various speakers had reported the results of their latest tests, the sum total of their conclusions being that Charlie's circulatory, respiratory, nervous, endocrine, lymphatic, digestive, and every other system anybody could think of were as normal as those of anyone sitting around the table. His bones were the same, his body chemistry was the same, his blood was a familiar grouping. His brain capacity and development were within the normal range for *Homo sapiens*, and evidence suggested that he had been right-handed. The genetic codes carried in his reproductive cells had been analyzed; a computer simulation of combining them with codes donated by an average human female had confirmed that the offspring of such a union would have inherited a perfectly normal set of characteristics.

Hunt tended to remain something of a passive observer of the proceedings, conscious of his status as an unofficial guest and wondering from time to time why he had been invited at all. The only reference made to him so far had been a tribute in Caldwell's opening remarks to the invaluable aid rendered by the Trimagniscope; apart from the murmur of agreement that had greeted this comment, no further mention had been made of either the instrument or its inventor. Lyn Garland had told him: "The meeting's on Monday, and Gregg wants you to be there to answer detailed questions on the scope." So here he was. Thus far, nobody had wanted to know anything detailed about the scope—only about the data it produced. Something gave him the uneasy feeling there was an ulterior motive lurking somewhere.

After dwelling on Charlie's computerized, mathematical sex life, the chair considered a suggestion, put forward by a Texas planetologist sitting opposite Hunt, that perhaps the Lunarians came from Mars. Mars had reached a later phase of planetary evolution than Earth and possibly had evolved intelligent life earlier, too. Then the arguments started. Martian exploration went right back to the 1970s; UNSA had been surveying the surface from satellites and manned bases for years. How come no sign of any Lunarian civilization had showed up? Answer: We've been on the Moon a hell of a lot longer than that and the first traces have only just shown up there. So you could expect discovery to occur later on Mars. Objection: If they came from Mars, then their civilization developed on Mars. Signs of a whole civilization should be far more obvious than signs of visits to a place like Earth's Moon—therefore the Lunarians should have been detected a lot sooner on Mars. Answer: Think about the rate of erosion on the Martian surface. The signs could be largely wiped out or buried. At least that could account for there not being any signs on Earth. Somebody then pointed out that this did not solve the problem—all it did was shift it to another place. If the Lunarians came from Mars, evolutionary theory was still in just as big a mess as ever.

So the discussion went on.

Hunt wondered how Rob Gray was getting on back at Westwood. They now had a training schedule to fit in on top of their normal daily data-collection routine. A week or so before, Caldwell had informed them that he wanted four engineers from Navcomms fully trained as Trimagniscope operators. His explanation, that this would allow round-the-clock operation of the scope and hence better productivity from it, had not left Hunt convinced; neither had his further assertion that Navcomms was going to buy itself some of the instruments but needed to get some in-house expertise while they had the opportunity.

Maybe Caldwell intended setting up Navcomms as an independent and self-sufficient scope-operating facility. Why would he do that? Was Forsyth-Scott or somebody else exerting pressure to get Hunt back to England? If this was a prelude to shipping him back, the scope would obviously stay in Houston. That meant that the first thing he'd be pressed into when he got back would be a panic to get the second prototype working. Big deal!

The meeting eventually accepted that the Martian-origin theory created more problems than it solved and, anyway, was pure speculation. Last rites in the form of "No substantiating evidence offered" were pronounced, and the corpse was quietly laid to rest under the epitaph *In Abeyance*, penned in the "Action" columns of the memoranda sheets around the table.

A cryptologist then delivered a long rambling ac-

count of the patterns of character groupings that occurred in Charlie's personal documents. They had already completed preliminary processing of all the individual papers, the contents of the wallet, and one of the
books; they were about half way through the second.
There were many tables, but nobody knew yet what they
meant; some structured lines of symbols suggested
mathematical formulas; certain page and section headings matched entries in the text. Some character strings
appeared with high frequency, some with less; some
were concentrated on a few pages, while others were
evenly spread throughout. There were lots of figures
and statistics. Despite the enthusiasm of the speaker, the
mood of the room grew heavy and the questions fewer.
They knew he was a bright guy; they wished he'd stop
telling them.

At length, Danchekker, who had been noticeably silent through most of the proceedings and appeared to
be growing increasingly impatient as they continued,
obtained leave from the chair to address the meeting.
He rose to his feet, clasped his lapels, and cleared his
throat. "We have devoted as much time as can be excused to exploring improbable and far-flung suggestions
which, as we have seen, turn out to be fallacious." He
spoke confidently, taking in the length of the table with
side-to-side swings of his body. "The time has surely
come, gentlemen, for us to dally no longer, but to concentrate our efforts on what must be the only viable line
of reasoning open to us. I state, quite categorically,
that the race of beings to whom we have come to refer
as the Lunarians originated here, on Earth, as did the
rest of us. Forget all your fantasies of visitors from
other worlds, interstellar travelers, and the like. The
Lunarians were simply products of a civilization that
developed here on our own planet and died out for reasons we have yet to determine. What, after all, is so
strange about that? Civilizations have grown and passed
away in the brief span of our more orthodox history,
and no doubt others will continue the pattern. This conclusion follows from comprehensive and consistent evi-

dence and from the proven principles of the various natural sciences. It requires no invention, fabrication, or supposition, but derives directly from unquestionable facts and the straightforward application of established methods of inference." He paused and cast his eyes around the table to invite comment.

Nobody commented. They already knew his arguments. Danchekker, however, seemed about to go through it all again. Evidently he had concluded that attempts to make them see the obvious by appealing to their powers of reason alone were not enough; his only resort then was insistent repetition until they either concurred or went insane.

Hunt leaned back in his chair, took a cigarette from a box lying nearby on the table, and tossed his pen down on his pad. He still had reservations about the professor's dogmatic attitude, but at the same time he was aware that Danchekker's record of academic distinction was matched by those of few people alive at the time. Besides, this wasn't Hunt's field. His main objection was something else, a truth he accepted for what it was and made no attempt to fool himself by rationalizing: Everything about Danchekker irritated him. Danchekker was too thin; his clothes were too old-fashioned—he carried them as if they had been hung on to dry. His anachronistic gold-rimmed spectacles were ridiculous. His speech was too formal. He had probably never laughed in his life. A skull vacuum-packed in skin, Hunt thought to himself.

"Allow me to recapitulate," Danchekker continued. "*Homo sapiens*—modern man—belongs to the phylum Vertebrata. So, also, do all the mammals, fish, birds, amphibians, and reptiles that have ever walked, crawled, flown, slithered, or swum in every corner of the Earth. All vertebrates share a common pattern of basic architecture, which has remained unchanged over millions of years despite the superficial, specialized adaptations that on first consideration might seem to divide the countless species we see around us.

"The basic vertebrate pattern is as follows: an internal skeleton of bone or cartilage and a vertebral column. The vertebrate has two pairs of appendages, which may be highly developed or degenerate, likewise a tail. It has a ventrally located heart, divided into two or more chambers, and a closed circulatory system of blood made up of red cells containing hemoglobin. It has a dorsal nerve cord which bulges at one end into a five-part brain contained in a head. It also has a body cavity that contains most of its vital organs and its digestive system. All vertebrates conform to these rules and are thereby related."

The professor paused and looked around as if the conclusion were too obvious to require summarizing. "In other words, Charlie's whole structure shows him to be directly related to a million and one terrestrial animal species, extinct, alive, or yet to come. Furthermore, *all* terrestrial vertebrates, including ourselves *and* Charlie, can be traced back through an unbroken succession of intermediate fossils as having inherited their common pattern from the earliest recorded ancestors of the vertebrate line"—Danchekker's voice rose to a crescendo—"from the first boned fish that appeared in the oceans of the Devonian period of the Paleozoic era, over four hundred million years ago!" He paused for this last to take hold and then continued. "Charlie is as human as you or I in every respect. Can there be any doubt, then, that he shares our vertebrate heritage and therefore our ancestry? And if he shares our ancestry, then there is no doubt that he also shares our places of origin. Charlie *is* a native of planet Earth."

Danchekker sat down and poured himself a glass of water.

A hubbub of mixed murmurings and mutterings ensued, punctuated by the rustling of papers and the clink of water glasses. Here and there, chairs creaked as cramped limbs eased themselves into more comfortable positions. A metallurgist at one end of the table was gesturing to the man seated next to her. The man shrugged, showed his empty palms, and nodded his head in Danchekker's direction. She turned and called to the professor.

"Professor Danchekker . . . Professor . . ." Her voice made itself heard. The background noise died away. Danchekker looked up. "We've been having a little argument here—maybe you'd like to comment. Why couldn't Charlie have come from a parallel line of evolution somewhere else?"

"I was wondering that, too," came another voice.

Danchekker frowned for a moment before replying.

"No. The point you are overlooking here, I think, is that the evolutionary process is fundamentally made up of random events. Every living organism that exists today is the product of a chain of successive mutations that has continued over millions of years. The most important fact to grasp is that each discrete mutation is in itself a purely random event, brought about by aberrations in genetic coding and the mixing of the sex cells from different parents. The environment into which the mutant is born dictates whether it will survive to reproduce its kind or whether it will die out. Thus, some new characteristics are selected for further improvement, while others are promptly eradicated and still others are diluted away by interbreeding.

"There are still people who find this principle difficult to accept—primarily, I suspect, because they are incapable of visualizing the implications of numbers and time scales beyond the ranges that occur in everyday life. Remember we are talking about billions of billions of combinations coming together over millions of years.

"A game of chess begins with only twenty playable moves to choose from. At every move the choice available to the player is restricted, and yet, the number of legitimate positions that the board could assume after only ten moves is astronomical. Imagine, then, the number of permutations that could arise when the game continues for a billion moves and at each move the player has a billion choices open to him. This is the game of evolution. To suppose that two such independent sequences could result in end products that are identical would surely be demanding too much of our credulity. The laws of chance and statistics are quite firm when applied to sufficiently large numbers of samples. The laws of thermodynamics, for example, are nothing more than expressions of the probable behavior of gas molecules, yet the numbers involved are so large that we feel quite safe in accepting the postulates as rigid rules; no significant departure from them has ever been observed. The probability of the parallel line of evolution that you suggest is less than the probability of heat flowing from the kettle to the fire, or of all the air molecules in this room crowding into one corner at the same time, causing us all to explode spontaneously. Mathematically speaking, yes—the possibility of parallelism is finite, but so indescribably remote that we need consider it no further."

A young electronics engineer took the argument up at this point.

"Couldn't God get a look in?" he asked. "Or at least, some kind of guiding force or principle that we don't yet comprehend? Couldn't the same design be produced via different lines in different places?"

Danchekker shook his head and smiled almost benevolently.

"We are scientists, not mystics," he replied. "One of the fundamental principles of scientific method is that new and speculative hypotheses do not warrant consideration as long as the facts that are observed are adequately accounted for by the theories that already exist. Nothing resembling a universal guiding force has ever been revealed by generations of investigation, and since the facts observed are adequately explained by the accepted principles I have outlined, there is no necessity to invoke or invent additional causes. Notions of guiding forces and grand designs exist only in the mind of the misguided observer, not in the facts he observes."

"But suppose it turns out that Charlie came from somewhere else," the metallurgist insisted. "What then?"

"Ah! Now, *that* would be an entirely different matter.

If it should be proved by some other means that Charlie did indeed evolve somewhere else, then we would be forced to accept that parallel evolution had occurred as an observed and unquestionable fact. Since this could not be explained within the framework of contemporary theory, our theories would be shown to be woefully inadequate. *That* would be the time to speculate on additional influences. *Then*, perhaps, your universal guiding force might find a rightful place. To entertain such concepts at this stage, however, would be to put the cart fairly and squarely before the horse. In so doing, we would be guilty of a breach of one of the most fundamental of scientific principles."

Somebody else tried to push the professor from a different angle.

"How about convergent lines rather than parallel lines? Maybe the selection principles work in such a way that different lines of development converge toward the same optimum end product. In other words, although they start out in different directions, they will both eventually hit on the same, best final design. Like . . ." He sought for an analogy. "Like sharks are fish and dolphins are mammals. They both came from different origins but ended up hitting on the same general shape."

Danchekker again shook his head firmly. "Forget the idea of perfection and best end products," he said. "You are unwittingly falling into this trap of assuming a grand design again. The human form is not nearly as perfect as you perhaps imagine. Nature does not produce best solutions—it will try *any* solution. The only test applied is that it be good enough to survive and reproduce itself. Far more species have proved unsuccessful and become extinct than have survived—far, far more. It is easy to contemplate a kind of preordained striving toward something perfect when this fundamental fact is overlooked—when looking back down the tree, as it were, with the benefit of hindsight from our particular successful branch and forgetting the countless other branches that got nowhere.

"No, forget this idea of perfection. The developments we see in the natural world are simply cases of something good enough to do the job. Usually, many conceivable alternatives would be as good, and some better.

"Take as an example the cusp pattern on the first lower molar tooth of man. It is made up of a group of five main cusps with a complex of intervening grooves and ridges that help to grind up food. There is no reason to suppose that this particular pattern is any more efficient than any one of many more that might be considered. This particular pattern, however, first occurred as a mutation somewhere along the ancestral line leading toward man and has been passed on ever since. The same pattern is also found on the teeth of the great apes, indicating that we both inherited it from some early common ancestor where it happened through pure chance.

"Charlie has human cusp patterns on all his teeth.

"Many of our adaptations are far from perfect. The arrangement of internal organs leaves much to be desired, owing to our inheriting a system originally developed to suit a horizontal and not an upright posture. In our respiratory system, for example, we find that the wastes and dirt that accumulate in the throat and nasal regions drain inside and not outside, as happened originally, a prime cause of many bronchial and chest complaints not suffered by four-footed animals. That's hardly perfection, is it?"

Danchekker took a sip of water and made an appealing gesture to the room in general.

"So, we see that any idea of convergence toward the ideal is not supported by the facts. Charlie exhibits all our faults and imperfections as well as our improvements. No, I'm sorry—I appreciate that these questions are voiced in the best tradition of leaving no possibility unprobed and I commend you for them, but really, we must dismiss them."

Silence enveloped the room at his concluding words. On all sides, everybody seemed to be staring thoughtfully through the table, through the walls, or through the ceiling.

Caldwell placed his hands on the table and looked around until satisfied that nobody had anything to add. "Looks like evolution stays put for a while longer," he grunted. "Thank you Professor."

Danchekker nodded without looking up.

"However," Caldwell continued, "the object of these meetings is to give everyone a chance to talk freely as well as listen. So far, some people haven't had much to say—especially one or two of the newcomers." Hunt realized with a start that Caldwell was looking straight at him. "Our English visitor, for example, whom most of you already know. Dr. Hunt, do you have any views that we ought to hear about . . . ?"

Next to Caldwell, Lyn Garland was making no attempt to conceal a wide smile. Hunt took a long draw at his cigarette and used the delay to collect his thoughts. In the time it took for him to coolly emit one long, diffuse cloud of smoke and flick his hand at the ashtray, all the pieces clicked together in his brain with the smooth precision of the binary regiments parading through the registers of the computers downstairs. Lyn's persistent cross-examinations, her visits to the Ocean, his presence here—Caldwell had found a catalyst.

Hunt surveyed the array of attentive faces. "Most of what's been said reasserts the accepted principles of comparative anatomy and evolutionary theory. Just to clear the record for anyone with misleading ideas, I've no intention of questioning them. However, the conclusion could be summed up by saying that since Charlie comes from the same ancestors as we do, he must have evolved on Earth the same as we did."

"That is so," threw in Danchekker.

"Fine," Hunt replied. "Now, all this is really your problem, not mine, but since you've asked me what I think, I'll state the conclusion another way. Since Charlie evolved on Earth, the civilization he was from evolved on Earth. The indications are that his culture was about as advanced as ours, maybe in one or two areas slightly more advanced. So, we ought to find no end of traces of his people. We don't. Why not?"

All heads turned toward Danchekker.

The professor sighed. "The only conclusion left open to us is that whatever traces were left have been erased by the natural processes of weathering and erosion," he said wearily. "There are several possibilities: A catastrophe of some sort could have wiped them out to the extent that there were no traces; or possibly their civilization existed in regions which today are submerged beneath the oceans. Further searching will no doubt produce solutions to this question."

"If any catastrophe as violent as that occurred so recently, we would already know about it," Hunt pointed out. "Most of what was land then is still land today, so I can't see them sinking into the ocean somewhere, either; besides, you've only to look at our civilization to see it's not confined to localized areas—it's spread all over the globe. And how is it that in spite of all the junk that keeps turning up with no trouble at all from primitive races from around the same time—bones, spears, clubs, and so on—nobody has ever found a single example of anything related to this supposed technologically advanced culture? Not a screw, or a piece of wire, or a plastic washer. To me, that doesn't make sense."

More murmuring broke out to mark the end of Hunt's critique.

"Professor?" Caldwell invited comment with a neutral voice.

Danchekker compressed his mouth into a grimace. "Oh, I agree, I agree. It is surprising—very surprising. But what alternative are you proposing?" His voice took on a note of sarcasm. "Do you suggest that man and all the animals came to Earth in some enormous celestial Noah's Ark?" He laughed. "If so, the fossil record of a hundred million years disproves you."

"Impasse." The comment came from Professor Schorn, an authority on comparative anatomy, who had arrived from Stuttgart a few days before.

"Looks like it," Caldwell agreed.

Danchekker, however, was not through. "Would Dr. Hunt care to answer my question?" he challenged. "Precisely what other place of origin is he suggesting?"

"I'm not suggesting anywhere in particular," Hunt replied evenly. "What I am suggesting is that perhaps a more open-minded approach might be appropriate at this stage. After all, we've only just found Charlie. This business will go on for years yet; there's bound to be a lot more information surfacing that we don't have right now. I think it's too early to be jumping ahead and predicting what the answers might be. Better just to keep on plodding along and using every scrap of data we've got to put together a picture of the place Charlie came from. It might turn out to be Earth. Then again, it might not."

Caldwell led him on further. "How would you suggest we go about that?"

Hunt wondered if this was a direct cue. He decided to risk it. "You could try taking a closer look at this." He drew a sheet of paper out from the folder in front of him and slid it across to the center of the table. The paper showed a complicated tabular arrangement of Lunarian numerals.

"What's that?" asked a voice.

"It's from one of the pocket books," Hunt replied. "I think the book is something not unlike a diary. I also believe that that"—he pointed at the sheet—"could well be a calendar." He caught a sly wink from Lyn Garland and returned it.

"Calendar?"

"How d'you figure that one?"

"It's all gobbledygook."

Danchekker stared hard at the paper for a few seconds. "Can you prove it's a calendar?" he demanded.

"No, I can't. But I have analyzed the number pattern and can state that it's made up of ascending groups that repeat in sets and subsets. Also, the alphabetic groups that seem to label the major sets correspond to the headings of groups of pages further on—remarkably like the layout of a diary."

"*Hmmph!* More likely some form of tabular page index."

"Could be," Hunt granted. "But why not wait and see? Once the language has unraveled a bit more, it should be possible to cross-check a lot of what's here with items from other sources. This is the kind of thing that maybe we ought to be a little more open-minded about. You say Charlie comes from Earth; I say he might. You say this is not a calendar; I say it might be. In my estimation, an attitude like yours is too inflexible to permit an unbiased appraisal of the problem. You've already made up your mind what you want the answers to be."

"Hear, hear!" a voice at the end of the table called.

Danchekker colored visibly, but Caldwell spoke before he could reply.

"You've analyzed the numbers—right?"

"Right."

"Okay, supposing for now it's a calendar—what more can you tell us?"

Hunt leaned forward across the table and pointed at the sheet with his pen.

"First, two assumptions. One: the natural unit of time on any world is the day—that is, the time it takes the planet to rotate on its axis . . ."

"Assuming it rotates," somebody tossed in.

"That was my second assumption. But the only cases we know of where there's no rotation—or where the orbital period equals the axial period, which amounts to the same thing—occur when a small body orbits close to a far more massive one and is swamped by gravitational tidal effects, like our Moon. For that to happen to a body the size of a planet, the planet would have to orbit very close to its parent star—too close for it to support any life comparable to our own."

"Seems reasonable," Caldwell said, looking around the table. Various heads were nodding assent. "Where do we go from there?"

"Okay," Hunt resumed. "Assuming it rotates and the day is its natural unit of time—if this complete table represents one full orbit around its sun, there are seventeen hundred days in its year, one entry for each."

"Pretty long," someone hazarded.

"To us, yes: at least, the year-to-day ratio is big. It could mean the orbit is large, the rotational period short, or perhaps a bit of both. Now look at the major number groups—the ones tagged with the heavy alphabetic labels. There are forty-seven of them. Most contain thirty-six numbers, but nine of them have thirty-seven—the first, sixth, twelfth, eighteenth, twenty-fourth, thirtieth, thirty-sixth, forty-second, and forty-seventh. That seems a bit odd at first sight, but so would our system to someone unfamiliar with it. It suggests that maybe somebody had to do a bit of fiddling with it to make it work."

"Mmm . . . like with our months."

"Exactly. This is just the sort of juggling you have to do to get a sensible fit of our months into our year. It happens because there's no simple relationship between the orbital periods of planet and satellite; there's no reason why there should be. I'm guessing that if this is a calendar that relates to some other planet, then the reason for this odd mix of thirty-sixes and thirty-sevens is the same as the one that causes problems with our calendar: That planet had a moon."

"So these groups are months," Caldwell stated.

"If it's a calendar—yes. Each group is divided into three subgroups—weeks, if you like. Normally there are twelve days in each, but there are nine long months, in which the middle week has thirteen days."

Danchekker looked for a long time at the sheet of paper, an expression of pained disbelief spreading slowly across his face.

"Are you proposing this as a serious scientific theory?" he queried in a strained voice.

"Of course not," Hunt replied. "This is all pure speculation. But it does indicate some of the avenues that could be explored. These alphabetic groups, for example, might correspond to references that the language people might dig from other sources—such as dates on documents, or date stamps on pieces of clothing or other equipment. Also, you might be able to find some independent way of arriving at the number of days in the year; if it turned out to be seventeen hundred, that would be quite a coincidence, wouldn't it?"

"Anything else?" Caldwell asked.

"Yes. Computer correlation analysis of this number pattern may show hidden superposed periodicities; for all we know, there could have been more than one moon. Also, it should be possible to compute families of curves giving possible relationships between planet-to-satellite mass ratios against mean orbital radii. Later on you might know enough more to be able to isolate one of the curves. It might describe the Earth-Luna system; then again, it might not."

"*Preposterous!*" Danchekker exploded.

"Unbiased?" Hunt suggested.

"There is something else that may be worth trying," Schorn interrupted. "Your calendar, if that's what it is, has so far been described in relative terms only—days per month, months per year, and so on. There is nothing that gives us any absolute values. Now—and this is a long shot—from detailed chemical analysis we are making some progress in building a quantitative model of Charlie's cell-metabolism cycles and enzyme processes. We may be able to calculate the rate of accumulation of waste materials and toxins in the blood and tissues, and from these results form an estimate of his natural periods of sleep and wakefulness. If, in this way, I could provide a figure for the length of the day, the other quantities would follow immediately."

"If we knew that, then we'd know the planet's orbital period," said somebody else. "But could we get an estimate of its mass?"

"One way might be by doing a structural analysis of Charlie's bone and muscle formations and then working out the power–weight ratios," another chipped in.

"That would give us the planet's mean distance from its sun," said a third.

"Only if it was like our Sun."

"You could get a check on the planet's mass from the glass and other crystalline materials in his equipment. From the crystal structure, we should be able to figure out the strength of the gravitational field they cooled in."

"How could we get a figure for density?"

"You still need to know the planetary radius."

"He's like us, so the surface gravity will be Earth-like."

"Very probable, but let's prove it."

"Prove that's a calendar first."

Remarks began pouring in from all sides. Hunt reflected with some satisfaction that at least he had managed to inject some spirit and enthusiasm into the proceedings.

Danchekker remained unimpressed. As the noise abated, he rose again to his feet and pointed pityingly to the single sheet of paper, still lying in the center of the table.

"All balderdash!" he spat. "There is the sum total of your evidence. There"—he slid his voluminous file, bulging with notes and papers, across beside it—"is mine, backed by libraries, data banks, and archives the world over. Charlie comes from Earth!"

"Where's his civilization, then?" Hunt demanded. "Removed in an enormous celestial garbage truck?"

Laughter from around the table greeted the return of Danchekker's own gibe. The professor darkened and seemed about to say something obscene. Caldwell held up a restraining hand, but Schorn saved the situation by interrupting in his calm, unruffled tone. "It would seem, ladies and gentlemen, that for the moment we must compromise by agreeing to a purely hypothetical situation. To keep Professor Danchekker happy, we must accept that the Lunarians evolved from the same ancestors as ourselves. To keep Dr. Hunt happy, we must assume they did it somewhere else. How we are to reconcile these two irreconcilables, I would not for one moment attempt to predict."

chapter nine

Hunt saw less and less of the Trimagniscope during the weeks that followed the progress meeting. Caldwell seemed to go out of his way to encourage the Englishman to visit the various UNSA labs and establishments nearby, to "see what's going on first-hand," or the offices in Navcomms HQ to "meet someone you might find interesting." Hunt was naturally curious about the Lunarian investigations, so these developments suited him admirably. Soon he was on familiar terms with most of the engineers and scientists involved, at least in the Houston vicinity, and he had a good idea of how their work was progressing and what difficulties they were encountering. He eventually acquired a broad overview of the activity on all fronts and found that, at least at the general level, the awareness of the whole picture that he was developing was shared by only a few privileged invidicuals within the organization.

Things were progressing in a number of directions. Calculations of structural efficiency, based on measurements of Charlie's skeleton and the bulk supported by it, had given a figure for the surface gravity of his home planet, which agreed within acceptable margins of error with figures deduced separately from tests performed on the crystals of his helmet visor and other components formed from a molten state. The gravity field at the surface of Charlie's home planet seemed to have been not much different from that of Earth; possibly it was slightly stronger. These results were accepted as being no more than rough approximations. Besides, nobody knew how typical Charlie's physical build had been of that of the Lunarians in general, so there was no firm indication of whether the planet in question had been Earth or somewhere else. The issue was still wide open.

On equipment tags, document headings, and appended to certain notes, the linguistics section had found examples of Lunarian words which matched exactly some of the labels on the calendar, just as Hunt had suggested they might. While this *proved* nothing, it did add further plausibility to the idea that these words indicated dates of some kind.

Then something else that seemed to connect with the calendar appeared from a totally unexpected direction. Site-preparation work in progress near Lunar Tycho Base Three turned up fragments of metal fabrications and structures. They looked like the ruins of some kind of installation. The more thorough probe that followed yielded no fewer than fourteen more bodies, or more accurately, bits of bodies from which at least fourteen individuals of both sexes could be identified. Clearly, none of the bodies was in anything approaching the condition of Charlie's. They had all been literally blown to pieces. The remains comprised little more than splinters of charred bone scattered among scorched tatters of spacesuits. Apart from suggesting that besides being physically the same as humans, the Lunarians had been every bit as accident-prone, these discoveries provided no new information—until the discovery of the wrist unit. About the size of a large cigarette pack, not including the wrist bracelet, the device carried on its upper face four windows that looked like miniature electronic displays. From their size and shape, the windows seemed to have been intended to display character data rather than pictures, and the device was thought to be a chronometer or a computing-calculating aid; maybe it was both—and other things besides.

After a perfunctory examination at Tycho Three the unit had been shipped to Earth along with some other items. It eventually found its way to the Navcomms laboratories near Houston, where the gadgets from Charlie's backpack were being studied. After some preliminary experimenting the casing was safely removed, but detailed inspection of the complex molecular circuits inside revealed nothing particularly meaningful. Having no better ideas, the Navcomms engineers resorted to applying low voltages to random points to see what happened. Sure enough, when particular sequences of binary patterns were injected into one row of contacts, an assortment of Lunarian symbols appeared across the windows. This left nobody any the wiser until Hunt, who happened to be visiting the lab, recognized one sequence of alphabetic sets as the months that appeared on the calendar. Hence, at least one of the functions performed by the wrist unit seemed closely related to the table in the diary. Whether or not this had anything to do with recording the passage of time remained to be seen, but at least odd things looked as if they were beginning to tie up.

The Linguistics section was making steady, if less spectacular progress toward cracking the language. Many of the world's most prominent experts were getting involved, some choosing to move to Houston, while others worked via remote data links. As the first phase of their assault, they amassed volumes of statistics on word and character distributions and matchings, and produced reams of tables and charts that looked as meaningless to everybody else as the language itself. After that it was largely a matter of intuition and guessing games played on computer display screens. Every now and again somebody spotted a more meaningful pattern, which led to a better guess, which led to a still more meaningful pattern—and so on. They produced lists of words in categories believed to correspond to nouns, adjectives, verbs, and adverbs, and later on added adjectival and adverbial phrases—fairly basic requirements for any advanced inflecting language. They began to develop a feel for the rules for deriving variants, such as plurals and verb tenses, from common roots, and for the conventions that governed the formation of word sequences. An appreciation of the rudiments of Lunarian grammar was emerging from all this, and the experts in Linguistics faced the future with optimism, suddenly confident that they were approaching the point where they would begin attempting to match the first English equivalents to selected samples.

The Mathematics section, organized on lines similar to Linguistics, was also finding things that were interesting. Part of the diary was made up of many pages of numeric and tabular material—suggesting, perhaps, a reference section of *Useful Information*. One of the pages was divided vertically, columns of numbers alternating with columns of words. A researcher noticed that one of the numbers, when converted to decimal, came out to 1836—the proton–electron mass ratio, a fundamental physical constant that would be the same anywhere in the Universe. It was suggested that the page might be a listing of equivalent Lunarian units of mass, similar to equivalence tables used for converting ounces to grams, grams to pounds . . . and so on. If so, they had stumbled on a complete record of the Lunarian system of measuring mass. The problem was that the whole supposition rested on the slender assumption that the figure 1836 did, in fact, denote the proton–electron mass ratio and was not merely a coincidental reference to something completely different. They needed a second source of information to check it against.

When Hunt talked to the mathematicians one afternoon, he was surprised to learn that they were unaware that the chemists and anatomists in other departments had computed estimates of surface gravity. As soon as he mentioned the fact, everybody saw the significance at once. If the Lunarians had adopted the practice that was common on Earth—using the same units to express mass and weight on their own planet—then the numbers in the table gave Lunarian weights. Furthermore, there was available to them at least one object whose weight they could estimate accurately: Charlie himself. Thus, since they already had an estimate of surface gravity, they could easily approximate how much Charlie would have weighed in kilograms back home. Only one piece of information was missing for a solution to the whole problem: a factor to convert kilograms to Lunarian weight units. Then Hunt speculated that there could well be among Charlie's personal documents an identity card, a medical card—something that recorded his weight in his own units. If so, that one number would tell them all they needed to know. The discussion ended abruptly, with the head of the mathematics section departing in great haste and a state of considerable excitement to talk to the head of the linguistics section. Linguistics agreed to make a special note if anything like that turned up. So far nothing had.

Another small group, tucked away in offices in the top of the Navcomms HQ building, was working on what was perhaps the most exciting discovery to come out of the books so far. Twenty pages, right at the end of the second book, showed a series of maps. They were all drawn to an apparently small scale, each one depicting extensive areas of the world's surface—but the world so depicted bore no resemblance to Earth. Oceans, continents, rivers, lakes, islands, and most other geographical features were easily distinguishable, but in no way could they be reconciled with Earth's surface, even allowing for the passage of fifty thousand years—which would have made little difference anyway, aside from the size of the polar ice caps.

Each map carried a rectangular grid of reference lines, similar to those of terrestrial latitude and longitude, with the lines spaced forty-eight units (decimal) apart. These numbers were presumed to denote units of Lunarian circular measure, since nobody could think of any other sensible way to dimension coordinates on the surface of a sphere. The fourth and seventh maps provided the key: the zero line of longitude to which all the other lines were referenced. The line to the east was tagged "528" and that to the west "48," showing that the full Lunarian circle was divided into 576 Lunarian degrees. The system was consistent with their duodecimal counting method and their convention of reading from right to left. The next step was to calculate the

percentage of the planet's surface that each map represented and to fit them together to form the complete
globe.

Already, however, the general scheme was clear. The
ice caps were far larger than those believed to have existed on Earth during the Pleistocene Ice Age, stretching in some places to within twenty (Earth) degrees of
the equator. Most of the seas around the equatorial belt
were completely locked in by coastlines and ice. An assortment of dots and symbols scattered across the land
masses in the ice-free belt and, more thinly, over the ice
sheets themselves, seemed to indicate towns and cities.

When Hunt received an invitation to come up and
have a look at the maps, the scientists working on them
showed him the scales of distance that were printed at
the edges. If they could only find some way of converting those numbers into miles, they would have the diameter of the planet. But nobody had told them about the
tables the mathematics section thought might be mass-
unit conversion factors. Maybe one of the other tables
did the same thing for units of length and distance? If
so, and if they could find a reference to Charlie's height
among his papers, the simple process of measuring him
would allow them to work out how many Earth meters
there were in a Lunarian mile. Since they already had a
figure for the planet's surface gravity, its mass and
mean density should follow immediately.

This was all very exciting, but all it proved was that
a world had existed. It did not prove that Charlie and
the Lunarians originated there. After all, the fact that a
man carries a London street map in his pocket doesn't
prove him to be a Londoner. So the work of relating
numbers derived from physical measurements of Charlie's body to the numbers on the maps and in the tables
could turn out to be based on a huge fallacy. If the diary came from the world shown on the maps but Charlie
came from somewhere else, then the system of measure-
ment deduced from the maps and tables in the diary
might be a totally different system from the one used to
record his personal characteristics in his papers, since

the latter system would be the system used in the somewhere else, not in the world depicted on the maps. It all got very confusing.

Finally, nobody claimed to have proved conclusively that the world on the maps wasn't Earth. Admittedly it didn't look like Earth, and attempts to derive the modern distribution of terrestrial continents from the land areas on the maps had met with no success at all. But the planet's gravity hadn't been all that much different. Maybe the surface of Earth had undergone far greater changes over the last fifty thousand years than had been previously thought? Furthermore, Danchekker's arguments still carried a lot of weight, and any theory that discounted them would have an awful lot of explaining to do. But by that time, most of the scientists working on the project had reached a stage where nothing would have surprised them any more, anyway.

"Got your message. Came straight over," Hunt announced as Lyn Garland ushered him into Caldwell's office. Caldwell nodded toward one of the chairs opposite his desk, and Hunt sat down. Caldwell glanced at Lyn, who was still standing by the door.

"It's okay," he said. She left, closing the door behind her.

Caldwell fixed Hunt with an expressionless stare for a few seconds, at the same time drumming his fingers on the desk. "You've seen a lot of the setup here during the past few months. What do you think of it?"

Hunt shrugged. The answer was obvious.

"I like it. Exciting things happen around here."

"You like exciting things happening, huh?" The executive director nodded, half to himself. He remained thoughtful for what seemed a long time. "Well, you've only seen part of what goes on. Most people have no idea how big UNSA is these days. All the things you see around here—the labs, the installations, the launch areas—that's just the backup. Our main business is up front." He gestured toward the photographs adorning one of the walls. "We have people right now exploring the Martian deserts, flying probes down through the clouds on Venus, and walking on the moons of Jupiter. In the deep-space units in California, they're designing ships that will make Vegas and even the Jupiter Mission ships look like paddleboats. Photon-drive robot probes that will make the first jump to the stars— some seven miles long! Think of it—seven miles long!"

Hunt did his best to react in the appropriate manner. The problem was, he wasn't sure what manner was appropriate. Caldwell never said or did anything without a reason. The reason for this turn of conversation was far from obvious.

"And that's only the beginning," Caldwell went on. "After that, men will follow the robots. Then—who knows? This is the biggest thing the human race has ever embarked on: USA, US Europe, Canada, the Soviets, the Australians—they're all in on it together. Where does a thing like that go once it starts moving, huh? Where does it stop?"

For the first time since his arrival at Houston, Hunt detected a hint of emotion in the American's voice. He nodded slowly, though still not comprehending.

"You didn't drag me here to give me a UNSA commercial," he said.

"No, I didn't," Caldwell agreed. "I dragged you over because it's time we had a serious talk. I know enough about you to know how the wheels go round inside your head. You are made out of the same stuff as the guys who are making all the things happen out there." He sat back in his chair and held Hunt's gaze with a direct stare. "I want you to quit messing around at IDCC and come over to us."

The statement caught Hunt like a right hook.

"What . . . ! To Navcomms!"

"Correct. Let's not play games. You're the kind of person we need, and we can give you the things you need. I know I don't have to make a big speech to explain myself."

Hunt's initial surprise lasted perhaps half a second. Already the computer in his head was churning out answers. Caldwell had been building toward this and testing him out for weeks. So, that was why he had moved in Navcomms engineers to take over running the scope. Had the thought been in his mind as long ago as that? Already Hunt had no doubt what the outcome of the interview would be. However, the rules of the game demanded that the set questions be posed and answered before anything final could be pronounced. Instinctively he reached for his cigarette case, but Caldwell preempted him and slid his cigar box across the desk.

"You seem pretty confident you've got what I need," Hunt said as he selected a Havana. "I'm not sure even I know what that is."

"Don't you . . . ? Or is it that you just don't like talking about it?" Caldwell stopped to light his own cigar. He puffed until satisfied, then continued: "New Cross to the *Journal of the Royal Society,* solo. Some achievement." He made a gesture of approval. "We like self-starters over here—sorta . . . traditional. What made you do it? He didn't wait for a reply "First electronics, then mathematics . . . after that nuclear physics, later on nucleonics. What's next Dr. Hunt? Where do you go from there?" He settled back and exhaled a cloud of smoke while Hunt considered the question.

Hunt raised his eyebrows in mild admiration. "You seem to have been doing your homework," he said.

Caldwell didn't answer directly but asked, simply, "How was your uncle in Lagos when you visited him on vacation last year? Did he prefer the weather to Worcester, England? Seen much of Mike from Cambridge lately? I doubt it—he joined UNSA; he's been at Hellas Two on Mars for the last eight months. Want me to go on?"

Hunt was too mature to feel indignant; besides, he liked to see a professional in action. He smiled faintly.

"Ten out of ten."

At once Caldwell's mood became deadly serious. He leaned forward and spread his elbows on the desk.

"I'll tell you where you go from here, Dr. Hunt," he said. "Out—out to the stars! We're on our way to the

stars over here! It started when Danchekker's fish first
crawled up out of the mud. The urge that made them do
it is the same as the one that's driven you all your life.
You've gone inside the atom as far as you can go;
there's only one way left now—out. That's what UNSA
has to offer that you can't refuse."

There was nothing Hunt could add. Two futures lay
spread out before him: One led back to Metadyne, the
other beckoned onwards toward infinity. He was as incapable of choosing the first as his species was of returning to the depths of the sea.

"What's your side of the deal, then?" he asked after
some reflection.

"You mean, what do you have that we need?"

"Yes."

"We need the way your brain works. You can think
sideways. You see problems from different angles that
nobody else uses. That's what I need to bust open this
Charlie business. Everybody argues so much because
they're making assumptions that seem obvious but that
they shouldn't be making. It takes a special kind of
mind to figure out what's wrong when things that anybody with common sense can see are true turn out to be
not true. I think you're the guy."

The compliments made Hunt feel slightly uncomfort-
able. He decided to move things along. "What do you
have in mind?"

"Well, the guys we have at present are top grade inside their own specialties," Caldwell replied. "Don't get
me wrong, these people are good—but I'd like them to
concentrate on doing the things they're best at. However, aside from all that, I need someone with an unspe-
cialized, and therefore impartial, outlook to coordinate
the findings of the specialists and integrate them into an
overall picture. If you like, I need people like Danchekker to paint the pieces of the puzzle, but I need someone like you to fit the pieces together. You've been
doing a bit of that, unofficially, for quite a while anyway; I'm saying, 'Let's make it official.' "

"How about the organization?" Hunt asked.

"I've thought about that. I don't want to alienate any of our senior people by subordinating them or any of their staffs to some new whiz kid. That's only good politics. Anyhow, I don't think you'd want it that way."

Hunt shook his head to show his agreement.

"So," Caldwell resumed, "what I figure is, the various departments and sections will continue to function as they do at present. Our relationship with outfits outside Navcomms will remain unaffected. However, all the conclusions that everybody has reached so far, and new findings as they turn up, will be referred to a centralized coordinating section—that's you. Your job will be to fit the bits together, as I said earlier. You'd build up your own staff as time goes on and the work load increases. You'd be able to request any particular items of information you find you need from the specialist functions; that way you'd be defining some of their objectives. As for your objectives, they're already spelled out: Find out who these Charlie people were, where they came from, and what happened to them. You report directly to me and get the whole problem off my back. I've got enough on my schedule without worrying about corpses." Caldwell threw out an arm to show that he was finished. "Well, what do you say?"

Hunt had to smile within himself. As Caldwell had said, there was really nothing to think about. He took a long breath and turned both hands upward. "As you said—an offer I can't refuse."

"So, you're in?"

"I'm in."

"Welcome aboard, then." Caldwell looked pleased. "This calls for a drink." He produced a flask and glasses from somewhere behind the desk. He poured the whiskey and passed a glass to his newest employee.

"When do you want it to start?" Hunt asked after a moment.

"Well, you probably need a couple of months or so to sort out formalities with IDCC. But why wait for formalities? You're on loan here from IDCC anyway and under my direction for the duration; also, we're paying for you. So what's wrong with tomorrow morning?"

"Christ!"

Caldwell's manner at once became brisk and businesslike.

"I'll allocate offices for you in this building. Rob Gray takes full charge of scope operations and keeps the engineers I've assigned to him as his permanent staff for as long as he's in Houston. That frees you totally. By the end of this week I want estimates of what you think you'll need in the way of clerical and secretarial staff, technical personnel, equipment, furniture, lab space, and computer facilities.

"By this time next week I want you to have a presentation ready for a meeting of section and department heads that I'm going to call, to tell them how you see yourself and them working together. Make it tactful. I won't issue any official notification of these changes until after the meeting, when everybody knows what's going on. Don't talk about it until then, except to myself and Lyn.

"Your outfit will be designed *Special Assignment Group L,* and your position, will be section head, Group L. The post is classed as 'Executive, grade four, civilian,' within the Space Arm. It carries all the appropriate benefits of free use of UNSA vehicles and aircraft, access to restricted files up to category three, and standard issues of clothing and accessories for duties overseas or off-planet. All that is in the *Executive Staff Manual*; details of reporting structures, admin procedures, and that kind of thing are in the *UNSA Corporate Policy Guide*. Lyn will get you copies.

"You'll have to get in touch with the federal authorities in Houston regarding permanent residence in the USA; Lyn knows the right people. Arrange transfer of your personal belongings from England at your own convenience and charge it to Navcomms. We'll help out finding you somewhere to live, but in the meantime stay on at the Ocean."

Hunt had the fleeting thought that had Caldwell been

born three thousand years previously, Rome might well have been built in a day.

"What's your current salary?" Caldwell asked.

"Twenty-five thousand European dollars."

"We'll make it thirty."

Hunt nodded mutely.

Caldwell paused and checked mentally for anything he might have overlooked. Finding nothing, he sat back and raised his glass. "Cheers, then, Vic."

It was the first time he had addressed Hunt informally.

"Cheers."

"To the stars."

"To the stars."

A low roar from a point outside the city reached the room. They glanced toward the window to see a column of light climbing into the blue as a Vega lifted off from a distant launch pad. A quite surge of excitement welled up in Hunt's veins as he took in the sight. It was a symbol of the ultimate expression of man's outward urge, and he was about to become part of it.

chapter ten

Demands for the services of Special Assignment Group L commenced as soon as the new unit officially went into operation, and they continued to increase rapidly in the weeks that followed. By the end of a month Hunt was swamped and forced to take on extra people at a faster rate than he had intended. Originally his idea had been to keep going with a skeleton staff for a while, at least until he formed a better idea of what was required. When Caldwell first announced the establishment of the

new group, there had been one or two instances of
petty jealousy and resentment, but the attitude that pre-
vailed in the end was that Hunt had contributed several
worthwhile ideas, and it seemed only sensible to get him
in on the team permanently. After a while, even the dis-
senters grudgingly began to concede that things seemed
to run more smoothly with Group L around. Some of
them eventually did a complete about-face and became enthusiastic supporters of the scheme, as they
came to appreciate that the communication channels to
Hunt's people worked in bidirectional mode, and for every bit of data they fed in, ten bits came back in the
other direction. As the oil thus added to Caldwell's jig-
saw-puzzle-solving machine began to prove effective,
the machine shifted fully into top gear, and suddenly
pieces started fitting together.

The mathematics section was still working on the
equations and formulas found in the books. Since mathematical relationships would remain true irrespective of
the conventions used to express them, their interpretation was a far less arbitrary affair than that of deciphering the Lunarian language. The mathematicans had
been stimulated by the discovery of the mass conversion
table. They turned their attention to the other tables
contained in the same book and soon found one that
listed many commonly used physical and mathematical
constants. From it they quickly picked out *pi* as well as
e, the base of natural logarithms, and one or two more,
but they still didn't understand the system of units well
enough to evaluate the majority.

Another set of tables turned out to be simple trigonometric functions; these were easily recognized once the
cartographers had provided the units of circular measure.
The headings of the columns of these tables gave the
Lunarian symbols for sine, cosine, tangent, and the like.
Once these were known, many of the mathematical expressions elsewhere started making more sense; some of
them fell out immediately as familiar trigonometric relationships. These in turn helped establish the conventions used to denote normal arithmetic operations and

that of exponentiation, which led to the identification of the equations of mechanical motion. Nobody was surprised when these equations revealed that Lunarian scientists had deduced the same laws as Newton. The mathematicians progressed to tables of elementary first integrals and standard forms of low-order differential equations. On later pages were expressions which they suspected might describe systems of resonance and damped oscillations. Here again, the uncertainty over units presented a problem; expressions of this type would be in a standard form that could apply equally well to electrical, mechanical, thermal, or many other types of physical phenomena. Until they knew more about Lunarian units, they could not be sure precisely what these equations meant, even if they succeeded in interpreting them mathematically.

Hunt remembered having noticed that many of the electrical subassemblies from Charlie's backpack had small metal labels mounted adjacent to plugs, sockets, and other input–output connections. He speculated that some of the symbols engraved on these labels might represent ratings in units of voltage, current, power, frequency, and so on. He spent a day in the electronics labs, produced a full report on these markings, and passed it on to Mathematics. Nobody had thought to tell them about it sooner.

The electronics technicians located the battery in the wrist unit from Tycho, took it to pieces, and with the assistance of an electrochemist from another department, worked out the voltage it had been designed to produce. Linguistics translated the markings on the casing, and that gave a figure for the Lunarian unit for electrical voltage. Well, it was a start.

Professors Danchekker and Schorn were in charge of the biological side of the research. Perhaps surprisingly, Danchekker exhibited no reluctance to cooperate with Group L and kept them fully updated with a regular flow of information. This was more the result of his deeply rooted sense of propriety than of any change of heart. He was a formalist, and if this procedure was what the formalities of the arrangement required, he would adhere to it rigidly. His refusal to budge one inch from his uncompromising views regarding the origins of the Lunarians, however, was total.

As promised, Schorn had set up investigations to determine the length of Charlie's natural day from studies of body chemistry and cell metabolism, but he was running into trouble. He was getting results, all right, but the results made no sense. Some tests gave a figure of twenty-four hours, which meant that Charlie could be from Earth; some gave thirty-five hours, which meant he couldn't be; and other tests came up with figures in between. Thus, if the aggregate of these results meant anything at all, it indicated that Charlie came from a score of different places all at the same time. Either it was crazy, or there was something wrong with the methods used, or there was more to the matter than they thought.

Danchekker was more successful in a different direction. From an analysis of the sizes and shapes af Charlie's blood vessels and associated muscle tissues, he produced equations describing the performance of Charlie's circulatory system. From these he then derived a set of curves that showed the proportions of body heat that would be retained and lost for any given body temperature and outside temperature. He came up with a figure for Charlie's normal body temperature from some of Schorn's figures that were not suspect and were based on the assumption that, as in the case of terrestrial mammals, the process of evolution would have led to Charlie's body regulating its temperature to such a level that the chemical reactions within its cells would proceed at their most efficient rates. By substituting this figure back into his original equations, Danchekker was able to arrive at an estimate of the outside temperature or, more precisely, the temperature of the environment in which Charlie seemed best adapted to function. Allowing for error, it came out at somewhere between two and nine degrees Celsius.

With Schorn's failure to produce a reliable indication

of the length of the Lunarian day, there was still no way of assigning any absolute values to the calendar, although sufficient corroborating evidence had been forthcoming from various sources to verify beyond reasonable doubt that it was indeed a calendar. As more clues to Lunarian electrical units were found by Electronics, an alternative approach to obtaining the elusive Lunarian unit of time suggested itself. If Mathematics could untangle the equations of electrical oscillation, they should be able to manipulate the quantities involved in such a way as to express the two constants denoting the dielectric permittivity and magnetic permeability of free space in Lunarian units. The ratio of these constants would yield the velocity of light, expressed in Lunarian units of distance per Lunarian units of time. The units for representing distance were understood already; therefore, those used for measuring time would be given automatically.

All this activity in UNSA naturally attracted widespread public attention. The discovery of a technologically advanced civilization from fifty thousand years in the past was not something that happened very often. Some of the headlines flashed around the World News Grid when the story was released, a few weeks after the original find, were memorable: MAN ON MOON BEFORE ARMSTRONG; some were hilarious: EXTINCT CIVILIZATION ON MARS; some were just wrong: CONTACT MADE WITH ALIEN INTELLIGENCE. But most summed up the situation fairly well.

In the months that followed, UNSA's public relations office in Washington, long geared to conducting steady and predictable dealings with the news media, reeled under a deluge of demands from hard-pressed editors and producers all over the globe. Washington struggled valiantly for a while, but in the end did the human thing, and delegated the problem to Navcomms' local PR department at Houston. The PR director at Houston found a ready-made clearinghouse of new information in the form of Group L, right on his doorstep, so still another dimension was added to Hunt's ever growing work load. Soon, press conferences, TV documentaries, filmed interviews, and reporters became part of his daily routine; so did the preparation of weekly progress bulletins. Despite the cold objectivity and meticulous phrasing of these bulletins, strange things seemed to happen to them between their departure from the offices of Navcomms and their arrival on the world's newspaper pages and wall display screens. Even stranger things happened in the minds of some people who read them.

One of the British Sunday papers presented just about all of the Old Testament in terms of the interventions of space beings as seen through the eyes of simple beholders. The plagues of Egypt were ecological disruptions deliberately brought about as warnings to the oppressors; flying saucers guided Moses through the Red Sea while the waters were diverted by nucleonic force fields; and the manna from heaven was formed from the hydrocarbon combustion products of thermonuclear propulsion units. A publisher in Paris observed the results, got the message, and commissioned a free-lancer to reexamine the life of Christ as a symbolic account of the apparent miracle workings of a Lunarian returning to Earth after a forty-eight-thousand-year meditation in the galactic wilderness.

"Authentic" reports that the Lunarians were still around abounded. They had built the pyramids, sunk Atlantis, and dug the Bosporus. There were genuine eyewitness accounts of Lunarian landings on Earth in modern times. Somebody had held a conversation with the pilot of a Lunarian spaceship two years before in the middle of the Colorado Desert. Every reference ever recorded to supernatural phenomena, apparitions, visitations, miracles, saints, ghosts, visions, and witches had a Lunarian connection.

But as the months passed and no dramatic revelations unfolded, the world began to turn elsewhere for new sensations. Reports of further findings became confined to the more serious scientific journals and proceedings of the professional societies. But the scientists on the project continued their work undisturbed.

Then a UNSA team erecting an optical observatory on the Lunar Farside detected unusual echoes on ultrasonics from about two hundred feet below the surface. They sank a shaft and discovered what appeared to be all that was left of the underground levels of another Lunarian base, or at any rate, some kind of construction. It was just a metal-walled box about ten feet high and as broad and as long as a small house; one end was missing, and about a quarter of the volume enclosed had filled up with dust and rock debris. In the space that was left at the end, they found the charred skeletons of eight more Lunarians, some pieces of furniture, a few items of technical equipment, and a heap of sealed metal containers. Whatever had formed the remainder of the structure that this gallery had been part of was gone without a trace.

The metal containers were later opened by the scientists at Westwood. Inside the cans was a selection of assorted foodstuffs, well preserved despite having been cooked. Presumably, whatever had done the cooking had also cooked the Lunarians. Most of the cans contained processed vegetables, meats, and sweet preparations; a few, however, yielded a number of fish, about the size of herrings and preserved intact.

When Danchekker's assistant dissected one of the fish and began looking inside, he couldn't make sense of what he found, so he called the professor down to the lab to ask what he made of it. Danchekker didn't go home until eight o'clock the next morning. A week later he announced to an incredulous Vic Hunt: "This specimen never swam in any of our oceans; it did not evolve from, nor is it in any way related to, any form of life that has ever existed on this planet!"

chapter eleven

The Apollo Seventeen Mission, in December 1972, had
marked the successful conclusion to man's first con-
certed effort to reach and explore first-hand a world
other than his own. After the Apollo program, NASA
activities were restricted, mainly as a result of the finan-
cial pressures exerted on the USA by the economic re-
cessions that came and went across the Western world
throughout that decade, by the politically inspired oil
crisis and various other crises manufactured in the Middle East and the lower half of Africa, and by the pro-
motion of the Vietnam War. During the mid and late
seventies, a succession of unmanned probes were dis-
patched to Mars, Venus, Mercury, and some of the
outer planets. When manned missions were resumed in
the 1980's, they focused on the development of various
types of space shuttle and on the construction of permanently manned orbiting laboratories and observatories,
the main objective being the consolidation of a firm
jumping-off point prior to resumed expansion outward.
Thus, for a period, the Moon was left once more on its
own, free to continue its billion-year contemplation of
the Universe without further interruption by man.

The information brought back by the Apollo astro-
nauts finally resolved the conflicting speculations concerning the Moon's nature and origins that had been
mooted by generations of Earth-bound observers. Soon
after the Solar System was formed, 4,500 million years
ago, give or take a few, the Moon became molten to
a considerable depth, possibly halfway to the center;
the heat was generated by the release of gravitational

energy as the Moon continued to accumulate. During the cooling that followed, the heavier, iron-bearing minerals sank toward the interior, while the less dense, aluminum-rich ones floated to the surface to form the highland crust. Continual bombardment by meteorites stirred up the mixture and complicated the process to some degree but by 4,300 million years ago the formation of the crust was virtually complete. The bombardment continued until 3,900 million years ago, by which time most of the familiar surface features already existed. From then until 3,200 million years ago, basaltic lavas flowed from the interior, induced in some places by remelting due to concentrations of radioactive heat sources below the surface, to fill in the impact basins and create the darker *maria*. The crust continued cooling to greater depths until molten material could no longer penetrate. Thereafter, all remained unchanging through the ages. Occasionally an additional impact crater appeared and falling dust gradually eroded the top millimeter of surface, but essentially, the Moon became a dead planet.

This history came from detailed observations and limited explorations of Nearside. Orbital observations of Farside suggested that much of the same story applied there also, and since this sequence was consistent with existing theory, nobody doubted its validity for many years after Apollo. Of course, details remained to be added, but the broad picture was convincingly clear. However, when man returned to the Moon in the strength and to stay, ground exploration of Farside threw up a completely different and totally unexpected story.

Although the surface of Farside looked much the same as Nearside to the distant observer, it proved at the microscopic level to have undergone something radically different in its history. Furthermore, as bases, launch sites, communications installations, and all the other paraphernalia that accompanied man wherever he went, began proliferating on Nearside, the methodical surface coverage that this entailed produced oddities there, too.

All the experiments performed on the rock samples brought back from the eight sites explored before the mid-seventies gave consistent results supporting the orthodox theories. When the number of sites grew to thousands, by far the majority of additional data confirmed them—but some curious exceptions were noted, exceptions which seemed to indicate that some of the features on Nearside ought, rightfully, to be on Farside.

None of the explanations hazarded were really conclusive. This made little difference to the executives and officers of UNSA, since by that time the pattern of Lunar activity had progressed from that of pure scientific research to one of intense engineering operations. Only the academic fraternity of a few universites found time to ponder and correspond on the spectral inconsistencies between dust samples. So for many years the well-documented problem of "lunar hemispheric anomalies" remained filed, along with a million and one other items, in the "Awaiting Explanation" drawer of science.

A methodical review of the current state of knowledge in any branch of science that might have a bearing on the Lunarian problem was a routine part of Group L's business. Anything to do with the Moon was, naturally, high on the list of things to check up on, and soon the group had amassed enough information to start a small library on the subject. Two junior physicists, who didn't duck quickly enough when Hunt was giving out assignments, were charged with the Herculean task of sifting through all this data. It took them some time for them to get around to the topic of hemispheric anomalies. When they did, they found reports of a series of dating experiments performed some years previously by a nucleologist named Kronski at the Max Planck Institute in Berlin. The data that appeared in those reports caused the two physicists to drop everything and seek out Hunt immediately.

After a long discussion, Hunt made a vi-phone call to a Dr. Saul Steinfield of the Department of Physics of the University of Nebraska, who specialized in Lunar phenomena. As a consequence of that call, Hunt made arrangements for the deputy head of group L to take charge for a few days, and he flew north to Omaha early the next morning. Steinfield's secretary met Hunt at the airport, and within an hour Hunt was standing in one of the physics department laboratories, contemplating a three-foot-diameter model of the Moon.

"The crust isn't evenly distributed," Steinfield said, waving toward the model. "It's a lot thicker on Farside than on Nearside—something that has been known for a long time, ever since the first artificial satellites were hung around the Moon in the nineteen sixties. The center of mass is about two kilometers away from the geometric center."

"And there's no obvious reason," Hunt mused.

Steinfield's flailing arm continued to describe wild circles around the sphere in front of them. "There's no reason for the crust to solidify a lot thicker on one side, sure, but that doesn't really matter, because that's not the way it happened. The material that makes up the Farside surface is much younger than anything anybody ever believed existed on the Moon in any quantity up until about, ah, thirty or so years back—one hell of a lot younger! But you know that—that's why you're here."

"You don't mean it was formed recently," Hunt stated.

Steinfield shook his head vigorously from side to side, causing the two tufts of white hair that jutted from the sides of his otherwise smooth head to wave about in a frenzy. "No. We can tell that it's about as old as the rest of the Solar System. What I mean is—it hasn't been where it is very long."

He caught Hunt's shoulder and half turned him to face a wall chart showing a sectional view through the Lunar center. "You can see it on this. The red shell is the original outer crust going right around—it's roughly circular, as you'd expect. On Farside—here—this blue stuff sits on top of it and wasn't added very long ago."

"On top of what used to be the surface."

"Exactly. Somebody dumped a couple of billion tons of junk down on the old crust—but only on this side."

"And that's been verified pretty conclusively?" Hunt asked, just to be doubly sure.

"Yeah . . . yeah. Enough bore holes and shafts have been sunk all over Farside to tell us pretty closely where the old surface was. I'll show you something over here . . ." A major section of the far wall comprised nothing but rows of small metal drawers, each with its own neatly lettered label, extending from floor to ceiling. Steinfield walked across the room, and stooped to scan the labels, at the same time mumbling to himself semi-intelligibly. With a sudden "That's it!" he pounced on one of the drawers, opened it, and returned bearing a closed glass container about the size of a small pickle jar. It contained a coarse piece of a light gray rocky substance that glittered faintly in places, mounted on a wire support.

"This is a fairly common KREEP basalt from Farside. It—"

" 'Creep' ?"

"Rich in potassium—that is, K—rare earth elements, and phosphorus: KREEP."

"Oh—I see."

"Compounds like this," Steinfield continued, "make up a lot of the highlands. This one solidified around 4.1 billion years ago. Now, by analyzing the isotope products produced by cosmic-ray exposure, we can tell how long it's been lying on the surface. Again, the figure for this one comes out at about 4,100 million years."

Hunt looked slightly puzzled. "But that's normal. It's what you'd expect, isn't it?"

"If it had been lying on the surface, yes. But this came from the bottom of a shaft over seven hundred feet deep! In other words, it was on the surface for all that time—then suddenly it's seven hundred feet down." Steinfield gestured toward the wall chart again. "As I said, we find the same thing all over Farside. We can estimate how far down the old surface used to be. Below it we find old rocks and structures that go way back, just like on Nearside; above it everything's a mess—the rock all got pounded up and lots of melting took place when the garbage came down, all the way up to what's now the surface. It's what you'd expect."

Hunt nodded his agreement. The energy released by that amount of mass being stopped dead in its tracks would have been phenomenal.

"And nobody knows where it came from?" he asked.

Steinfield repeated his head-shaking act. "Some people say that a big meteorite shower must have got in the way of the Moon. That may be true—it's never been argued conclusively one way or the other. The composition of the garbage isn't really like a lot of meteorites, though—it's closer to the Moon itself. It's as if they were made out of the same stuff—that's why it looks the same from higher up. You have to look at the microstructure to see the things I've been talking about."

Hunt examined the specimen curiously for a while in silence. At length he laid it carefully on the top of one of the benches. Steinfield picked it up and returned it to its drawer.

"Okay," Hunt said as Steinfield rejoined him. "Now, what about the Farside surface?"

"Kronski and company."

"Yes—as we disccussed yesterday."

"The Farside surface craters were made by the tail end of the garbage-dumping process, unlike the Nearside craters, which came from meteorite impacts oh . . . a few billion years back. In rock samples from around the rims of Farside craters we find that things like the activity levels of long half-life elements are very low— for instance, aluminum twenty-six and chlorine thirty-six; also the rates of absorption of hydrogen, helium, and inert gases from the Solar wind. Things like that tell us that those rocks haven't been lying there very long; and since they got where they were by being thrown out of the craters, the craters haven't been there very long, ei-

ther." Steinfield made an exaggerated empty-handed
gesture. "The rest you know. People like Kronski have
done all the figuring and put them at around fifty thousand years old—yesterday!" He waited for a few seconds. "There must be a Lunarian connection somewhere. The number sounds like too much of a
coincidence to me."

Hunt frowned for a while and studied the detail of
the Farside hemisphere of the model. "And yet, you
must have known about all this for years," he said,
looking up. "Why the devil did you wait for us to call
you?"

Steinfield showed his hands again and held the pose
for a second or two. "Well, you UNSA people are
pretty smart cookies. I figured you already knew about
all this."

"We should have picked it up sooner, I admit," Hunt
agreed. "But we've been rather busy."

"Guess so," Steinfield murmured. "Anyhow, there's
even more to it. I've told you all the consistent things.
Now I'll tell you some of the funny things . . . ." He
broke off as if just struck by a new thought. "I'll tell you
about the funny things in a second. How about a cup of
coffee?"

"Great."

Steinfield lit a Bunsen burner, filled a large laboratory beaker from the nearest tap, and positioned it on a
tripod over the flame. Then he squatted down to rum-
mage in the cupboard beneath the bench and at last
emerged triumphantly with two battered enamel mugs.

"First funny thing: The distribution of samples that
we dig up on Farside that have a history of recent radioactive exposure doesn't match the distribution or
strength of the activity sources. There ought to be
sources clustered in places where there aren't."

"How about the meteorite storm including some
highly active meteorites?" Hunt suggested.

"No, won't wash," Steinfield answered, looking along
a shelf of glass jars and eventually selecting one that
contained a reddish-brown powder and was labeled

"Ferric Oxide." "If there were meteorites like that, bits of them should still be around. But the distribution of active elements in the garbage is pretty even—about normal for most rocks." He began spooning the powder into the mugs. Hunt inclined his head apprehensively in the direction of the jar.

"Coffee doesn't seem to last long around here if you leave it lying around in coffee jars," Steinfield explained. He nodded toward a door that led into the room next-door and bore the sign "RESEARCH STUDENTS." Hunt nodded understandingly.

"Vaporized?" Hunt tried.

Again Steinfield shook his head.

"In that case they wouldn't have been in proximity to the rock long enough to produce the effects observed." He opened another jar marked "Disodium Hydrogen Phosphate." "Sugar?"

"Second funny thing," Steinfield continued. "Heat balance. We know how much mass came down, and from the way it fell, we can figure its kinetic energy. We also know from statistical sampling how much energy needed to be dissipated to account for the melting and structural deformations; also, we know how much energy gets produced by underground radioactivity and where. Problem: The equations don't balance; you'd need more energy to make what happened happen than there was available. So, where did the extra come from? The computer models of this are very complex and there could be errors in them, but that's the way it looks right now."

Steinfield allowed Hunt to digest this while he picked up the beaker with a pair of tongs and proceeded to fill the mugs. Having safely completed this operation, he began filling his pipe, still silent.

"Any more?" Hunt asked at last, reaching for his own cigarette case.

Steinfield nodded affirmatively. "Nearside exceptions. Most of the Nearside craters fit with the classic model: old. However, there are some scattered around that don't fit the pattern; cosmic-ray dating puts them at approximately the same age as those on Farside. The usual explanation is that some strays from the recent Farside bombardment overshot around to the Nearside . . ." He shrugged. "But there are peculiarities in some instances that don't really support that."

"Like?"

"Like some of the glasses and breccia formations show heating patterns that aren't consistent with recent impact . . . I'll show you what I mean later."

Hunt turned this new information over in his mind as he lit a cigarette and sipped his drink. It tasted like coffee, anyway.

"And that's the last funny thing?"

"Yep, that's about the broad outline. No, wait a minute—last funny thing plus one. How come none of the meteorites in the shower hit Earth? Plenty of eroded remains of terrestrial meteorite craters have been identified and dated. All the computer simulations say that there should be a peak of abnormal activity at around this time, judging from how big the heap of crud that hit the Moon must have been. But there aren't any signs of one, even allowing for the effects of the atmosphere."

Hunt and Steinfield spent the rest of that day and all of the next sifting through figures and research reports that went back many years. Hunt did not sleep at all during the following night, but smoked a pack of cigarettes and consumed a gallon of coffee while he stared at the walls of his hotel room and twisted the new information into every contortion his mind could devise.

Fifty thousand years ago the Lunarians were on the Moon. Where they come from didn't really matter for the time being; that was another question. At about the same time an intense meteorite storm obliterated the Farside surface. Did the storm wipe out the Lunarians on the Moon? Possibly—but that wouldn't have had any effect on them back on whatever planet they had come from. If all the UNSA people on Luna were wiped out, it wouldn't make any lasting difference to Earth. So, what happened to the rest of the Lunarians? Why hadn't anybody seen them since? Had something else happened to them that was more widespread than whatever happened on the Moon? Could the something else have caused the meteorite storm? Could a second something else have both caused the first and extinguished the Lunarians in other places? Perhaps there was no connection? Unlikely.

Then there were the inconsistencies that Steinfield had talked about . . . . An absurd idea came from nowhere, which Hunt rejected impatiently. But as the night wore on, it kept coming back again with growing insistence. Over breakfast he decided that he had to know the story that lay below those billions of tons of rubble. There had to be some way of extracting enough information to reconstruct the characteristics of the surface just before the bombardment commenced. He put the question to Steinfield later on that morning, back in the lab.

Steinfield shook his head firmly. "We tried for over a year to make a picture like that. We had twelve programmers working on it. They got nowhere. It's too much of a mess down there—all ploughed up. All you get is garbage."

"How about a partial picture?" Hunt persisted. Was there any way that a contour map could be calculated, showing just the distribution on radiation sources immediately prior to the bombardment?"

"We tried that, too. You do get a degree of statistical clustering, yes. But there's no way we could tell where each individual sample was when it got irradiated. They would have been thrown miles by the impacts; a lot of them would have been bounced all over the place by repeat impacts. Nobody ever built a computer that could unscramble all that entropy. You're up against the second law of thermodynamics; if you ever built one, it wouldn't be a computer at all—it would be a refrigerator."

"What about a chemical approach? What techniques are available that might reveal where the prebombardment craters were? Could their 'ghosts' still be detected a thousand feet down below the surface?"

"No way!"

"There has to be some way of reconstructing what the surface used to look like."

"Did you ever try reconstructing a cow from a truckload of hamburger?"

They talked about it for another two days and into the nights at Steinfield's home and Hunt's hotel. Hunt told Steinfield why he needed the information. Steinfield told Hunt he was crazy. Then one morning, back at the laboratory, Hunt exclaimed, "The Nearside exceptions!"

"Huh?"

"The Nearside craters that date from the time of the storm. Some of them could be right from the beginning of it."

"So?"

"They didn't get buried like the first craters on Farside. They're intact."

"Sure—but they won't tell you anything new. They're from recent impacts, same as everything that's on the surface of Farside."

"But you said some of them showed radiation anomalies. That's just what I want to know more about."

"But nobody ever found any suggestion of what you're talking about."

"Maybe they weren't looking for the right things. They never had any reason to."

The physics department had a comprehensive collection of Lunar rock samples, a sizeable proportion of which comprised specimens from the interiors and vicinities of the young, anomalous craters on Nearside. Under Hunt's persistent coercion, Steinfield agreed to conduct a specially devised series of tests on them. He estimated that he would need a month to complete the work.

Hunt returned to Houston to catch up on developments there and a month later flew back to Omaha. Steinfield's experiments had resulted in a series of computer-generated maps showing anomalous Nearside craters. The craters divided themselves into two classes on the maps: those with characteristic irradiation patterns and those without.

"And another thing," Steinfield informed him. "The first class, those that show the pattern, have also got another thing in common that the second class hasn't got: glasses from the centers were formed by a different process. So now we've got anomalous anomalies on Nearside, too!"

Hunt spent a week in Omaha and then went directly to Washington to talk to a group of government scientists and to study the archives of a department that had ceased to exist more than fifteen years before. He then returned to Omaha once again and showed his findings to Steinfield. Steinfield persuaded the university authorities to allow selected samples from their collection to be loaned to the UNSA Mineralogy and Petrology Laboratories in Pasadena, California, for further testing of an extremely specialized nature, suitable equipment for which existed at only a few establishments in the world.

As a direct consequence of these tests, Caldwell authorized the issue of a top-priority directive to the UNSA bases at Tycho, Crisium, and some other Lunar locations, to conduct specific surveys in the areas of certain selected craters. A month after that, the first samples began arriving at Houston and were forwarded immediately to Pasadena; so were the large numbers of samples collected from deep below the surface of Farside.

The outcome of all this activity was summarized in a memorandum stamped "SECRET" and written on the anniversary of Hunt's first arrival in Houston.

9 September 2028

TO: G. Caldwell
      Executive Director
      Navigation and Communications
      Division

FROM: Dr. V. Hunt
      Section Head
      Special Assignment Group L

ANOMALIES OF LUNAR CRATERING

(1) <u>Hemispheric Anomalies</u>
For many years, radical differences have been known to exist between the nature and origins of Lunar Nearside and Farside surface features.

   (a) Nearside
Original Lunar surface from 4 billion years ago. Nearly all surface cratering caused by explosive release of kinetic energy by meteorite impacts. Some younger—e.g., Copernicus, 850 million years old.

   (b) Farside
Surface comprises large mass of recently added material to average depth circa 300 meters. Craters formed during final phase of this bombardment. Dating of these events coincides with Lunarian presence. Origin of bombardment uncertain.

(2) <u>Nearside Exceptions</u>
Known for approx. the last thirty years that some Nearside craters date from same period as those on Farside. Current theory ascribes them to overshoots from Farside bombardment.

(3) <u>Conclusion From Recent Research at Omaha and Pasadena</u>
All Nearside exceptions previously attributed to meteoritic impacts. This belief now considered incorrect. Two classes of exceptions now distinguished:

(a) Class I Exceptions
Confirmed as meteoritic
impacts occurring 50,000
years ago.

(b) Class II Exceptions
Differing from Class I in
irradiation history, formation
of glasses, absence of
impact corroboration and
positive results to tests
for elements hyperium, bonnevillium, genevium. Example:
Crater Lunar Catalogue
reference MB 3076/K2/E currently classed as meteoritic.
Classification erroneous.
Crater MB 3076/K2/E was made
by a nucleonic bomb. Other
cases confirmed. Investigations continuing.

(4) Farside Subsurface
Intensive sampling from depths
approximating that of the original
crust indicate widespread nucleonic detonations prior to
meteorite bombardment. Thermonuclear and fission reactions also
suspected but impossible to
confirm.

(5) Implications
(a) Sophisticated weapons used on
Luna at or near time of
Lunarian presence, mainly on
Farside. Lunarian involvement
implied but not proved.

(b) If Lunarians involved, possibility of more widespread
conflict embracing Lunarian
home planet. Possible cause
of Lunarian extinction.

> (c) Charlie was a member of more
> than a small, isolated expedi-
> tion to our Moon. A signifi-
> cant Lunarian presence on
> the Moon is indicated. Mainly
> concentrated on Farside.
> Practically all traces since
> obliterated by meteorite
> storm.

chapter twelve

Front page feature of the New York *Times,*
14 October 2028:

LUNARIAN PLANET LOCATED
Did Nuclear War Destroy Minerva?

Sensational new announcements by UN Space Arm
Headquarters, Washington, D.C., at last positively
identify the home planet of the Lunarian civilization,
known to have achieved space flight and reached
Earth's Moon fifty thousand years ago. Information
pieced together during more than a year of intense
work by teams of scientists based at the UNSA Navigation and Communications Division Headquarters,
Houston, Texas, shows conclusively that the Lunarians came from an Earth-like planet that once existed
in our own Solar System.

A tenth planet, christened Minerva after the Roman
goddess of wisdom, is now known to have existed approximately 250 million miles from the Sun between
the orbits of Mars and Jupiter, in the position now
occupied by the Asteroid Belt, and is firmly estab-

lished as having been the center of the Lunarian civilization.

In a further startling announcement, a UNSA spokesman stated that data collected recently at the Lunar bases, following research at the University of Nebraska, Omaha, and the UNSA Mineralogy and Petrology Laboratories, Pasadena, California, indicate that a large-scale nuclear conflict took place on the Moon at the time the Lunarians were there. The possibility that Minerva was destroyed in a full-scale nuclear holocaust of interplanetary dimensions cannot be ruled out.

Nucleonic Bombs Used at Crisium

Investigations in recent months at the University of Nebraska and Pasadena give positive evidence that nucleonic bombs have caused craters on the Moon previously attributed to meteorite impacts. H-bomb and A-bomb effects are also suspected but cannot be confirmed.

Dr. Saul Steinfield of the Department of Physics at the University of Nebraska explained: "For many years we have known that Lunar Farside craters are very much younger than most of the craters on Nearside. All the Farside craters, and a few of the Nearside ones, date from about the time of the Lunarians, and have always been thought to be meteoritic. Most of them, including all Farside ones, are. We have now proved, however, that some of the Nearside ones were made by bombs—for example, a few on the northern Periphery of Mare Crisium and a couple near Tycho. So far, we've identified twenty-three positively and have a long list to check out."

Further evidence collected from deep below the Farside surface indicates heavier bombing there than on Nearside. Obliteration of the original Farside surface by a heavy meteorite storm immediately after these events, accounts for only meteorite craters being found there today and makes detailed reconstruction of exactly what took place unlikely. "The evidence for higher activity on Farside is mainly statistical," said Steinfield yesterday. "There's no way you could figure anything specifiic—for example, an actual crater count—under all that garbage."

The new discoveries do not explain why the meteorite storm happened at this time. Professor Pierre Guillemont of the Hale Observatory commented: "Clearly, there could be a connection with the Lunarian presence. Personally, I would be surprised if the agreement in dates is just a coincidence, although that, of course, is possible. For the time being, it must remain an unanswered question."

Clues from ILIAD Mission

Startling confirmation that Minerva disintegrated to form the Asteroid Belt has been received from space. Examination of Asteroid samples carried out on board the spacecraft *Iliad,* launched from Luna fifteen months ago to conduct a survey of parts of the Belt, shows many Asteroids to be of recent origin. Data beamed back to Mission Control Center at UNSA Operational Command Headquarters, Galveston, Texas, gives cosmic-ray exposure times and orbit statistics pinpointing Minerva's disintegration at fifty thousand years ago.

Earth scientists are eagerly awaiting arrival of the first Asteroid material to be sent back from *Iliad,* which is due at Luna in six weeks time.

Lunarian Origin Mystery

Scientists do not agree that Lunarians necessarily originated on Minerva. Detailed physical examinations of "Charlie" (*Times,* 7 November 2027) shows Lunarian anatomy identical to that of humans and incapable of being the product of a separate evolutionary process, according to all accepted theory. Conversely, absence of traces of Lunarian history on Earth seems to rule out any possibility of terrestrial origins. This remains the main focus of controversy among the investigators.

In an exclusive interview, Dr. Victor Hunt, the British-born UNSA nucleonics expert coordinating Lunarian investigations from Houston, explained to a *Times* reporter: "We know quite a lot about Minerva now—its size, its mass, its climate, and how it rotated and orbited the Sun. Upstairs we've built a six-foot scale model of it that shows you every continent, ocean, river, mountain range, town, and city. Also, we know it supported an advanced civilization. We also know a lot about Charlie, including his place of birth, which is given on several of his personal documents as a town easily identified on Minerva. But that doesn't prove very much. My deputy was born in Japan, but both his parents come from Brooklyn. So until we know a lot more than we do, we can't even say for sure that the Minervan civilization and the Lunarian civilization were one and the same.

"It's possible the Lunarians originated on Earth and either went to live on Minerva or made contact with another race who were there already. Maybe the Lunarians originated on Minerva. We just don't know. Whichever alternative you choose, you've got problems."

Alien Marine Life Traced to Minerva

Professor Christian Danchekker, an eminent biologist at Westwood Laboratories, Houston, and also involved in Lunarian research from the beginning, confirmed that the alien species of fish discovered among foodstocks in the ruin of a Lunarian base on Lunar Farside several months ago (*Times,* 6 July 2028) appear to have been a life form native to Minerva. Markings on the containers in which the fish were preserved show that they came from a well-defined group of equatorial islands on Minerva. According to Professor Danchekker: "There is no question whatsoever that this species evolved on a planet other than Earth. It seems clear that the fish belong to an evolutionary line that developed on Minerva, and they were caught there by members of a group of colonists from Earth who established an extension of their civilization there."

The professor described the suggestion that the Lunarians might also be natives of Minerva as "ludicrous."

Despite a wealth of new information, therefore, much remains to be explained about recent events in the Solar System. Almost certainly, the next twelve months will see further exciting developments.

(See also the Special Supplement by our Science Editor on page 14.)

chapter thirteen

Captain Hew Mills, UN Space Arm, currently attached to the Solar System Exploration Program mission to the moons of Jupiter, stood gazing out of the transparent dome that surmounted the two-story Site Operations Control building. The building stood just clear of the ice, on a rocky knoll overlooking the untidy cluster of domes, vehicles, cabins, and storage tanks that went to make up the base he commanded. In the dim gray background around the base, indistinct shadows of rock buttresses and ice cliffs vanished and reappeared through the sullen, shifting vapors of the methane–ammonia haze. Despite his above-average psychological resilience and years of strict training, an involuntary shudder ran down his spine as he thought of the thin triple wall of the dome—all that separated him from this foreboding, poisonous, alien world, cold enough to freeze him as black as coal and as brittle as glass in seconds. Ganymede, largest of the moons of Jupiter, was, he thought, an awful place.

"Close-approach radars have locked on. Landing sequence is active. Estimated time to touchdown: three minutes, fifty seconds." The voice of the duty controller at one of the consoles behind Mills interrupted his broodings.

"Very good, Lieutenant," he acknowledged. "Do you have contact with Cameron?"

"There's a channel open on screen three, sir."

Mills moved around in front of the auxiliary console. The screen showed an empty chair and behind it an interior view of the low-level control room. He pressed the call button, and after a few seconds the face of Lieutenant Cameron moved into the viewing angle.

"The brass are due in three minutes," Mills advised. "Everything okay?"

"Looking good, sir."

Mills resumed his position by the wall of the dome and noted with satisfaction the three tracked vehicles lurching into line to take up their reception positions. Minutes ticked by.

"Sixty seconds," the duty controller announced. "Descent profile normal. Should make visual contact any time now."

A patch of fog above the landing pads in the central area of the base darkened and slowly materialized into the blurred outline of a medium-haul surface transporter, sliding out of the murk, balanced on its exhausts with its landing legs already fully extended. As the transporter came to rest on one of the pads and its shock absorbers flexed to dispose of the remaining momentum, the reception vehicles began moving forward. Mills nodded to himself and left the dome via the stairs that led down to ground level.

Ten minutes later, the first reception vehicle halted outside the Operations Control building and an extending tube telescoped out to dock with its airlock. Major Stanislow, Colonel Peters, and a handful of aides walked through into the outer access chamber, where they were met by Mills and a few other officers. Mutual introductions were concluded, and without further preliminaries the party ascended to the first floor and proceeded through an elevated walkway into the adjacent dome, constructed over the head of number-three shaft. A labyrinth of stairs and walkways brought them eventually to number-three high-level airlock anteroom. A capsule was waiting beyond the airlock. For the next four minutes they plummeted down, down, deep into the ice crust of Ganymede.

They emerged through another airlock into number-three low-level anteroom. The air vibrated with the humming and throbbing of unseen machines. Beyond the anteroom, a short corridor brought them at last to the low-level control room. It was a maze of consoles and equipment cubicles, attended by perhaps a dozen operators, all intent on their tasks. One of the longer walls, constructed completely from glass, gave a panoramic view down over the workings in progress outside the control room. Lieutenant Cameron joined them as they lined up by the glass to take in the spectacle beyond.

They were looking out over the floor of an enormous cathedral, over nine hundred feet long and a hundred feet high, hewn and melted out of the solid ice. Its rough-formed walls glistened white and gray in the glare of countless arc lights. The floor was a litter of steel-mesh roadways, cranes, gantries, girders, pipes, tubes, and machinery of every description. The left-side wall, stretching away to the far end of the tunnel, carried a lattice of ladders, scaffolding, walkways, and cabins that extended up to the roof. All over the scene, scores of figures in ungainly heavy-duty spacesuits bustled about in a frenzy of activity, working in an atmosphere of pressurized argon to eliminate any risk of explosion from methane and the other gases released from the melted ice. But all eyes were fixed on the right-hand wall of the tunnel.

For almost the entire length, a huge, sweeping wall of smooth, black metal reared up from the floor and curved up and over, out of sight above their heads to be lost below the roof of the cavern. It was immense—just a part of something vast and cylindrical, lying on its side, the whole of which must have stretched far down into the ice below floor level. At the near end, outside the control room, a massive, curving wing flared out of the cylinder and spanned the cavern above their heads like a bridge, before disappearing into the ice high on the far left. At intervals along the base of the wall, where metal and ice met, a series of holes six feet or so across marked the ends of the network of pilot tunnels that had been driven all around and over and under the object.

It was far larger than a Vega. How long it had lain there, entombed beneath the timeless ice sheets of Ganymede, nobody knew. But the computations of field-vector resultants collected from the satellites had been right; there certainly had been something big down here—and it hadn't been just ore deposits.

"Ma-an," breathed Stanislow, after staring for a long time. "So that's it, huh?"

"That is big!" Peters added with a whistle. The aides echoed the sentiments dutifully.

Stanislow turned to Mills. "Ready for the big moment, then, Captain?"

"Yes, sir," Mills confirmed. He indicated a point about two hundred feet away where a group of figures was gathered close to the wall of the hull, surrounded by an assortment of equipment. Beside them a rectangular section of the skin about eight feet square had been cut away. "First entry point will be there—approximately amidships. The outer hull is double layered; both layers have been penetrated. Inside is an inner hull . . ." For the benefit of the visitors, he gestured toward a display positioned near the observation window showing the aperture in close-up. "Preliminary drilling shows that it's a single layer. The valves that you can see projecting from the inner hull were inserted to allow samples of the internal atmosphere to be taken before opening it up. Also, the cavity behind the access point has been argon-flooded."

Mills turned to Cameron before going on to describe

further details of the operation. "Lieutenant, carry out a final check of communications links, please."

"Aye, aye, sir." Cameron walked back to the supervisory console at the end of the room and scanned the array of screens.

"Ice Hole to Subway. Come in, please."

The face of Commander Stracey, directing activities out near the hull, moved into view, encased in its helmet. "All checks completed and go," he reported. "Standing by, ready to proceed."

"Ice Hole to Pithead. Report transmission quality."

"All clear, vision and audio," responded the duty controller from the dome far above them.

"Ice Hole to Ganymede Main." Cameron addressed screen three, which showed Foster at Main Base, situated seven hundred miles away to the south.

"Clear."

"Ice Hole to Jupiter Four. Report, please."

"All channels clear and checking positive." The last acknowledgment came from the deputy mission director on screen four, speaking from his nerve center in the heart of the mile-long Jupiter Mission Four command ship, at that moment orbiting over two thousand miles up over Ganymede.

"All channels positive and ready to proceed, sir," Cameron called to Mills.

"Carry on, then, Lieutenant."

"Aye, aye, sir."

Cameron passed the order to Stracey, and out by the hull the ponderous figures lumbered into action, swinging forward a rock-drill supported from an overhead gantry. The group by the window watched in silence as the bit chewed relentlessly into the inner wall. Eventually the drill was swung back.

"Initial penetration complete," Stracey's voice informed them. "Nothing visible inside."

An hour later, a pattern of holes adorned the exposed expanse of metal. When lights were shone through and a TV probe inserted, the screen showed snatches of a large compartment crammed with ducts and machinery.

Shortly afterward, Stracey's team began cutting out the panel with torches. Mills invited Peters and Stanislow to come and observe the operations first-hand. The trio left the control room, descended to the lower floor, and a few minutes later emerged, clad in spacesuits, through the airlock onto the tunnel floor. As they arrived at the aperture, the rectangle of metal was just being swung aside.

The spotlights confirmed the general impression obtained via the drill holes. When preliminary visual examinations were completed, two sergeants who had been standing by stepped forward. Communications lines were plugged into their backpacks and they were handed TV cameras trailing cables, flashlights, and a pouch of tools and accessories. At the same time, other members of the team were smoothing over the jagged edges of the hole with pads of adhesive plastic to prevent tearing of the lines. An extending aluminum ladder was lowered into the hole and secured. The first sergeant to enter turned about on the edge of the hole, carefully located the top rung with his feet, and inch by inch disappeared down into the chamber. When he had found a firm footing, the second followed.

For twenty minutes they clambered through the mechanical jungle, twisting and turning among the chaotic shadows cast by the lights pouring in through the hole above. Progress was slow; they had difficulty finding level surfaces to move on, since the ship appeared to be lying on its side. But foot by foot, the lines continued to snake sporadically down into the darkness. Eventually the sergeants stopped before the noseward bulkhead of the compartment. The screens outside showed their way barred by a door leading through to whatever lay forward; it was made of a steely-gray metal and looked solid. It was also about ten feet high by four wide. A long conference produced the decision that there was no alternative but for them to return to where the hole had been cut to collect drills, torches, and all the other gadgetry needed to go through the whole drilling, purging, argon-filling, and cutting routine all over again. From the look of the door, it could be a long job. Mills, Stanislow, and Peters went back to the control room, collected the remainder of their party, and went to the surface installations for lunch. They returned three hours later.

Behind the bulkhead was another machinery compartment, as confusing as the first but larger. This one had many doors leading from it—all closed. The two sergeants selected one at random in the ceiling above their heads, and while they were cutting through it, others descended into the first and second compartments to position rollers for minimizing the drag of their trailing cables, which was beginning to slow them down appreciably. When the door was cut, a second team relieved the first.

They used another ladder to climb up through the door and found themselves standing on what was supposed to be the wall of a long corridor running toward the nose of the ship. A succession of closed doors, beneath their feet and over their heads, passed across the screens outside. Over two hundred feet of cabling had disappeared into the original entry point.

"We're just passing the fifth bulkhead since entering the corridor," the commentary on the audio channel informed the observers. "The walls are smooth, and appear to be metallic, but covered with a plastic material. It's coming away in most places. The floor up one side is black and looks rubbery. There are lots of doors in both walls, all big like the first one. Some have . . ."

"Just a second, Joe," the voice of the speaker's companion broke in. "Swing the big light down here . . . by your feet. See, the door you're standing on slides to the side. It's not closed all the way."

The screens showed a pair of standard-issue heavy-duty UNSA boots, standing on a metal panel in the middle of a pool of light. The boots shuffled to one side to reveal a black gap, about twelve inches wide, running down one side of the panel. They then stepped off the panel and onto the surrounding area as their owner evidently inspected the situation.

"You're right," Joe's voice announced at last. "Let's see if it'll budge."

There then followed a jumbled sequence of arms, legs, walls, ceilings, lightness, and darkness as TV cameras and lamps exchanged hands and were waved about. When a stable picture resulted, it showed two heavily clad arms braced across the gap. Eventually:

"No dice. Stuck solid."

"How about the jack?"

"Yeah, maybe. Pass it down, willya?"

A long dialogue followed during which the jack was maneuvered into place and expanded. It slipped off. Muttered curses. Another try. And then:

"It's moving! Come on, baby . . . let's have a bit more light . . . I think it'll go easy now . . . See if you can get a foot against it . . ."

On the monitors the gray slab graunched gradually out of the picture. A black, bottomless pit fell away beneath.

"The door is about two-thirds open," a breathless voice resumed. "It's gummed up there and won't go any further. We're gonna have a quick looksee around from up here, then we'll have to come back to get another ladder. Can somebody have one ready at the door that leads up into this corridor?"

The camera closed in on the pitch-black oblong. A few seconds later a circle of light appeared in the scene, picking out part of the far wall. The light began moving around inside and the camera followed. Banks of what appeared to be electronic equipment . . . corners of cubicles . . . legs of furniture . . . sections of bulkhead . . . moved through the circle.

"There's a lot of loose junk down at that end . . . Move the light around a bit . . ." Several colored cylinders in a heap, about the size of jelly jars . . . something like a braided belt, lying in a tangle . . . a small gray box with buttons on one face . . .

"What was that? Go over a bit, Jerry . . . No, a bit more to the left."

Something white. A bar of white.

"*Jeez!* Look at that! Jerry, will you look at that?"

The skull, grinning up out of the pool of eerie white light, startled even the watchers out in the tunnel. But it was the size of the skeleton that stunned them; no man had ever boasted a chest that compared with those massive hoops of bone. But besides that, even the most inexpert among the observers could see that whatever the occupants of this craft had been, they bore no resemblance to man.

The stream of data taken in by the cameras flashed back to preprocessors in the low-level control room, and from there via cable to the surface of Ganymede. After encoding by the computers in the Site Operations Control building, it was relayed by microwave repeaters seven hundred miles to Ganymede Main Base, restored to full strength, and redirected up to the orbiting command ship. Here, the message was fed into the message exchange and scheduling processor complex, transformed into high-power laser modulations, and slotted into the main outgoing signal beam to Earth. For over an hour the data streaked across the Solar System, covering 186,000 miles every second, until the sensors of the long-range relay beacon, standing in Solar orbit not many million miles outside that of Mars, fished it out of the void, a microscopic fraction of its original power. Retransmission from here found the Deep Space Link Station, lodged in Trojan equilibrium with Earth and Luna, and eventually a synchronous communications satellite hanging high over the central USA, which beamed it down to a ground station near San Antonio. A landline network completed the journey to UNSA Mission Control, Galveston, where the information was greedily consumed by the computers of Operational Command Headquarters.

The Jupiter Four command ship had taken eleven months to reach the giant planet. Within four hours of the event, the latest information to be gathered by the mission was safely lodged in the data banks of UN Space Arm.

chapter fourteen

The discovery of the giant spaceship, frozen under the ice field of Ganymede, was a sensation but, in a sense, not something totally unexpected. The scientific world had more or less accepted as fact that an advanced civilization had once flourished on Minerva; indeed, if the arguments of the orthodox evolutionists were accepted, at least two planets—Minerva and Earth—had supported high-technology civilizations to some extent at about the same time. It did not come as a complete surprise, therefore, that man's persistent nosing around the Solar System should uncover more evidence of its earlier inhabitants. What did surprise everybody was the obvious anatomical difference between the Ganymeans—as the beings on board the ship soon came to be called—and the common form shared by the Lunarians and mankind.

To the still unresolved question of whether the Lunarians and the Minervans had been one and the same or not, there was immediately added the further riddle: Where had the Ganymeans come from, and had they any connection with either? One bemused UNSA scientist summed up the situation by declaring that it was about time UNSA established an Alien Civilizations Division to sort out the whole damn mess!

The pro-Danchekker faction quickly interpreted the new development as full vindication of evolutionary theory and of the arguments they had been promoting all along. Clearly, two planets in the Solar System had evolved intelligent life at around the same period in the past; the Ganymeans had evolved on Minerva and the

Lunarians had evolved on Earth. They came independently from different lines and that was why they were different. Lunarian pioneers made contact with the Ganymeans and settled on Minerva—that was how Charlie had come to be born there. Extreme hostilities broke out between the two civilizations at some point, resulting in the extinction of both and the destruction of Minerva. The reasoning was consistent, plausible, and convincing. Against it, the single objection—that no evidence of any Lunarian civilization on Earth had ever been detected—began to look more lonely and more feeble every day. Deserters left the can't-be-of-Earth-origin camp in droves to join Danchekker's growing legions. Such was his gain in prestige and credibility that it seemed perfectly natural for his department to assume responsibility for conducting the preliminary evaluation of the data coming in from Jupiter.

Despite his earlier skepticism, Hunt too found the case compelling. He and a large part of Group L's staff spent much time searching every available archive and record from such fields as archeology and paleontology for any reference that could be a pointer to the one-time existence of an advanced race on Earth. They even delved into the realms of ancient mythology and combed various pseudoscientific writings to see if anything could be extracted that was capable of substantiation, that suggested the works of superbeings in the past. But always the results were negative.

While all this was going on, things began to happen in an area where progress had all but ground to a halt for many months. Linguistics had run into trouble: The meager contents of the documents found about Charlie's person simply had not contained enough information to make great inroads into deciphering a whole new, alien language. Of the two small books, one—that containing the maps and tables and resembling a handy pocket reference—together with the loose documents, had been translated in parts and had yielded most of the fundamental data about Minerva and quite a lot about Charlie. The second book contained a series of dated entries in handwritten script, but despite repeated attempts, it had obstinately defied decoding.

This situation changed dramatically some weeks after the opening up of the underground remains of the devastated Lunarian base on Lunar Farside. Among the pieces of equipment included in that find had been a metal drum, containing a series of glass plates, rather like the magazines of some slide projectors. Closer examination of the plates revealed them to be simple projection slides, each holding a closely packed matrix of microdot images which, under a microscope, were seen to be pages of printed text. Constructing a system of lamps and lenses to project them onto a screen was straightforward, and in one fell swoop Linguistics became the owners of a miniature Lunarian library. Results followed in months.

Don Maddson, head of the linguistics section, rummaged through the litter of papers and files that swamped the large table standing along the left-hand wall of his office, selected a loosely clipped wad of typed notes, and returned to the chair behind his desk.

"There's a set of these on its way up to you," he said to Hunt, who was sitting in the chair opposite. "I'll leave you to read the details for yourself later. For now, I'll just sum up the general picture."

"Fine," Hunt said. "Fire away."

"Well, for a start, we know a bit more about Charlie. One of the documents found in a pouch on the backpack appears to be something like army pay records. It gives an abbreviated history of some of the things he did and a list of the places he was posted to—that kind of thing."

"Army? Was he in the army, then?"

Maddson shook his head. "Not exactly. From what we can gather, they didn't differentiate much between civilian and military personnel in terms of how their society was structured. It's more like everybody belonged to different branches of the same big organization."

"A sort of last word in totalitarianism?"

"Yeah, that's about it. The State ran just about everything; it dominated every walk of life and imposed a rigid discipline everywhere. You went where you were sent and did what you were told to do; in most cases, that meant into industry, agriculture, or the military forces. Whatever you did, the State was your boss anyway—that's what I meant when I said they were all different branches of the same big organization."

"Okay. Now, about the pay records?"

"Charlie was born on Minerva, we know that. So were his parents. His father was some kind of machine operator; his mother worked in industry, too, but we can't make out the exact occupation. The records also tell us where he went to school, for how long, where he took his military training—everybody seemed to go through some kind of military training—and where he learned about electronics. It tells us all the dates, too."

"So he was something like an electronics engineer, was he?" Hunt asked.

"Sort of. More of a maintenance engineer than a design or development engineer. He seems to have specialized in military equipment—there's a long list of postings to combat units. The last one is interesting . . ." Maddson selected a sheet and passed it across to Hunt. "That's a translation of the last page of postings. The final entry gives the name of a place and, alongside it, a description which, when translated literally, means 'off-planet.' That's probably the Lunarian name for whatever part of our Moon he was sent to."

"Interesting," Hunt agreed. "You've found out quite a lot more about him."

"Yep, we've got him pretty well taped. If you convert their dates into our units, he was about thirty-two years old at the date of his last posting. Anyhow, that's all really incidental; you can read the details. I was going to run over the picture we're getting of the kind of world he was born into." Maddson paused to consult his notes again. Then he resumed: "Minerva was a dying world. At the time we're talking about, the last cold period of the Ice Age was approaching its peak.

I'm told that ice ages are Solar-System-wide phenomena; Minerva was a lot farther from the Sun than here, so as you can imagine, things were pretty bleak there."

"You've only got to look at the size of those ice caps," Hunt commented.

"Yes, exactly. And it was getting worse. The Lunarian scientists figured they had less than a hundred years to go before the ice sheets met and blanketed the whole planet completely. Now, as you'd expect, they had studied astronomy for centuries—centuries before Charlie's time, that is—and they'd known for a long time that things were going to get worse before they got better. So, they'd reached the conclusion, way back, that the only way out was to escape to another world. The problem, of course, was that for generations after they got the idea, nobody knew anything about how to do something about it. The answer had to lie somewhere along the line of better science and better technology. It became kind of a racial goal—the one thing that mattered, that generation after generation worked toward—the development of the sciences that would get them to places they knew existed, before the ice wiped out the whole race."

Maddson pointed to another pile of papers on the corner of his desk. "This was the prime objective that the State was set up to achieve, and because the stakes were so high, everything was subordinated to that objective. Hence, from birth to death the individual was subordinated to the needs of the State. It was implied in everything they wrote and drummed into them from the time they were knee-high. Those papers are a translation of a kind of catechism they had to memorize at school; it reads like Nazi stuff from the nineteen thirties." He stopped at that point and looked at Hunt expectantly.

Hunt looked puzzled. After a moment he said, "This doesn't quite make sense. I mean—how could they be striving to develop space flight if they were colonists from Earth? They must have already developed it."

Maddson gave an approving nod. "Thought you might say that."

"But . . . it's bloody silly."

"I know. It implies they must have evolved on Minerva from scratch—unless they came from Earth, forgot everything they knew, and had to learn it all over. But that also sounds crazy to me."

"Me. too." Hunt thought for a long time. At last he shook his head with a sigh. "Doesn't make sense. Anyhow, what else is there?"

"Well, we've got the general picture of a totally authoritarian State, demanding unquestioning obedience from the individual and controlling just about everything that moves. Everything needs a license; there are travel licenses, off-work licenses, sick-ration licenses—even procreation licenses. Everything is in short supply and rationed by permits—food, every kind of commodity, fuel, light, accommodation—you name it. And to keep everybody in line, the State operates a propaganda machine like you never dreamed of. To make things worse, the whole planet was desperately short of every kind of mineral. That slowed them down a lot. Despite their concentrated effort, their rate of technological progress was probably not as fast as you'd think. Maybe a hundred years didn't give them as long as it sounds." Maddson turned some sheets, scanned the next one briefly, and then went on. "To make matters worse still, they also had a big political problem."

"Go on."

"Now, we're assuming that as their civilization developed, it followed similar lines to ours—first tribes, then villages, towns, nations, and so on. Seems reasonable. So, somewhere along the way they started discovering the different sciences, same as we did. As you'd expect, the same ideas started occuring to different people in different places at around the same time—like, we've gotta get outa this place. As these ideas became accepted, the Lunarians seem to have figured also that there just weren't sufficient resources for more than a few lucky ones to make it. No way were they going to get a whole planet full of people out."

"So they fought about it," Hunt offered.

"That's right. The way I picture it, lots of nations grew up, all racing each other, as well as the ice, to get the technological edge. Every other one was a rival, so they fought it out. Another thing that made them fight was the mineral shortage, especially the shortage of metallic ores." Maddson pointed at a map of Minerva mounted above the table. "See those dots on the ice sheets? Most of them were a combination of fortress and mining town. They dug right down through the ice to get at the deposits, and the army was there to make sure they kept the stuff."

"And that was the way life was. Mean people, eh?"

"Yeah, for generation after generation." Maddson shrugged. "Who knows? Maybe if we were freezing over fast, we'd be forced in the same direction. Anyhow, the situation had complications. They had the problem of having to divide their efforts and resources between two different demands all the time: first, developing a technology that would support mass interplanetary travel and, second, armaments and the defense organization to protect it—and there weren't a lot of resources to divide in the first place. Now, how would you solve a problem like that?"

Hunt pondered for a while.

"Cooperate?" he tried.

"Forget it. They didn't think that way."

"Only one other strategy possible, then: Wipe out the opposition first and then concentrate everything on the main objective."

Maddson nodded solidly. "That is exactly what they did. War, or near war, was pretty well a natural way of life all through their history. Gradually the smaller fish were eliminated until, by the time we get to Charlie, there are only two superpowers left, each dominating one of the two big equatorial continental land masses . . ." He pointed at the map again. ". . . Cerios and

Lambia. From various references, we know Charlie was a Cerian."

"All set for the big showdown, then."

"Check. The whole planet was one big fortress–factory. Every inch of surface was covered by hostile missiles; the sky was full of orbiting bombs that could be dropped anywhere. We get the impression that relative to the pattern of our own civilization, their armaments programs had taken a bigger share than space research and had progressed faster." Maddson shrugged again. "The rest you can guess."

Hunt nodded slowly and thoughtfully. "It all fits," he mused. "It must have been a huge con, though. I mean, even from whichever side won, only a handful would have been able to get away in the end; I suppose they'd have been the ruling clique and its minions. Christ! No wonder they needed good propaganda; they—"

Hunt stopped in midsentence and looked at Maddson with a curious expression. "Just a minute—there's something else in all this that doesn't add up." He paused to collect his thoughts. "They had already developed interplanetary travel—how else did they get to our Moon?"

"We wondered that," Maddson said. "The only thing we could think of was that maybe they'd already figured on making for Earth eventually—that had to be the obvious choice. Maybe they were capable of sending a scouting group to stake the place out, but didn't have full-scale mass-transportation capacity yet. Probably they weren't too far away from their goal when they blew it. Perhaps if they'd pooled their marbles at that point instead of starting a crazy war over it, things might have been different."

"Sounds plausible," Hunt agreed. "So Charlie could have been part of a reconnaissance mission sent on ahead, only the opposition had the same idea and they bumped into each other. Then they started blowing holes in our Moon. Disgraceful."

A short silence ensued.

"There's another thing I don't get, either," Hunt said, rubbing his chin.

"What's that?"

"Well, the opposition—the Lambians. Everybody in Navcomms is going around saying that the war that clobbered Minerva was fought between colonists from Earth—that must be Charlie's lot, the Cerians—and an alien race that belonged to Minerva—the Ganymeans, who, from what you said, would be the Lambians. We said a moment ago that this idea of the Cerians being from Earth doesn't make sense, because if they had originated there, they wouldn't be trying to develop space flight. We can't be one hundred percent certain of that because something unusual could have happened, such as the colony being cut off for a few thousand years for some reason. But you can't say that about the Lambians; they couldn't have been neck-and-neck rivals trying to develop space flight."

"They already had it, for sure," Maddson completed for him. "We sure as hell found them on Ganymede."

"Quite. And that ship was no beginner's first attempt, either. You know, I'm beginning to think that whoever the Lambians were, they weren't Ganymeans."

"I think you're right," Maddson confirmed. "The Ganymeans were a totally different biological species. Wouldn't you expect that if they were the opposition in Lambia, somehow it would show up in the Lunarian writings? But it doesn't. Everything we've examined suggests that the Cerians and the Lambians were simply different nations of the same race. For example, we've found extracts from what appear to be Cerian newspapers, which included political cartoons showing Lambian figures; the figures are drawn as human forms. That wouldn't be so if the Lambians looked anything like the Ganymeans must have looked."

"So it appears the Ganymeans had nothing to do with the war," Hunt concluded.

"Right."

"So where do they fit in?"

Maddson showed his empty palms. "That's the funny

thing. They don't seem to fit anywhere—at least, we haven't even found anything that looks like a reference to them."

"Maybe they're just a big red herring, then. I mean, we've only supposed that they came from Minerva; nothing actually demonstrates that they did. Perhaps they never had anything to do with the place at all."

"Could well be. But I can't help feeling that . . ."

The chime on Maddson's desk display console interrupted the discussion. He excused himself and touched a button to accept the call.

"Hi, Don," said the face of Hunt's assistant, upstairs in Group L's offices. "Is Vic there?" He sounded excited. Maddson swiveled the unit around to point in Hunt's direction.

"It's for you," he said needlessly.

"Vic," said the face without preamble. "I've just had a look at the reports of the latest tests that came in from Jupiter Four two hours ago. That ship under the ice and the big guys inside it—they've completed the dating tests." He drew a deep breath. "It looks like maybe we can forget the Ganymeans in all this Charlie business. Vic, if all the figures are right, that ship has been sitting there for something like twenty-five *million* years!"

chapter fifteen

Caldwell moved a step closer to inspect more carefully the nine-foot-high plastic model standing in the middle of one of the laboratories of the Westwood Biological Institute. Danchekker gave him plenty of time to take in the details before continuing.

"A full-size replica of a Ganymean skeleton," he

said. "Built on the strength of the data beamed back from Jupiter. The first indisputable form of intelligent alien life ever to be studied by man." Caldwell looked up at the towering frame, pursed his lip in a silent whistle, and walked in a slow circle around and back to where the professor was standing. Hunt simply stood and swept his eyes up and down the full length of the model in wordless fascination.

"That structure is in no way related to that of any animal ever studied on Earth, living or extinct," Danchekker informed them. He gestured toward it. "It is based on a bony internal skeleton, walks upright as a biped, and has a head on top—as you can see; but apart from such superficial similarities, it has clearly evolved from completely unfamiliar origins. Take the head as an obvious example. The arrangement of the skull cannot be reconciled in any way with that of known vertebrates. The face has not receded back into the lower skull, but remains a long, down-pointing snout that widens at the top to provide a broad spacing for the eyes and ears. Also, the back of the skull has enlarged to accommodate a developing brain, as in the case of man, but instead of assuming a rounded contour, it bulges back above the neck to counterbalance the protruding face and jaw. And look at the opening through the skull in the center of the forehead; I believe that this could have housed a sense organ that we do not possess— possibly an infrared detector inherited from a nocturnal, carnivorous ancestor."

Hunt moved forward to stand next to Caldwell and peered intently at the shoulders. "These are unlike anything I've ever come across, too," he commented. "They're made up of . . . kind of overlappping plates of bone. Nothing like ours at all."

"Quite," Danchekker confirmed. "Probably adapted from the remains of ancestral armor. And the rest of the trunk is also quite alien. There is a dorsal spine with an arrangement of ribs below the shoulder plates, as you can see, but the lowermost rib—immediately above the body cavity—has developed into a massive hoop of bone with a diametral strut stretching forward from an enlarged spinal vertebra. Now, notice the two systems of smaller linked bones at the sides of the hoop . . ." He pointed them out. "They were probably used to assist with breathing by helping to expand the diaphragm. To me, they look suspiciously like the degenerate remnants of a paired-limb structure. In other words, although this creature, like us, had two arms and walked on two legs, somewhere in his earlier ancestry were animals with three pairs of appendages, not two. That in itself is enough to immediately rule out any kinship with every vertebrate of this planet."

Caldwell stooped to examine the pelvis, which comprised just an arrangement of thick bars and struts to contain the thigh sockets. There was no suggestion of the splayed dish form of the lower human torso.

"Must've had peculiar guts, too," he offered.

"It could be that the internal organs were carried more by suspension from the hoop above than by support from underneath," Danchekker suggested. He stepped back and indicated the arms and legs. "And last, observe the limbs. Both lower limbs have two bones as do ours, but the upper arm and thigh are different—they have a double-bone arrangement as well. This would have resulted in vastly improved flexibility and the ability to perform a whole range of movements that could never be duplicated by a human being. And the hand has six digits, two of them opposing; thus its owner effectively enjoyed the advantages of having two thumbs. He would have been able to tie his shoes easily with one hand."

Danchekker waited until Caldwell and Hunt had fully studied every detail of the skeleton to their satisfaction. When they looked toward him again, he resumed: "Ever since the age of the Ganymeans was verified, there has been a tendency for everybody to discount them as merely a coincidental discovery and having no direct bearing on the Lunarian question. I believe, gentlemen, that I am now in a position to demonstrate that they had a very real bearing indeed on the question."

Hunt and Caldwell looked at him expectantly. Danchekker walked over to a display console by the wall of the lab, tapped in a code, and watched as the screen came to life to reveal a picture of the skeleton of a fish. Satisfied, he turned to face them.

"What do you notice about that?" he asked.

Caldwell stared obediently at the screen for a few seconds while Hunt watched in silence.

"It's a funny fish," Caldwell said at last. "Okay—you tell me."

"It is not obvious at first sight," Danchekker replied, "but by detailed comparison it is possible to relate the structure of that fish, bone for bone, to that of the Ganymean skeleton. They're both from the same evolutionary line."

"That fish is one of those that were found on the Lunarian base on Farside," Hunt said suddenly.

"Precisely, Dr. Hunt. The fish dates from some fifty thousand years ago, and the Ganymean skeleton from twenty-five million or so. It is evident from anatomical considerations that they are related and come from lines that branched apart from a common ancestral life form somewhere in the very remote past. It follows that they share a place of origin. We already know that the fish evolved in the oceans of Minerva; therefore, the Ganymeans also came from Minerva. We thus have proof of something that has been merely speculation for some time. All that was wrong with the earlier assumption was our failure to appreciate the gap in time between the presence of the Ganymeans on Minerva, and that of the Lunarians."

"Okay," Caldwell accepted. "The Ganymeans came from Minerva, but a lot earlier than we thought. What's the big message and why did you call us over here?"

"In itself, this conclusion is interesting but no more," Danchekker answered. "But it looks pale by comparison with what comes next. In fact"—he shot a glance at Hunt—"the rest tells us all we need to know to resolve the whole question once and for all."

The two regarded him intently.

The professor moistened his lips, then went on: "The Ganymean ship has been opened up fully, and we now have an extremely comprehensive inventory of practically everything it contained. The ship was constructed for large freight-carrying capacity and was loaded when it met with whatever fate befell it on Ganymede. The cargo that it was carrying, in my opinion, constitutes the most sensational discovery ever to be made in the history of paleontology and biology. You see, that ship was carrying, among other things, a large consignment of botanical and zoological specimens, some alive and in cages, the rest preserved in canisters. Presumably the stock was part of an ambitious scientific expedition or something of that nature, but that really doesn't matter for now. What does matter is that we now have in our possession a collection of animal and plant trophies the like of which has never before been seen by human eyes: a comprehensive cross section of many forms of life that existed on Earth around the late Oligocene and early Miocene periods, twenty-five million years ago!"

Hunt and Caldwell stared at him incredulously. Danchekker folded his arms and waited.

"Earth!" Caldwell managed, with difficulty, to form the word. "Are you telling me that the ship had been to Earth?"

"I can see no alternative explanation," Danchekker returned. "Without doubt, the ship was carrying a variety of animal forms that have every appearance of being identical to species that have been well-known for centuries as a result of the terrestrial fossil record. The biologists on the Jupiter Four Mission are quite positive of their conclusions, and from the information they have sent back, I see no reason to doubt their opinions." Danchekker moved his hand back to the keyboard. "I will show you some examples of the kind of thing I mean," he said.

The picture of the fish skeleton vanished and was replaced by one of a massive, hornless, rhinoceroslike creature. In the background stood an enormous opened canister from which the animal had presumably been removed. The canister was lying in front of what looked like a wall of ice, surrounded by cables, chains, and parts of a latticework built of metal struts.

The *Baluchitherium*, gentlemen," Danchekker informed them, "or something so like it that the difference escapes me. This animal stood eighteen feet high at the shoulder and attained a bulk in excess of that of the elephant. It is a good example of the *titanoheres*, or titanic beasts, that were abundant in the Americas during the Oligocene but which died out fairly rapidly soon afterward."

"Are you saying that baby was alive when the ship ditched?" Caldwell asked in a tone of disbelief.

Danchekker shook his head. "Not this particular one. As you can see, it has come to us in practically as good a condition as when it was alive. It was taken from that container in the background, in which it had been packed and preserved to keep for a long time. Fortunately, whoever packed it was an expert. However, as I said earlier, there were cages and pens in the ship that originally held live specimens, but by the time they were discovered they had deteriorated to skeleton condition, as had the crew. There were six of this particular species in the pens."

The professor changed the picture to show a small quadruped with spindly legs.

"*Mesohippus*—ancestor of the modern horse. About the size of a collie dog and walking on a three-toed foot with the center toe highly elongated, clearly foreshadowing the single-toed horse of today. There is a long list of other examples such as these, every one immediately recognizable to any student of early terrestrial life forms."

Speechless, Hunt and Caldwell continued to watch as the view changed once more. This time it showed something that at first sight suggested a medium-sized ape from the gibbon or chimpanzee family. Closer examination, however, revealed differences that set it apart from the general category of ape. The skull construction was lighter, especially in the area of the lower jaw, where the chin had receded back to fall almost below the tip of the nose. The arms were proportionately somewhat on the short side for an ape, the chest broader and flatter, and the legs longer and straighter. Also, the opposability of the big toe had gone.

Danchekker allowed plenty of time for these points to register before continuing with his commentary.

"Clearly, the creature you now see before you belongs to the general anthropoid line that includes both man and the great apes. Now, remember, this specimen dates from around the early Miocene period. The most advanced anthropoid fossil from around that time so far found on Earth was discovered during the last century in East Africa and is known as *Proconsul*. *Proconsul* is generally accepted as representing a step forward from anything that had gone before, but he is definitely an ape. Here, on the other hand, we have a creature from the same period in time, but with distinctly more pronounced humanlike characteristics than *Proconsul*. In my opinion, this is an example of something that occupies a position corresponding to that of *Proconsul*, but on the other side of the split that occurred when man and ape went their own separate ways—in other words, a direct ancestor to the human line!" Danchekker concluded with a verbal flourish and gazed at the other two men expectantly. Caldwell stared back with widening eyes, and his jaw dropped as impossible thoughts raced through his mind.

"Are you telling . . . that the Charlie guys could have . . . from that?"

"Yes!" Danchekker snapped off the screen and swung back to face them triumphantly. "Established evolutionary theory is as sound as I've insisted all along. The notion that the Lunarians might have been colonists from Earth turns out indeed to be true, but not in the sense that was intended. There are no traces of their civilization to be found on Earth, because it never existed on Earth—but neither was it the product of any parallel process of evolution. The Lunarian civilization developed independently on Minerva from the same ancestral stock as we did and all other terrestrial verte-brates—from ancestors that were transported to Mi-nerva, twenty-five million years ago, by the Gany-means!" Danchekker thrust out his jaw defiantly and clasped the lapels of his jacket. "And that, Dr. Hunt, would seem to be the solution to your problem!"

chapter sixteen

The trail behind this rapid succession of new devel-opments was by this time littered with the abandoned carcases of dead ideas. It reminded the scientists forci-bly of the pitfalls that await the unwary when specula-tion is given too free a rein and imagination is allowed to float further and further aloft from the firm grounds of demonstrable proof and scientific rigor. The reaction against this tendency took the form of a generally cooler reception to Danchekker's attempted abrupt wrapping up of the whole issue than might have been expected. So many blind alleys had been exhausted by now, that any new suggestion met with instinctive skepticism and demands for corroboration.

The discovery of early terrestrial animals on the Gany-mean spaceship proved only one thing conclusive-ly: that there were early terrestrial animals on the Ganymean spaceship. It didn't prove beyond doubt that other consignments had reached Minerva safely, or in-deed, that this particular consignment was ever intended for Minerva. For one thing, Jupiter seemed a strange place to find a ship that had been bound for Minerva from Earth. All it proved, therefore, was that this con-signment hadn't got to wherever it was supposed to go.

Danchekker's conclusions regarding the origins of the

Ganymeans, however, were fully endorsed by a committee of experts on comparative anatomy in London, who confirmed the affinity between the Ganymean skeleton and the Minervan fish. The corollary to this deduction—that the Lunarians too had evolved on Minerva from displaced terrestrial stock—although neatly accounting for the absence of Lunarian traces on Earth and for the evident lack of advanced Lunarian space technology, required a lot more in the way of substantiating evidence.

In the meantime, Linguistics had been busy applying their newfound knowledge from the microdot library to the last unsolved riddle among Charlie's papers, the notebook containing the handwritten entries. The story that emerged provided vivid confirmation of the broad picture already deduced in cold and objective terms by Hunt and Steinfield; it was an account of the last days of Charlie's life. The revelations from the book lobbed yet another intellectual grenade in among the already disarrayed ranks of the investigators. But it was Hunt who finally pulled the pin.

Clasping a folder of loose papers beneath his arm, Hunt strolled along the main corridor of the thirteenth floor of the Navcomms Headquarters building, toward the linguistics section. Outside Don Maddson's office he stopped to examine with curiosity a sign bearing a string of two-inch-high Lunarian characters that had been pinned to the door. Shrugging and shaking his head, he entered the room. Inside, Maddson and one of his assistants were sitting in front of the perpetual pile of litter on the large side table away from the desk. Hunt pulled up a chair and joined them.

"You've been through the translations," Maddson observed, noting the contents of the folder as Hunt began arranging them on the table.

Hunt nodded. "Very interesting, this. There are a few points I'd like to go over just to make sure I've got it straight. Some parts just don't made sense."

"We should've guessed," Maddson sighed resignedly. "Okay, shoot."

"Let's work through the entries in sequence," Hunt suggested. "I'll stop when we get to the odd bits. "By the way . . . " He inclined his head in the direction of the door. "What's the funny sign outside?"

Maddson grinned proudly. "It's my name in Lunarian. Literally it means *Scholar Crazy-Boy*. Get it? *Don Mad-Son*. See?"

"Oh, Christ," Hunt groaned. He returned his attention to the papers.

"You've expressed the Lunarian-dated entries simply as consecutive numbers starting at Day One, but subdivisions of their day are converted into our hours."

"Check," Maddson confirmed. "Also, where there's doubt about the accuracy of the translation, the phrase is put in parentheses with a question mark. That helps keep things simple."

Hunt selected his first sheet. "Okay," he said. "Let's start at the beginning." He read aloud:

"Day One. As expected, today we received full (mobilization alert?) orders. Probably means a posting somewhere. Koriel . . . This is Charlie's pal who turns up later, isn't it?"

"Correct."

" *. . . thinks it could be to one of the (ice nests far-intercept?).* What's that?"

"That's an awkward one," Maddson replied. "It's a composite word; that's the literal translation. We think it could refer to a missile battery forming part of an outer defense perimeter, located out on the ice sheets."

"Mmm—sounds reasonable. Anyhow, *Hope so. It would be a change to get away from the monotony of this place. Bigger food ration in (ice-field combat zones?).* Now . . ." Hunt looked up. "He says, 'the monotony of this place.' How sure are we that we know where 'this place' is?"

"Pretty sure," Maddson replied with a firm nod. "The name of a town is written above the date at the top of the entry. It checks with the name of a coastal town on Cerios and also with the place given in his pay book for his last posting but one."

"So you're sure he was on Minerva when he wrote this?"

"Sure, we're sure."

"Okay. I'll skip the next bit that talks about personal thoughts.

Day Two. Koriel's hunches have proved wrong for once. We're going to Luna."

Hunt looked up again, evidently considering this part important. "How do you know he means Earth's Moon there?"

"Well, one reason is that the word he uses there is the same as the last place the pay book says he was posted to. We guess it means Luna because that's where we found him. Another reason is that later on, as you'll have read, he talks about being sent specifically to a base called Seltar. Now, we've found a reference among some of the things turned up on Farside to a list of bases on place 'X,' and the name *Seltar* appears on the list. X is the same word that is written in the pay book and in the entry you've just read. Implication: X is a Lunarian name for Earth's Moon."

Hunt thought hard for a while.

"He arrived at Seltar, too, didn't he?" he said at last. "So if he knew where he was being sent as early as that, and you're certain he was being sent to the Moon, and he got where he was supposed to go . . . that rules out the other possibility that occurred to me. There's no way he could have been scheduled for Luna but re-routed somewhere else at the last minute without the entry in the pay book being changed, is there?"

Maddson shook his head. "No way. Why'd you want to make up things like that anyhow?"

"Because I'm looking for ways to get around what comes later. It gets crazy."

Maddson looked at Hunt curiously but suppressed his question. Hunt looked down at the papers again.

"Days Three and Four describe news reports of the fighting on Minerva. Obviously a large-scale conflict had already broken out there. It looks as if nuclear weapons were being used by then—that bit near the end of Day Four, for instance: *It looks like the Lambians have succeeded in confusing the (sky nets?) over Paverol*— That's a Cerian town, isn't it? *Over half the city vaporized instantly.* That doesn't sound like a limited skirmish. What's a sky net—some kind of electronic defense screen?"

"Probably," Maddson agreed.

"Day Five he spent helping to load the ships. From the descriptions of the vehicles and equipment, it sounds as if they were embarking a large military force of some kind." Hunt scanned rapidly down the next sheet. "Ah, yes—this is where he mentions Seltar. *We're going with the Fourteenth Brigade to join the Annihilator emplacement at Seltar.* There's something crazy about this Annihilator. But we'll come back to that in a minute.

"Day Seven. Embarked four hours ago as scheduled. Still sitting here. Takeoff delayed, since whole area under heavy missile attack. Hills inland all on fire. Launching pits intact but situation overhead confused. Unneutralized Lambian satellites still covering our flight path.

"Later. Received clearance for takeoff suddenly, and the whole flight was away in minutes. Didn't delay in planetary orbit at all—still not very healthy—so set course at once. Two ships reported lost on the way up. Koriel is taking bets on how many ships from our flight touch down on Luna. We're flying inside a tight defense screen but must stand out clearly on Lambian search radars. There's a bit about Koriel flirting with one of the girls from a signals unit—quite a character, this Koriel, wasn't he . . . ? More war news received en route . . . Now—this is the part I meant." Hunt found the entry with his finger.

"Day Eight. In Lunar orbit at last!" He laid the sheet down on the table and looked from one linguist to the other. " *'In Lunar orbit at last.'* Now, you tell me: Exactly how did that ship travel from Minerva to our

Moon in under two of our days? Either there is some form of propulsion that UNSA ought to be finding out about, or we've been very wrong about Lunarian technology all along. But it doesn't fit. If they could do that, they didn't have any problem about developing space flight; they were way ahead of us. But I don't believe it—everything says they had a problem."

Maddson made a show of helplessness. He knew it was crazy. Hunt looked inquiringly at Maddson's assistant, who merely shrugged and pulled a face.

"You're sure he means Lunar orbit—*our* Moon?"

"We're sure." Maddson was sure.

"And there's no doubt about the date he shipped out?" Hunt persisted.

"The embarkation date is stamped in the pay book, and it checks with the date of the entry that says he shipped out. And don't forget the wording on Day—where was it?—here, Day Seven. *'Embarked four hours ago as scheduled'*— See, 'as scheduled.' No suggestion of a change in timetable."

"And how certain is the date he reached Luna?" asked Hunt.

"Well that's a little more difficult. Just going by the dates of the notes, they're one Lunarian day apart, all right. Now, it's possible that he used a Minervan time scale on Minerva, but switched to some local system when he got to Luna. If so, it's a big coincidence that they tally like they do, but"—he shrugged—"it's possible. The thing that bothers me about that idea, though, is the absence of any entries between the ship-out date and the arrival-at-Luna date. Charlie seems to have written his diary regularly. If the voyage took months, like you're saying it should have, it looks funny to me that there's nothing at all between those dates. It's not as if he'd have been short of free time."

Hunt reflected for a few moments on these possibilities. Then he said, "There's worse to come. Let's press on for now." He picked up the notes and resumed:

"Landed at last, five hours ago. (Expletive) what a mess! The landscape below as we came in on the (ap-

proach run?) was glowing red in places all around Seltar for miles. There were lakes of molten rock, bright orange, some with walls of rocks plunging straight into them where whole mountains have been blown away. The base is covered deep in dust, and some of the surface installations have been crushed by flying debris. The defenses are holding out, but the outer perimeter is (torn to shreds?). Most important—[unreadable] diameter dish of the Annihilator is intact and it is operational. The last group of ships in our flight was wiped out by an enemy strike coming in from deep space. Koriel has been collecting on all sides."

Hunt laid the paper down and looked at Maddson. "Don," he said, "how much have you been able to piece together about this Annihilator thing?"

"It was a kind of superweapon. There was more information in some of the other texts. Both sides had them, sited on Minerva itself and, from what you're reading right now, on Luna too." He added as an afterthought, "Maybe on other places as well."

"Why on Luna? Any ideas?"

"Our guess is that the Cerians and the Lambians must have developed space-flight technology further than we thought," Maddson said. "Perhaps both sides had selected Earth as their target destination for the big move, and they both sent advance parties to Luna to set up a bridgehead and . . . protect the investment."

"Why not on Earth itself, then?"

"I dunno."

"Let's stick with it for now, anyway," Hunt said. "How much do we know about what these Annihilators were?"

"From the description *dish*, apparently it was some kind of radiation projector. From other clues, they fired a high-energy photon beam probably produced by intense matter–antimatter reaction. If so, the term *Annihilator* is particularly apt; it carries a double meaning."

"Okay." Hunt nodded. "That's what I thought. Now it goes silly." He consulted his notes. "Day Nine they were getting organized and repairing battle damage.

What about Day Ten, then, eh?" He resumed reading:

"Day Ten. Annihilator used for the first time today. Three fifteen-minutes blasts aimed at Calvares, Paneris, and Sellidorn. Now, they're all Lambian cities, right?"

"So they have this Annihilator emplacement, sitting on our Moon, happily picking off cities on the surface of Minerva?"

"Looks like it," Maddson agreed. He didn't look very happy.

"Well, I don't believe it," Hunt declared firmly. "I don't believe they had the ability to register a weapon that accurately over that distance, and even if they could, I don't believe they could have held the beam narrow enough not to have burned up the whole planet. And I don't believe the power density at that range could have been high enough to do any damage at all." He looked at Maddson imploringly. "Christ, if they had technology like that, they wouldn't have been trying to perfect interplanetary travel—they'd have been all over the bloody Galaxy!"

Maddson gestured wide with his arms. "I just translate what the words tell me. You figure it out."

"It goes completely daft in a minute," Hunt warned. "Where was I, now . . . ?"

He continued to read aloud, describing the duel that developed between the Cerian Annihilator at Seltar and the last surviving Lambian emplacement on Minerva. With a weapon firing from far out in space and commanding the whole Minervan surface, the Cerians held the key that would decide the war. Destroying it was obviously the first priority of the Lambian forces and the prime objective of their own Annihilator on Minerva. The Annihilators required about one hour to recharge between firings, and Charlie's notes conveyed vividly the tension that built up in Seltar as they waited, knowing that an incoming blast could arrive at any second. All around Seltar the battle was building up to a frenzy as Lambian ground and space-borne forces hurled everything into knocking out Seltar before it could score on its distant target. The skill in operating the weapon lay in computing and compensating for the distortions induced in the aiming system by enemy electronic countermeasures. In one passage, Charlie detailed the effects of a near miss from Minerva that lasted for sixteen minutes, during which time it melted a range of mountains about fifteen miles from Seltar, including the Twenty-second and Nineteenth Armored Divisions and the Forty-fifth Tactical Missile Squadron that had been positioned there.

"This is it," Hunt said, waving one of the sheets in the air. "Listen to this. *We've got it! Four minutes ago we fired a concentrated burst at maximum power. The announcement has just come over the loudspeaker down here that it scored a direct hit. Everyone is laughing and clapping each other on the back. Some of the women are crying with relief.* That," said Hunt, slapping the papers down on the table and slumping back in his chair with exasperation, "is bloody ridiculous! Within four minutes of firing they had confirmation of a hit! How? How is God's name could they have? We know that when Minerva and Earth were at their closest, the distance between them would have been one hundred fifty to one hundred sixty million miles. The radiation would have taken something like thirteen minutes to cover that distance, and there would have to be at least another thirteen minutes before anybody on Luna could possibly know about where it struck. So, even with the planets at their closest positions, they'd have needed at least twenty-six minutes to get that report. Charlie says they got it in under four! That is absolutely, one-hundred-percent impossible! Don, how sure are you of those numbers?"

"As sure as we are of any other Lunarian time units. If they're wrong, you might as well tear up that calendar you started out with and go all the way back to square one."

Hunt stared at the page for a long time, as if by sheer power of concentration he could change the message contained in the neatly formatted sheets of typescript. There was only one thing that these figures could mean, and it put them right back to the beginning. At length he carried on:

"The next bit tells how the whole Seltar area came under sustained bombardment. A detachment including Charlie and Koriel was sent out overland to man an emergency command post about eleven miles from Seltar Base . . . I'll skip the details of that . . . Yes, here's the next bit that worries me. Under Day Twelve: *Set off on time in a small convoy of two scout cars and three tracked trucks. The journey was weird—miles of scorched rocks and glowing pits. We could feel the heat inside the truck. Hope the shielding was good. Our new home is a dome, and underneath it are levels going down about fifty feet. Army units dug in the hills all around. We have landline contact with Seltar, but they seem to have lost touch with Main HQ at Gorda. Probably means all long-distance landlines are out and our comsats are destroyed. Again no broadcasts from Minerva. Lots of garbled military traffic. They must have assumed (frequency priority?). Today was the first time above surface for many days. The face of Minerva looks dirty and blotchy.* There," Hunt said. "When I first read that, I thought he was referring to a video transmission. But thinking about it, why would he say it that way in that context? Why right after 'the first time above surface for many days'? But he couldn't have seen any detail of Minerva from where he was, could he?"

Could have used a pretty ordinary telescope," Maddson's assistant suggested.

"Could have, I suppose," Hunt reflected. "But you'd think there'd be more important things to worry about than star gazing in the middle of all that. Anyhow, he goes on: *About two-thirds is blotted out by huge clouds of brown and gray, and coastal outlines are visible only in places. There is a strange red spot glowing through, somewhere just north of the equator, with black spreading out from it hour by hour. Koriel reckons it's a city on fire, but it must be a tremendous blaze to be visible through all that. We've been watching it move across all*

*day as Minerva rotates. Huge explosions over the ridge
where Seltar Base is."*

The narrative continued and confirmed that Seltar
was totally destroyed as the fighting reached its climax.
For two days the whole area was systematically
pounded, but miraculously the underground parts of the
dome remained intact, although the upper levels were
blown away. Afterward the scattered survivors from the
military units occupying the surrounding hills began
straggling back, some in vehicles and many on foot, to
the dome, which by this time was the only inhabitable
place left for miles.

The expected waves of victorious Lambian troop-
ships and armored columns failed to materialize. From
the regular pattern of incoming salvos, the Cerian officers slowly realized that there was nothing left of the
enemy army that had moved forward into the mountains
around Seltar. In the fighting with the Cerian defenses,
the Lambians had suffered immense losses and their
survivors had pulled out, leaving missile batteries pro-
grammed to fire robot mode to cover their withdrawal.

On Day Fifteen, Charlie wrote: *Two more red spots
on Minerva, one northeast of the first and the other
well south. The first has elongated from northwest to
southeast. The whole surface is now just a mass of dirty
brown with huge areas of black mixing in with it. Nothing at all on radio or video from Minerva; everything
blotted out by atmospherics.*

There was nothing further to be done at Seltar. The
inhabitable parts of what had been the dome were
packed with survivors and wounded; already many were
having to live in the assortment of vehicles huddled
around outside it. Supplies of food and oxygen, never
intended for more than a small company, would give
only a temporary respite. The only hope, slender as it
was, lay in reaching HQ Base at Gorda overland—a
journey estimated to require twenty days.

On Day Eighteen, the departure from the dome was
recorded as follows: *Formed up in two columns of vehicles. Ours moved out half an hour ahead of the second*

*as a small advanced scouting group. We reached a ridge
about three miles from the dome and could see the
main column finish loading and begin lining up. That
was when the missiles hit. The first salvo caught them
all out in the open. They didn't have a chance. We
trained our receivers on the area for a while, but there
was nothing. The only way we'll ever get off this death
furnace is if there are ships left at Gorda. As far as I
know, there are 340 of us, including over a hundred
girls. The column comprises five scout cars, eight tracked
trucks, and ten heavy tanks. It will be a grim journey.
Even Koriel isn't taking bets on how many get there.*

*Minerva is just a black, smoky ball, difficult to pick
out against the sky. Two of the red spots have joined up
to form a line stretching at an angle across the equator.
Must be hundreds of miles long. Another red line is
growing to the north. Every now and then, parts of
them glow orange through the smoke clouds for a few
hours and then die down again. Must be a mess there.*

The column moved slowly through the desert of
scorched gray dust, and its numbers shrank rapidly as
wounds and radiation sickness took their toll. On Day
Twenty-six they encountered a Lambian ground force
and for three hours fought furiously among the crags
and boulders. The battle ended when the remaining
Lambian tanks broke cover and charged straight into
the Cerian position, only to be destroyed right on the
perimeter line by Cerian women firing laser artillery at
point-blank range. After the battle there were 165 Cerians left, but not enough vehicles to carry them.

After conferring, the Cerian officers devised a plan
to continue the journey leapfrog fashion. Half the
company would be moved half a day's distance forward
and left there with one truck to use as living accommodation, while the remaining vehicles returned to collect
the group left behind. So it would go on all the way to
Gorda. Charlie and Koriel were among the first group
lifted on ahead.

*Day Twenty-eight. Uneventful drive. Set up camp in
a shady gorge and watched the convoy about-face again*

*and begin its long haul back for the others. They should
be back this time tomorrow. Nothing much to do until
then. Two died on the drive, so there are fifty-eight of
us here. We take turns to rest and eat inside the truck.
When it's not your turn, you make yourself as comfortable as you can sitting among the rocks. Koriel is fu-
rious. He's just spent two hours sitting outside with four
of the artillery girls. He says whoever designed spacesuits should have thought of situations like that.*

The convoy never returned.

Using the single remaining truck, the group continued the same tactic as before, ferrying one party on
ahead, dumping them, and returning for the rest. By
Day Thirty-three, sickness, mishaps, and one suicide
had depleted the numbers such that all the survivors
could be carried in the truck at once, so the leapfrog-
ging was discontinued. Driving steadily, they estimated
they would reach Gorda on Day Thirty-eight. On Day
Thirty-seven, the truck broke down. The spare parts
needed to repair it were not available.

Many were weak. It was clear that an attempt to
reach Gorda on foot would be so slow that nobody
would make it.

*Day Thirty-seven. Seven of us—four men (myself,
Koriel, and two of the combat troopers) and three
girls—are going to make a dash for Gorda while the
others stay put in the truck and wait for a rescue party.
Koriel is cooking a meal before we set out. He has been
saying what he thinks of life in the infantry—doesn't
seem to think much of it at all.*

Some hours after they left the truck, one of the troopers climbed a crag to survey the route ahead. He slipped,
gashed his suit, and died instantly from explosive decompression. Later on, one of the girls hurt her leg and
lagged farther and farther behind as the pain worsened.
The Sun was sinking and there was no time for slowing
down. Everybody in the group wrestled with the same
equation in his mind—one life or twenty-eight?—but
said nothing. She solved the problem for them by quietly closing her air valve when they stopped to rest.

Day Thirty-eight. Just Koriel and me now—like the old days. The trooper suddenly doubled up, vomiting violently inside his helmet. We stood and watched while he died, and could do nothing. Some hours later, one of the girls collapsed and said she couldn't go on. The other insisted on staying with her until we send help from Gorda. Couldn't really argue—they were sisters. That was some time ago. We've stopped for a breather; I am getting near my limit. Koriel is pacing up and down impatiently and wants to get moving. That man has the strength of twelve [?lions?].

Later. Stopped at last for a couple of hours sleep. I'm sure Koriel is a robot—just keeps going and going. Human tank. Sun very low in sky. Must make Gorda before Lunar night sets in.

Day Thirty-nine. Woke up freezing cold. Had to turn suit heating up to maximum—still doesn't feel right. Think it's developing a fault. Koriel says I worry too much. Time to be on the move again. Feel stiff all over. Seriously wondering if I'll make it. Haven't said so.

Later. The march has been a nightmare. Kept falling down. Koriel insisted that the only chance we had was to climb up out of the valley we were in and try a short-cut over a high ridge. I made it about halfway up the cleft leading toward the ridge. Every step up the cleft I could see Minerva sitting right over the middle of the ridge, gashes of orange and red all over it, like a (macabre?) face, taunting. Then I collapsed. When I came to, Koriel had dragged me inside a pilot digging of some sort. Maybe someone was going to put an outpost of Gorda here. That was a while ago now. Koriel has gone on and says help will be back before I know it. Getting colder all the time. Feet numb and hands stiff. Frost starting to form in helmet—difficult to see.

Thinking about all the people strung out back there with night coming down, all like me, wondering if they'll be picked up. If we can hold out we'll be all right. Koriel will make it. If it were a thousand miles to Gorda, Koriel would make it.

Thinking about what has happened on Minerva and wondering if, after all this, our children will live on a sunnier world—and if they do, if they will ever know what we did.

Thinking about things I've never really thought about before. There should be better ways for people to spend their lives than in factories, mines, and army camps. Can't think what, though—that's all we've ever known. But if there is warmth and color and light somewhere in this Universe, then maybe something worthwhile will come out of what we've been through.

Too much thinking for one day. Must sleep for a while now.

Hunt found he had read right through to the end, absorbed in the pathos of those final days. His voice had fallen to a sober pitch. A long silence ensued.

"Well, that's it," he concluded, a little more briskly. "Did you notice that bit right at the end? In the last few lines he was talking about seeing the surface of Minerva again. Now, they might have used telescopes earlier on, but in the situation he was in there, they'd hardly be lugging half an observatory along with them, would they?"

Maddson's assistant looked thoughtful. "How about that periscope video gadget that was in the helmet?" he suggested. "Maybe there's something wrong in the translation. Couldn't he be talking about seeing a transmission through that?"

Hunt shook his head. "Can't see it. I've heard of people watching TV in all sorts of funny places, but never halfway up a bloody mountain. And another thing: He described it as sitting up above the ridge. That implies it's really out there. If it were a view on video, he'd never have worded it that way. Right, Don?"

Maddson nodded wearily. "Guess so," he said. "So, where do we go from here?"

Hunt looked from Maddson to the assistant and back again. He leaned his elbows on the edge of the table and rubbed his face and eyeballs with his fingers. Then he sighed and sat back.

"What do we know for sure?" he asked at last. "We know that those Lunarian spaceships got to our Moon in under two days. We know that they could accurately aim a weapon, sited on our Moon, at a Minervan target. We also know that the round trip for electromagnetic waves was much shorter than it could possibly have been if we've been talking about the right place. Finally, we can't prove but we think that Charlie could stand on our Moon and see quite clearly the surface features of Minerva. Well, what does that add up to?"

"There's only one place in the Universe that fits all those numbers," Maddson said numbly.

"Exactly—and we're standing on it! Maybe there was a planet called Minerva outside Mars, and maybe it had a civilization on it. Maybe the Ganymeans took a few animals there and maybe they didn't. But it doesn't really matter any more, does it? Because the only planet Charlie's ship could possibly have taken off from, and the only planet they could have aimed that Annihilator at, and the only planet he could have seen in detail from Luna—is this one!

"They *were* from Earth all along!

"Everyone will be jumping off the roof and out of every window in the building when this gets around Navcomms."

chapter seventeen

With the first comprehensive translation of the hand-written notebook, the paradox was complete. Now there were two consistent and apparently irrefutable bodies of evidence, one proving that the Lunarians must have evolved on Earth, and the other proving that they couldn't have.

All at once the consternation and disputes broke out afresh. Lights burned through the night at Houston and elsewhere as the same inevitable chains of reasoning were reeled out again and yet again, the same arrays of facts scrutinized for new possibilities or interpretations. But always the answers came out the same. Only the notion of the Lunarians having been the product of a parallel line of evolution appeared to have been abandoned permanently; more than enough theories were in circulation already without anyone having to invoke this one. The Navcomms fraternity disintegrated into a myriad of cliques and strays, scurrying about to ally first with this idea and then with that. As the turmoil subsided, the final lines of defense fortified themselves around four main camps.

The Pure Earthists accepted without reservation the deductions from Charlie's diary, and held that the Lunarian civilization had developed on Earth, flourished on Earth, and destroyed itself on Earth and that was that. Thus, all references to Minerva and its alleged civilization were nonsense; there never had been any civilization on Minerva apart from that of the Ganymeans, and that was too far in the remote past to have any bearing on the Lunarian issue. The world depicted on Charlie's maps was Earth, not Minerva, so there had to be a gross error somewhere in the calculations that put it at 250 million miles from the Sun. That this corresponded to the orbital radius of the Asteroids was just coincidence; the Asteroids had always been there, and anything from *Iliad* that said they hadn't was suspect and needed double-checking.

That left only one question unexplained: Why didn't Charlie's maps look like Earth? To answer this one, the Earthists launched a series of commando raids against the bastions of accepted geological theory and methods of geological dating. Drawing on the hypothesis that continents had been formed initially from a single granitic mass that had been shattered under the weight of immense ice caps and pushed apart by polar material rushing in to fill the gaps, they pointed to the size of the ice caps shown on the maps and stressed how much larger they were than anything previously supposed to have existed on Earth. Now, if in fact the maps showed Earth and not Minerva, that meant that the Ice Age on Earth had been far more severe than previously thought, and its effects on surface geography correspondingly more violent. Add to this the effects of the crustal fractures and vulcanism as described in Charlie's observations of Earth (not Minerva), and there was, perhaps, enough in all that to account for the transformation of Charlie's Earth into modern Earth. So, why were there no traces to be found today of the Lunarian civilization? Answer: It was clear from the maps that most of it had been concentrated on the equatorial belt. Today that region was completely ocean, dense jungle, or drifting desert—adequate to explain the rapid erasure of whatever had been left after the war and the climatic cataclysm.

The Pure Earthist faction attracted mainly physicists and engineers, quite happy to leave the geologists and geographers to worry about the bothersome details. Their main concern was that the sacred principle of the constancy of the velocity of light should not be thrown into the melting pot of suspicion along with everything else.

By entrenching themselves around the idea of Earth origins, the Pure Earthists had moved into the positions previously defended fanatically by the biologists. Now that Danchekker had led the way by introducing his fleet of Ganymean Noah's Arks, the biologists abruptly turned about-face and rallied behind their new assertion of Minervan origin from displaced terrestrial ancestors. What about Charlie's Minerva–Luna flight time and the loop delay around the Annihilator fire-control system? Something was screwed up in the interpretation of Minervan time scales that accounted for both these. Okay, how could Charlie see Minerva from Luna? Video transmissions. Okay, how could they aim the Annihilator over that distance? They couldn't. The dish at Seltar was only a remote-control tracking station. The weapon itself was mounted in a satellite orbiting Minerva.

The third flag flew over the Cutoff Colony Theory. According to this, an early terrestrial civilization had colonized Minerva, and then declined into a Dark Age during which contact with the colony was lost. The deteriorating conditions of the Ice Age later prompted a recovery on both planets, with the difference that Minerva faced a life-or-death situation and began the struggle to regain the lost knowledge in order that a return to Earth might be made. Earth, however, was going through lean times of its own and, when the advance parties from Minerva eventually made contact, didn't react favorably to the idea of another planetful of mouths to feed. Diplomacy having failed, the Minervans set up an invasion beachhead on Luna. The Annihilator at Seltar had thus been firing at targets on Earth; the translators had been misled by identical place-names on both planets—like Boston, New York, Cambridge, and a hundred other places in the USA, many of the towns on Minerva had been named after places on Earth when the original colony was first established.

The defenders of these arguments drew heavily from the claims of the Pure Earthists to account for the absence of Lunarian relics on Earth. In addition, they produced further support from the unlikely domain of the study of fossil corals in the Pacific. It had been known for a long time that analysis of the daily growth rings of ancient fossil corals provided a measure of how many days there had been in the year at various times in the past, and from this how fast the forces of tidal friction were slowing down the rotation of the Earth about its axis. These researches showed, for example, that the year of 350 million years ago contained about four hundred days. Ten years previously, work conducted at the Darwin Institute of Oceanography in Australia, using more refined and more accurate techniques, had revealed that the continuity from ancient to modern had not been as smooth as supposed. There was a confused period in the recent past—at about fifty thousand years before—during which the curve was discontinuous, and a comparatively abrupt lengthening in the day had occurred. Furthermore, the rate of deceleration was measurably greater after this discontinuity than it had been before. Nobody knew why this should have happened, but it seemed to indicate a period of violent climatic upheaval, as the corals had taken generations to settle down to a stable growth pattern afterward. The data seemed to indicate that widespread changes had taken place on Earth around this mysterious point in time, probably accompanied by global flooding, and all in all there *could* be enough behind the story to explain the complete disappearance of any record of the Lunarians' existence.

The fourth main theory was that of the Returning Exiles, which found these attempts to explain the disappearance of the terrestrial Lunarians artificial and inadequate. The basic tenet of this theory was that there could be only one satisfactory reason for the fact that there were no signs of Lunarians on Earth: There had never been any Lunarians on Earth worth talking about. Thus, they had evolved on Minerva as Danchekker maintained and had evolved an advanced civilization, unlike their contemporary brothers on Earth, who remained backward. Eventually, compelled by the Ice Age threat of extinction, the two superpowers of Cerios and Lambia had emerged and begun the race toward the Sun in the way described by Linguistics. Where Linguistics had gone wrong, however, was that by the time of Charlie's narrative, these events were already historical; the goal was already achieved. The Lambians had drawn ahead by a small margin and had already commenced building settlements on Earth, several of them named after their own towns on Minerva. The Cerians followed hard on their heels and established a fire base on Luna, the objective of course being to knock out the Lambian outposts on Earth before moving in themselves.

This theory did not explain the flight time of Charlie's ship, but its supporters attributed the difficulty to unknown differences between Minervan and local (Lunar) dating systems. On the other hand, it required only a few pilot Lambian bases to have been set up on Earth by the time of the war; thus, whatever remained of these after the Cerian assault, could credibly have vanished in fifty thousand years.

And as the battle lines were drawn up and the first ranging shots started whistling up and down the corridors of Navcomms, in no-man's-land sat Hunt. Somehow, he was convinced, everybody was right. He knew the competence of the people around him and had no doubt in their ability to get their figures right. If, after weeks or months of patient effort, one of them pronounced that x was 2, then he was quite prepared to believe that, in all probability, 2 it would turn out to be. Therefore, the paradox had to be an illusion. To try to argue which side was right and which was wrong was missing the whole point. Somewhere in the maze, probably so fundamental that nobody had even thought to question it, there had to be a fallacy—some wrong assumption that seemed so obvious they didn't even realize they were making it. If they could just get back to fundamentals and identify that single fallacy, the paradox would vanish and everything that was being argued would slide smoothly into a consistent, unified whole.

chapter eighteen

"You want me to go to Jupiter?" Hunt repeated slowly, making sure he had heard correctly.

Caldwell stared back over his desk impassively. "The Jupiter Five Mission will depart from Luna in six weeks time," he stated. "Danchekker has gone about as far as he can go with Charlie. What details are left to be found out can be taken care of by his staff at Westwood. He's got better things he'd like to be doing on Ganymede. There's a whole collection of alien skeletons there, plus a shipload of zoology from way back that nobody's ever seen the like of before. It's got him excited. He wants to get his hands on them. Jupiter Five is going right there, so he's getting together a biological team to go with it."

Hunt already knew all this. Nevertheless, he went through the motions of digesting the information and checking through it for any point he might have missed. After an appropriate pause he replied:

"That's fine—I can see *his* angle. But what does it have to do with me?"

Caldwell frowned and drummed his fingers, as if he had been expecting this question to come, while hoping it wouldn't.

"Consider this an extension of your assignment," he said at last. "From all the arguing that's going on around this place, nobody seems to be able to agree just how the Ganymeans fit into the Charlie business. Maybe they're a big part of the answer, maybe they're not. Nobody knows for sure."

"True." Hunt nodded.

Caldwell took this as all the confirmation he needed. "Okay," he said with a gesture of finality. "You've done a good job so far on the Charlie side of the picture; maybe it's time to balance things up a bit and give you a crack at the other side, too. Well"—he shrugged—"the information's not here—it's on Ganymede. In six weeks time, *J Five* shoves off for Ganymede. It makes sense to me that you go with it."

Hunt's brow remained creased in an expression that indicated he still didn't quite see everything. He posed the obvious question. "What about the job here?"

"What about it? Basically you correlate information that comes from different places. The information will still keep coming from the places whether you're in Houston or on board *Jupiter Five*. Your assistant is capable of stepping in and keeping the routine background research and cross-checking running smoothly in Group L. There's no reason why you can't continue to be kept updated on what's going on if you're out there. Anyhow, a change of scene never did anybody any harm. You've been on this job a year and a half now."

"But we're talking about a break of years, maybe."

"Not necessarily. *Jupiter Five* is a later design than *J Four*; it will make Ganymede in under six months. Also, a number of ships are being ferried out with the Jupiter Five Mission to start building up a fleet that will be based out there. Once a reserve's been established, there will be regular two-way traffic with Earth. In other words, once you've had enough of the place we'll have no problem getting you back."

Hunt reflected that nothing ever seemed to stay normal for very long when Caldwell was around. He felt no inclination to argue with this new directive. On the contrary, the prospect excited him. But there was something that didn't quite add up in the reasons Caldwell was giving. Hunt had the same feeling he had experienced on previous occasions that there was an ulterior motive lurking beneath the surface somewhere. Still, that didn't really matter. Caldwell seemed to have made up his mind, and Hunt knew from experience that when Caldwell made up his mind that something would be so, then by some uncanny power of preordination, so it would inevitably turn out to be.

Caldwell waited for possible objections. Seeing that none were forthcoming, he concluded: "When you joined us, I told you your place in UNSA was out front. That statement implied a promise. I always keep promises."

For the next two weeks Hunt worked frantically, reorganizing the operation of Group L and making his own personal preparations for a prolonged absence from Earth. After that, he was sent to Galveston for two weeks.

By the third decade of the twenty-first century, commercial flight reservations to Luna could be made through any reputable travel agent, for seats either on regular UNSA ships or on chartered ships crewed by UNSA officers. The standards of comfort provided on passenger flights were high, and accommodation at the larger Lunar bases was secure, enabling Lunar travel to become a routine chore in the lives of many businessmen and a memorable event for more than a few casual visitors, none of whom needed any specialized knowledge or training. Indeed, one enterprising consortium, comprising of a hotel chain, an international airline, a travel-tour operator, and an engineering corporation, had commenced the construction of a Lunar holiday resort, which was already fully booked for the opening season.

Places like Jupiter, however, were not yet open to the public. Persons detailed for assignments with the UNSA deep-space missions needed to know what they were doing and how to act in emergency situations. The ice sheets of Ganymede and the cauldron of Venus were no places for tourists.

At Galveston, Hunt learned about UNSA spacesuits and the standard items of ancillary equipment; he was taught the use of communication equipment, survival kits, emergency life support systems, and repair kits; he practiced test routines, radiolocation procedures, and equipment-fault diagnostic techniques. "Your life could depend on this little box," one instructor told the group. "You could wind up in a situation where it fails and the only person inside a hundred miles to fix it is you." Doctors lectured on the rudiments of space medicine and recommended methods of dealing with oxygen starvation, decompression, heat stroke, and hypothermia. Physiologists described the effects on bone calcium of long periods of reduced body weight, and showed how a correct balance could be maintained by a specially selected diet and drugs. UNSA officers gave useful hints that covered the whole gamut of staying alive and sane in alien environments, from navigating afoot on a hostile surface using satellite beacons as reference points, to the art of washing one's face in zero gravity.

And so, just over four weeks after his directive from Caldwell, Hunt found himself fifty feet below ground level at pad twelve of number-two terminal complex twenty miles outside Houston, walking along one of the access ramps that connected the wall of the silo to the gleaming hull of the Vega. An hour later, the hydraulic rams beneath the platform supporting the tail thrust the ship slowly upward and out, to stand clear on the roof of the structure. Within minutes the Vega was streaking into the darkening void above. It docked thirty minutes later, two and a half seconds behind schedule, with the half-mile-diameter transfer satellite *Kepler*.

On *Kepler* the passengers traveling on to Luna— including Hunt, three propulsion-systems experts keen to examine the suspected Ganymean gravity drives, four communications specialists, two structural engineers, and Danchekker's team, all destined to join Jupiter Five—transferred to the ugly and ungainly Capella class moonship that would carry them for the remainder of the journey from Earth orbit to the Lunar surface. The voyage lasted thirty hours and was uneventful. After they had been in Lunar orbit for twenty minutes, the announcement came over the loudspeaker that the craft had been cleared for descent.

Shortly afterward, the unending procession of plains, mountains, crags, and hills that had been marching across the cabin display screen slowed to a halt and the view started growing perceptibly larger. Hunt recognized the twin ring-walled plains of Ptolemy and Albategnius, with its central conical mountain and Crater Klein interrupting its encircling wall, before the ship swung northward and these details were lost off the top of the steadily enlarging image. The picture stabilized, now centered upon the broken and crumbling mountain wall that separated Ptolemy from the southern edge of the Plain of Hipparchus. What had previously looked like smooth terrain resolved itself into a jumble of rugged cliffs and valleys, and in the center, glints of sunlight began to appear, reflected from the metal structures of the vast base below.

As the outlines of the surface installations materialized out of the gray background and expanded to fill the screen, a yellow glow in the center grew, gradually transforming into the gaping entrance to one of the underground moonship berths. There was a brief impression of tiers of access levels stretching down out of sight and huge service gantries swung back to admit the ship. Rows of brilliant arc lights flooded the scene before the exhaust from the braking motors blotted out the view. A mild jolt signaled that the landing legs had made contact with Lunar rock, and silence fell abruptly inside the ship as the engines were cut. Above the squat nose of the moonship, massive steel shutters rolled together to seal out the stars. As the berth filled with air, a new world of sound impinged on the ears of the ship's occupants. Shortly afterward, the access ramps slid smoothly from the walls to connect the ship to the reception bays.

Thirty minutes after clearing arrival formalities, Hunt emerged from an elevator high atop one of the viewing domes that dominated the surface of Ptolemy Main Base. For a long time he gazed soberly at the harsh desolation in which man had carved this oasis of life. The streaky blue and white disk of Earth, hanging motionless above the horizon, suddenly brought home to him the remoteness of places like Houston, Reading, Cambridge, and the meaning of everything familiar, which until so recently he had taken for granted. In his wanderings he had never come to regard any particular place as home; unconsciously he had always accepted any part of the world to be as much home as any other. Now, all at once, he realized that he was away from home for the first time in his life.

As Hunt turned to take in more of the scene below, he saw that he was not alone. On the far side of the dome a lean, balding figure stood staring silently out over the wilderness, absorbed in thoughts of its own.

Hunt hesitated for a long time. At last he moved slowly across to stand beside the figure. All around them the mile-wide clutter of silver-gray metallic geometry that made up the base sprawled amid a confusion of pipes, girders, pylons, and antennae. On towers above, the radars swept the skyline in endless circles, while the tall, praying-mantislike laser transceivers stared unblinkingly at the heavens, carrying the ceaseless dialogues between the base computers and unseen communications satellites fifty miles up. In the distance beyond the base, the rugged bastions of Ptolemy's mountain wall towered above the plain. From the blackness above them, a surface transporter was sliding toward the base on its landing approach.

Eventually Hunt said: "To think—a generation ago, all this was just desert." It was more a thought voiced than a statement.

Danchekker did not answer for a long time. When he did, he kept his eyes fixed outside.

"But man dared to dream . . ." he murmured slowly. After a pause he added, "And what man dares to dream today, tomorrow he makes come true."

Another long silence followed. Hunt took a cigarette from his case and lit it. "You know," he said at last, blowing a stream of smoke slowly toward the glass wall of the dome, "it's going to be a long voyage to Jupiter. We could get a drink down below—one for the road, as it were."

Danchekker seemed to turn the suggestion over in his mind for a while. At length he shifted his gaze back within the confines of the dome and turned to face Hunt directly.

"I think not, Dr. Hunt," he said quietly.

Hunt sighed and made as if to turn.

"However, . . ." The tone of Danchekker's voice checked him before he moved. He looked up. "If your metabolism is capable of withstanding the unaccustomed shock of nonalcoholic beverages, a strong coffee might, ah, perhaps be extremely welcome."

It was a joke. Danchekker had actually cracked a joke!

"I'll try anything once," Hunt said as they began walking toward the door of the elevator.

chapter nineteen

Embarkation on the orbiting Jupiter Five command ship was not scheduled to take place until a few days later. Danchekker would be busy making final arrangements for his team and their equipment to be ferried up from the Lunar surface. Hunt, not being involved in these undertakings, prepared an itinerary of places to visit during the free time he had available.

The first thing he did was fly to Tycho by surface transporter to observe the excavations still going on around the areas of some of the Lunarian finds, and to meet at last many of the people who up until then had existed only as faces on display screens. He also went to see the deep mining and boring operations in progress not far from Tycho, where engineers were attempting to penetrate to the core regions of the Moon. They believed that concentrations of rich metal-bearing ores might be found there. If this turned out to be so, within decades the Moon could become an enormous spaceship factory, where parts prefabricated in processing and forming plants on the surface would be ferried up for final assembly in Lunar orbit. The economic advantages of constructing deep-space craft here and from Lunar materials, without having to lift everything up out of Earth's gravity pit to start with, promised to be enormous.

Next, Hunt visited the huge radio and optical observatories of Giordano Bruno on Farside. Here, sensitive receivers, operating fully shielded from the perpetual interference from Earth, and gigantic telescopes, freed from any atmosphere and not having to contend with distortions induced by their own weights, were pushing the frontiers of the known Universe way out beyond the limits of their Earth-bound predecessors. Hunt sat fascinated in front of the monitor screens and resolved planets of some of the nearer stars; he was shown one nine times the size of Jupiter, and another that described a crazy figure-eight orbit about a double star. He gazed deep into the heart of the Andromeda Galaxy, and out at distant specks on the very threshold of detection. Scientists and physicists described the strange new picture of the Cosmos that was beginning to emerge from their work here and explained some of the exciting advances in concepts of space–time mechanics, which indicated that feasible methods could be devised for deforming astronomic geodesics in such a way that the limitations once thought to apply to extreme effective velocities could be avoided. If so, interstellar travel would become a practical proposition; one of the scientists confidently predicted that man would cross the Galaxy within fifty years.

Hunt's final stop brought him back to Nearside—to the base at Copernicus near which Charlie had been found. Scientists at Copernicus had been studying descriptions of the terrain over which Charlie had traveled and the accompanying sketched maps; the information contained in the notebook had been transmitted up from Houston. From the traveling times, distances, and estimates of speed quoted, they suspected that Charlie's journey had begun somewhere on Farside and had brought him, by way of the Jura Mountains, Sinus Iridum, and Mare Imbrium, to Copernicus. Not everybody subscribed to this opinion, however; there was a problem. For some unaccountable reason, the directions and compass points mentioned in Charlie's notes bore no relationship to the conventional lunar north–south that derived from its axis of rotation. The only route for Charlie's journey that could be interpreted to make any sense at all was the one from Farside across Mare Imbrium, but even that only made sense if a completely new direction was assumed for the north–south axis.

Attempts to locate Gorda had so far met with no positive success. From the tone of the final entries in the diary, it could not have been very far from the spot where Charlie was found. About fifteen miles south of this point was an area covered by numerous overlapping craters, all confirmed as being meteoritic and of recent origin. Most researchers concluded that this must have been the site of Gorda, totally obliterated by a freak concentration of meteorites in the as yet unexplained storm.

Before leaving Copernicus, Hunt accepted an invitation to drive out overland and visit the place of Charlie's discovery. He was accompanied by a Professor Alberts from the base and the crew of the UNSA survey vehicle.

The survey vehicle lumbered to a halt in a wide gorge, between broken walls of slate-gray rock. All around it, the dust had been churned into a bewildering pattern of grooves and ridges by Caterpillar tracks, wheels, landing gear, and human feet—evidence of the intense activity that had occurred there over the last eighteen months. From the observation dome of the upper cabin, Hunt recognized the scene immediately; he had first seen it in Caldwell's office. He identified the large mound of rubble against the near wall of the gorge, and above it the notch leading into the cleft.

A voice called from below. Hunt rose to his feet, his movements slow and clumsy in his encumbering spacesuit, and clambered through the floor hatch and down a short ladder to the control cabin. The driver was stretching back in his seat, taking a long drink from a flask of hot coffee. Behind him, the sergeant in command of the vehicle was at a videoscreen, reporting back to base via comsat that they had reached their destination without mishap. The third crew member, a corporal who was to accompany Hunt and Alberts outside and who was already fitted out, was helping the professor secure his helmet. Hunt took his own helmet from the storage rack by the door and fixed it in place. When the three were ready, the sergeant supervised the final checkout of life-support and communications systems and cleared them to pass, one by one, through the airlock to the outside.

"Well, there you are, Vic. Really on the Moon now." Alberts's voice came through the speaker inside Hunt's helmet. Hunt felt the spongy dust yield beneath his boots and tried a few experimental steps up and down.

"It's like Brighton Beach," he said.

"Okay, you guys?" asked the voice of the UNSA corporal.

"Okay."

"Sure."

"Let's go, then."

The three brightly colored figures—one orange, one red, and one green—began moving slowly along the well-worn groove that ran up the center of the mound of rubble. At the top they stopped to gaze down at the survey vehicle, already looking toylike in the gorge below.

They moved into the cleft, climbing between vertical walls of rocks that closed in on both sides as they approached the bend. Above the bend the cleft straightened, and in the distance Hunt could see a huge wall of jagged buttresses towering over the foothills above them—evidently the ridge described in Charlie's note. He could picture vividly the scene in this very place so long ago, when two other figures in spacesuits had toiled onward and upward, their eyes fixed on that same feature. Above it, the red and black portent of a tormented planet had glowered down on their final agony like . . .

Hunt stopped, puzzled. He looked up at the ridge again, then turned to stare at the bright disk of Earth, shining far behind his right shoulder. He turned to look one way, then back again the other.

"Anything wrong?" Alberts, who had continued on a few paces, had turned and was staring back at him.

"I'm not sure. Hang on there a second." Hunt moved up alongside the professor and pointed up and ahead toward the ridge. "You're more familiar with this place than I am. See that ridge up ahead there— At any time in the year, could the Earth ever appear in a position over the top of it?"

Alberts followed Hunt's pointing finger, glanced briefly back at the Earth, and shook his head decisively behind his facepiece.

"Never. From the Lunar surface, the position of Earth is almost constant. It does wobble about its mean position a bit as a result of libration, but not by anything near that much." He looked again. "Never anywhere near there. That's an odd question. Why do you ask?"

"Just something that occurred to me. Doesn't really matter for now."

Hunt lowered his eyes and saw an opening at the base of one of the walls ahead. "That must be it. Let's carry on up to it."

The hole was exactly as he remembered from innumerable photographs. Despite its age, the shape betrayed its artificial origin. Hunt approached almost reverently and paused to finger the rock at one side of the opening with his gauntlet. The score marks had obviously been made by something like a drill.

"Well, that's it," came the voice of Alberts, who was standing a few feet back. "Charlie's Cave, we call it— more or less exactly as it must have been when he and his companion first saw it. Rather like treading in the sacred chambers of one of the pyramids, isn't it?"

"That's one way of putting it." Hunt ducked down to peer inside, pausing to fumble for the flashlight at his belt as the sudden darkness blinded him temporarily.

The rockfall that originally had covered the body had been cleared, and the interior was roomier than he expected. Strange emotions welled inside him as he stared at the spot where, millennia before the first page of history had been written, a huddled figure had painfully scrawled the last page of a story that Hunt had read so recently in an office in Houston, a quarter of a million miles away. He thought of the time that had passed since those events had taken place—of the empires that had grown and fallen, the cities that had crumbled to dust, and the lives that had sparkled briefly and been swallowed into the past—while all that time, unchanging, the secret of these rocks had lain undisturbed. Many minutes passed before Hunt reemerged and straightened up in the dazzling sunlight.

Again he frowned up toward the ridge. Something tantalizing was dancing elusively just beyond the fringes of the thinking portions of his mind, as if from the subconscious shadows that lay below, something insistent was shrieking to be recognized. And then it was gone.

He clipped the flashlight back into position on his belt and walked across to rejoin Alberts, who was studying some rock formations on the opposite wall.

chapter twenty

The giant ships that would fly on the fifth manned mission to Jupiter had been under construction in Lunar orbit for over a year. Besides the command ship, six freighters, each capable of carrying thirty thousand tons of supplies and equipment, gradually took shape high above the surface of the Moon. During the final two months before scheduled departure, the floating jumbles of machinery, materials, containers, vehicles, tanks, crates, drums, and a thousand other items of assorted engineering that hung around the ships like enormous Christmas-tree ornaments, were slowly absorbed inside. The Vega surface shuttles, deep-space cruisers, and other craft also destined for the mission began moving

in over a period of several weeks to join their respective
mother ships. At intervals throughout the last week, the
freighters lifted out of Lunar orbit and set course for
Jupiter. By the time its passengers and final comple-
ment of crew were being ferried up from the Lunar surface, only the command ship was left, hanging alone in
the void. As H hour approached, the gaggle of service
craft and attendant satellites withdrew and a flock of
escorts converged to stand a few miles off, cameras
transmitting live via Luna into the World News Grid.

As the final minutes ticked by, a million viewscreens
showed the awesome mile-and-a-quarter-long shape
drifting almost imperceptibly against the background of
stars; the serenity of the spectacle seemed somehow to
forewarn of the unimaginable power waiting to be un-
leashed. Exactly on schedule, the flight-control computers completed their final-countdown-phase checkout,
obtained "Go" acknowledgment from the ground control master processor, and activated the main thermonuclear drives in a flash that was visible from Earth.

The Jupiter Five Mission was under way.

For the next fifteen minutes the ship gained speed
and altitude through successively higher orbits. Then,
shrugging off the restraining pull of Luna with effortless
ease, *Jupiter Five* soared out and away to begin over-
taking and marshaling together its flock of freighters, by
this time already strung out across a million miles of
space. After a while the escorts turned back toward
Luna, while on Earth the news screens showed a steadily diminishing point of light, being tracked by the orbiting telescopes. Soon even that had vanished, and only
the long-range radars and laser links were left to continue their electronic exchanges across the widening
gulf.

Aboard the command ship, Hunt and the other
UNSA scientists watched on the wall screen in mess
twenty-four as the minutes passed by and Luna con-
tracted into a full disk, partly eclipsing that of Earth
beyond. In the days that followed, the two globes waned
and fused into a single blob of brilliance, standing out in

the heavens to signpost the way they had come. As days turned into weeks, even this shrank to become just another grain of dust among millions until, after about a month, they could pick it out only with difficulty.

Hunt found that it took time to adjust to the idea of living as part of a tiny man-made world, with the cosmos stretching away to infinity on every side and the distance between them and everything that was familiar increasing at more than ten miles every second. Now they depended utterly for survival on the skills of those who had designed and built the ship. The green hills and blue skies of Earth were no longer factors of survival and seemed to shed some of their tangible attributes, almost like the aftermath of a dream that had seemed real. Hunt came to think of reality as a relative quantity—not something absolute that can be left for a while and then returned to. The ship became the only reality; it was the things left behind that ceased, temporarily, to exist.

He spent hours in the viewing domes along the outer hull, slowly coming to terms with the new dimension being added to his existence, gazing out at the only thing left that was familiar: the Sun. He found reassurance in the eternal presence of the Sun, with its limitless flood of life-giving warmth and light. Hunt thought of the first sailors, who had never ventured out of sight of land; they too had needed something familiar to cling to. But before long, men would turn their prow toward the open gulf and plunge into the voids between the galaxies. There would be no Sun to reassure them then, and there would be no stars at all; the galaxies themselves would be just faint spots, scattered all the way to infinity.

What strange new continents were waiting on the other side of those gulfs?

Danchekker was spending one of his relaxation periods in a zero-gravity section of the ship, watching a game of 3-D football being played between two teams of off-duty crew members. The game was based on American-style football and took place inside an enormous sphere of transparent, rubbery plastic. Players hurtled up, down, and in all directions, rebounding off the wall and off each other in a glorious roughhouse directed—vaguely—at getting the ball through two circular goals on opposite sides of the sphere. In reality, the whole thing was just an excuse to let off steam and flex muscles beginning to go soft during the long, monotonous voyage.

A steward tapped the scientist on the shoulder and informed him that a call was waiting in the videobooth outside the recreation deck. Danchekker nodded, unclipped the safety loop of his belt from the anchor pin attached to the seat, clipped it around the handrail, and with a single effortless pull, sent himself floating gracefully toward the door. Hunt's face greeted him, speaking from a quarter of a mile away.

"Dr. Hunt," he acknowledged. "Good morning—or whatever it happens to be at the present time in this infernal contraption."

"Hello, Professor," Hunt replied. "I've been having some thoughts about the Ganymeans. There are one or two points I could use your opinion on; could we meet somewhere for a bite to eat, say inside the next half hour or so?"

"Very well. Where did you have in mind?"

"Well, I'm on my way to the restaurant in E section right now. I'll be there for a while."

"I'll join you there in a few minutes." Danchekker cut off the screen, emerged from the booth, and hauled himself back into the corridor and along it to an entrance to one of the transverse shafts leading "down" toward the axis of the ship. Using the handrails, he sailed some distance toward the center before checking himself opposite an exit from the shaft. He emerged through a transfer lock into one of the rotating sections, with simulated G, at a point near the axis where the speed differential was low. He launched himself back along another rail and felt himself accelerate gently, to land thirty feet away, on his feet, on a part of the structure that had sudddenly become the floor. Walking normally, he followed some signs to the nearest tube access point, pressed the call button, and waited about twenty seconds for a capsule to arrive. Once inside, he keyed in his destination and within seconds was being whisked smoothly through the tube toward E section of the ship.

The permanently open self-service restaurant was about half full. The usual clatter of cutlery and dishes poured from the kitchens behind the counter at one end, where a trio of UNSA cooks were dishing out generous helpings of assorted culinary offerings ranging from UNSA eggs and UNSA beans to UNSA chicken legs and UNSA steaks. Automatic food dispensers with do-it-yourself microwave cookers had been tried on *Jupiter Four* but hadn't proved popular with the crew. So the designers of *Jupiter Five* had gone back to the good old-fashioned methods.

Carrying their trays, Hunt and Danchekker threaded their way between diners, card players, and vociferous debating groups and found an empty table against the far wall. They sat down and began transferring their plates to the table.

"So, you've been entertaining some thoughts concerning our Ganymean friends," Danchekker commented as he began to butter a roll.

"Them and the Lunarians," Hunt replied. "In particular, I like your idea that the Lunarians evolved on Minerva from terrestrial animal species that the Ganymeans imported. It's the only thing that accounts acceptably for no traces of any civilization showing up on Earth. All these attempts people are making to show it might be different don't convince me much at all."

"I'm very gratified to hear you say so," Danchekker declared. "The problem, however, is proving it."

"Well, that's what I've been thinking about. Maybe we shouldn't have to."

Danchekker looked up and peered inquisitively over his spectacles. He looked intrigued. "Really? How, might I ask?"

"We've got a big problem trying to figure out anything about what happened on Minerva because we're fairly sure it doesn't exist any more except as a million chunks of geology strewn around the Solar System. But the Lunarians didn't have that problem. They had it in one piece, right under their feet. Also, they had progressed to an advanced state of scientific knowledge. Now, what must their work have turned up—at least to some extent?"

A light of comprehension dawned in Danchekker's eyes.

"Ah!" he exclaimed at once. "I see. If the Ganymean civilization had flourished on Minerva first, then Lunarian scientists would surely have deduced as much." He paused, frowned, then added: "But that does not get you very far, Dr. Hunt. You are no more able to interrogate Lunarian scientific archives than you are to reassemble the planet."

"No, you're right," Hunt agreed. "We don't have any detailed Lunarian scientific records—but we do have the microdot library. The texts it contains are pretty general in nature, but I couldn't help thinking that if the Lunarians discovered an advanced race had been there before them, it would be big and exciting news, something everybody would know about; you've only got to look at the fuss that Charlie has caused on Earth. Perhaps there were references through all of their writings that pointed to such a knowledge—if we knew how to read them." He paused to swallow a mouthful of sausage. "So, one of the things I've been doing over the last few weeks is going through everything we've got with a fine-tooth comb to see if anything could point to something like that. I didn't expect to find firm proof of anything much—just enough for us to be able to say with a bit more confidence that we think we know what planet we're talking about."

"And did you find very much?" Danchekker seemed interested.

"Several things," Hunt replied. "For a start, there are stock phrases scattered all through their language that refer to the Giants. Phrases like 'As old as the Giants' or 'Back to the year of the Giants' . . . like we'd say maybe, 'Back to the year one.' In another place there's a passage that begins 'A long time ago, even before the time of the Giants' . . . There are lots of things like that. When you look at them from this angle, they all suddenly tie together." Hunt paused for a second to allow the professor time to reflect on these points, then resumed: "Also, there are references to the Giants in another context, one that suggests superpowers or great knowledge—for example, 'Gifted with the wisdom of the Giants.' You see what I mean—these phrases indicate the Lunarians felt a race of giant beings—and probably one that was advanced technologically—had existed in the distant past."

Danchekker chewed his food in silence for a while.

"I don't want to sound overskeptical," he said at last, "but all this seems rather speculative. Such references could well be to nothing more than mythical creations—similar to our own heroes of folklore."

"That occurred to me, too," Hunt conceded. "But thinking about it, I'm not so sure. The Lunarians were the last word in pragmatism—they had no time for romanticism, religion, matters of the spirit, or anything like that. In the situation they were in, the only people who could help them were themselves, and they knew it. They couldn't afford the luxury and the delusion of inventing gods, heroes, and Father Christmases to work their problems out for them." He shook his head. "I don't believe the Lunarians made up any legends about these Giants. That would have been too much out of character."

"Very well," Danchekker agreed, returning to his meal. "The Lunarians were aware of the prior existence of the Ganymeans. I suspect, however, that you had more than that in mind when you called."

"You're right," Hunt said. "While I was going through the texts, I pulled together some other bits and pieces that are more in your line."

"Go on."

"Well, supposing for the moment that the Ganymeans did ship a whole zoo out to Minerva, the Lunarian biologists later on would have had a hell of a problem making any sense out of what they found all around them, wouldn't they? I mean, with two different groups of animals loose about the place, totally unrelated—and bearing in mind that they couldn't have known what we know about terrestrial species . . ."

"Worse than that, even," Danchekker supplied. "They would have been able to trace the native Minervan species all the way back to their origins; the imported types, however, would extend back through only twenty-five million years or so. Before that, there would have been no record of any ancestors from which they could have descended."

"That's precisely one of the things I wanted to ask you," Hunt said. He leaned forward and rested his elbows on the table. "Suppose you were a Lunarian biologist and knew only the facts he would have know. What sort of picture would it have added up to?"

Danchekker stopped chewing and thought for a long time, his eyes staring far beyond where Hunt was sitting. At length he shook his head slowly.

"That is a very difficult question to answer. In that situation one might, I suppose, speculate that the Ganymeans had introduced alien species. But on the other hand, that is what a biologist from Earth would think; he would be conditioned to expect a continuous fossil record stretching back over hundreds of millions of years. A Lunarian, without any such conditioning, might not regard the absence of a complete record as in any way abnormal. If that was part of the accepted way of things in the world in which he had grown up . . ."

Danchekker's voice faded away for a few seconds. "If I were a Lunarian," he said suddenly, his voice decisive, "I would explain what I saw thus: Life began in the distant past on Minerva, evolved through the accepted process of mutation and selection, and branched into many diverse forms. About twenty-five million years ago, a particularly violent series of mutations occurred in a short time, out of which emerged a new family of forms, radically different in structure from anything before. This family branched to produce its own divergency of species, living alongside the older models, and culminating in the emergence of the Lunarians themselves. Yes, I would explain the new appearances in that way. It's similar to the appearance of insects on Earth—a whole family in itself, structurally dissimilar to anything else." He thought it over again for a second and then nodded firmly. "Certainly, compared to an explanation of that nature, suggestions of forced interplanetary migrations would appear very farfetched indeed."

"I was hoping you'd say something like that." Hunt nodded, satisfied. "In fact, that's very much what they appear to have believed. It's not specifically stated in anything I've read, but odds and ends from different places add up to that. But there's something odd about it as well."

"Oh?"

"There's a funny word that crops up in a number of places that doesn't have a direct English equivalent; it means something between 'manlike' and 'man-related.' They used it to describe many animal types."

"Probably the animals descended from the imported types and related to themselves," Danchekker suggested.

"Yes, exactly. But they also used the same word in a totally different context—to mean 'ashore,' 'on land' . . . anything to do with dry land. Now, why should a word become synonymous with two such different meanings?"

Danchekker stopped eating again and furrowed his brow.

"I really can't imagine. Is it important?"

"Neither could I, and I think it is. I've done a lot of cross-checking with Linguistics on this, and it all adds up to a very peculiar thing: 'Manlike' and 'dry-land' became synonymous on Minerva because they did in fact mean the same thing. All the land animals on Minerva were new models. We coined the word *terrestoid* to describe them in English."

"*All* of them? You mean that by Charlie's time there

were none of the original Minervan species left at all?"
Danchekker sounded amazed.

"That's what we think—not on land, anyway. There
was a full fossil record of plenty of types all the way
up to, and including the Ganymeans, but nothing after
that—just terrestoids."

"And in the sea?"

"That was different. The old Minervan types continued right through—hence your fish."

Danchekker gazed at Hunt with an expression that
almost betrayed open disbelief.

"How extraordinary!" he exclaimed.

The professor's arm had suddenly become paralyzed
and was holding a fork in midair with half a roast po-
tato impaled on the end. "You mean that all the native
Minervan land life disappeared—just like that?"

"Well, during a fairly short time, anyway. We've
been asking for a long time what happened to the Ganymeans. Now it looks more as if the question should be
phrased in even broader terms: What happened to the
Ganymeans and all their land-dwelling relatives?"

chapter twenty-one

For weeks the two scientists debated the mystery of the
abrupt disappearance of the native Minervan land
dwellers. They ruled out physical catastrophe on the assumption that anything of that kind would have destroyed the terrestoid types as well. The same conclusion applied to climatic cataclysm.

For a while they considered the possibility of an epidemic caused by microorganisms imported with the immigrant animals, one against which the native species

enjoyed no inherited, in-built immunity. In the end they dismissed this idea as unlikely on two counts; first, an epidemic sufficiently virulent in its effects to wipe out each and every species of what must have numbered millions, was hard to imagine; second, all information received so far from Ganymede suggested that the Ganymeans had been considerably farther ahead in technical knowledge that either the Lunarians or mankind—surely they could never have made such a blunder.

A variation on this theme supposed that germ warfare had broken out, escalated, and got out of control. Both the previous objections carried less weight when viewed in this context; in the end, this explanation was accepted as possible. That left only one other possibility: some kind of chemical change in the Minervan atmosphere to which the native species hadn't been capable of adapting but the terrestoids had. But what?

While the pros and cons of these alternatives were still being evaluated on *Jupiter Five*, the laser link to Earth brought details of a new row that had broken out in Navcomms. A faction of Pure Earthists had produced calculations showing that the Lunarians could never have survived on Minerva at all, let alone flourished there; at that distance from the Sun it would simply have been too cold. They also insisted that water could never have existed on the surface in a liquid state and held this fact as proof that wherever the world shown on Charlie's maps had been, it couldn't have been anywhere near the Asteroids.

Against this attack the various camps of Minerva-ists concluded a hasty alliance and opened counterfire with calculations of their own, which invoked the greenhouse effect of atmospheric carbon dioxide to show that a substantially higher temperature could have been sustained. They demonstrated further that the percentage of carbon dioxide required to produce the mean temperature that they had already estimated by other means, was precisely the figure arrived at by Professor Schorn in his deduction of the composition of the Minervan atmosphere from an analysis of Charlie's cell metabolism and respiratory system. The land mine that finally demolished the Pure Earthist position was Schorn's later pronouncement that Charlie exhibited several physiological signs implying adaptation to an abnormally high level of carbon dioxide.

Their curiosity stimulated by all this sudden interest in the amount of carbon dioxide in the Minervan atmosphere, Hunt and Danchekker devised a separate experiment of their own. Combining Hunt's mathematical skill with Danchekker's knowledge of quantitative molecular biology, they developed a computer model of generalized Minervan microchemical behavior potentials, based on data derived from the native fish. It took them over three months to perfect. Then they applied to the model a series of mathematical operators that simulated the effects of different chemical agents in the environment. When he viewed the results on the screen in one of the console rooms Danchekker's conclusion was quite definite: "Any air-breathing life form that evolved from the same primitive ancestors as this fish and inherited the same fundamental system of microchemistry, would be extremely susceptible to a family of toxins that includes carbon dioxide—far more so than the majority of terrestrial species."

For once, everything added up. About twenty-five million years ago, the concentration of carbon dioxide in the atmosphere of Minerva apparently increased suddenly, possibly through some natural cause that had liberated the gas from chemical combination in rocks, or possibly as a result of something the Ganymeans had done. This could also explain why the Ganymeans had brought in all the animals. Perhaps their prime objective had been to redress the balance by covering the planet with carbon-dioxide-absorbing, oxygen-producing terrestrial green plants; the animals had been included simply to preserve a balanced ecology in which the plants could survive. The attempt failed. The native life succumbed, and the more highly resistant immigrants flourished and spread out over a whole new world denuded of alien competition. Nobody knew for sure that it had been so on Minerva. Possibly nobody ever would.

And nobody knew what had become of the Ganymeans. Perhaps they had perished along with their cousins. Perhaps, when their efforts proved futile, they had abandoned Minerva to its new inhabitants and left the Solar System completely to find a new home elsewhere. Hunt hoped so. For some strange reason he had developed an inexplicable affection for this mysterious race. In one of the Lunarian texts he had come across a verse that began: "Far away among the stars, where the Giants of old now live . . ." He hoped it was true.

And so, quite suddenly, at least one chapter in the early history of Minerva had been cleared up. Everything now pointed to the Lunarians and their civilization as having developed on Minerva and not on Earth. It explained the failure of Schorn's early attempt to fix the length of the day in Hunt's calendar by calculating Charlie's natural periods of sleep and wakefulness. The ancestors of the Lunarians had arrived from Earth carrying a deeply rooted metabolic rhythm evolved around a twenty-four hour cycle. During the twenty-five million years that followed, some of the more flexible biological processes in their descendants adapted successfully to the thirty-five-hour day of Minerva, while others changed only partially. By Charlie's time, all the Lunarians' physiological clocks had gotten hopelessly out of synchronization; no wonder Schorn's results made no sense. But the puzzling numbers in Charlie's notebook still remained to be accounted for.

In Houston, Caldwell read Hunt and Danchekker's joint report with deep satisfaction. He had realized long before that to achieve results, the abilities of the two scientists would have to be combined and focused on the problem at hand instead of being dissipated fruitlessly in the friction of personal incompatibility. How could he manipulate into being a situation in which the things they had in common outweighed their differences? Well, what did they have in common? Starting with the simplest and most obvious thing—they were both human beings from planet Earth. So where would this fundamental truth come to totally overshadow anything else? Where but on the barren wastes of the Moon or a hundred million miles out in the emptiness of space? Everything seemed to be working out better then he had dared hope.

"It's like I always said," Lyn Garland stated coyly when Hunt's assistant showed her a copy of the report. "Gregg's a genius with people."

The arrival in Ganymede orbit of the seven ships from Earth was a big moment for the Jupiter Four veterans, especially those whose tour of duty was approaching an end and who could now look forward to going home soon. In the weeks to come, as the complex program of maneuvering supplies and equipment between the ships and the surface installations unfolded, the scene above Ganymede would become as chaotic as that above Luna had been during departure preparations. The two command ships would remain standing off ten miles apart for the next two months. Then *Jupiter Four*, accompanied by two of the recently arrived freighters, would move out to take up station over Callisto and begin expanding the pilot base already set up there. *Jupiter Five* would remain at Ganymede until joined by *Saturn Two*, which was at that time undergoing final countdown for Lunar lift-out and due to arrive in five months. After rendezvous above Ganymede, one of the two ships (exactly which was yet to be decided) would set course for the ringed planet, on the farthest large-scale manned probe yet attempted.

The long-haul sailing days of *Jupiter Four* were over. Too slow by the standards of the latest designs, it would probably be stripped down to become a permanent orbiting base over Callisto. After a few years it would suffer the ignoble end of being dismantled and cannibalized for surface constructions.

With all the hustle and traffic congestion that erupted in the skies over Ganymede, it was three days before the time came for the group of UNSA scientists to be ferried to the surface. After months of getting used to the pattern of life and the company aboard the ship, Hunt felt a twinge of nostalgia as he packed his belongings in his cabin and stood in line waiting to board the Vega moored alongside in the cavernous midships docking bay. It was probably the last he would see of the inside of this immense city of metal alloys; when he returned to Earth, it would be aboard one of the small, fast cruisers ferried out with the mission.

An hour later *Jupiter Five,* festooned in a web of astronautic engineering, was shrinking rapidly on the cabin display in the Vega. Then the picture changed suddenly and the sinister frosty countenance of Ganymede came swelling up toward them.

Hunt sat on the edge of his bunk inside a Spartan room in number-three barrack block of Ganymede Main Base and methodically transferred the contents of his kit bag into the aluminum locker beside him. The air-extractor grill above the door was noisy. The air drawn in through the vents set into the lower walls was warm, and tainted with the smell of engine oil. The steel floor plates vibrated to the hum of heavy machinery somewhere below. Propped up against a pillow on the bunk opposite, Danchekker was browsing through a folder full of facsimiled notes and color illustrations and chattering excitedly like a schoolboy on Christmas Eve.

"Just think of it, Vic, another day and we'll be there. Animals that actually walked the Earth twenty-five million years ago! Any biologist would give his right arm for an experience like this." He held up the folder. "Look at that. I do believe it to be a perfectly preserved example of *Trilophodon*—a four-tusked Miocene mammoth over fifteen feet high. Can you imagine anything more exciting than that?"

Hunt scowled sourly across the room at the collection of pin-ups adorning the far wall, bequeathed by an earlier UNSA occupant.

"Frankly, yes," he muttered. "But equipped rather differently than a bloody *Trilophodon.*"

"Eh? What's that you said?" Danchekker blinked un-comprehendingly through his spectacles. Hunt reached for his cigarette case.

"It doesn't matter, Chris," he sighed.

chapter twenty-two

The flight northward to Pithead lasted just under two hours. On arrival, the group from Earth assembled in the officers' mess of the control building for coffee, during which scientists from Jupiter Four updated them on Ganymean matters.

The Ganymean ship had almost certainly been destined for a large-scale, long-range voyage and not for anything like a limited exploratory expedition. Several hundred Ganymeans had died with their ship. The quantity and variety of stores, materials, equipment, and livestock that they had taken with them indicated that wherever they had been bound, they had meant to stay.

Everything about the ship, especially its instrumentation and control systems, revealed a very advanced stage of scientific knowledge. Most of the electronics were still a mystery, and some of the special-purpose components were unlike anything the UNSA engineers had even seen. Ganymean computers were built using a mass-integration technology in which millions of components were diffused, layer upon layer, into a single monolithic silicon block. The heat dissipated inside was removed by electronic cooling networks interwoven with the functional circuitry. In some examples, believed to form parts of the navigation system, component packing densities approached that of the human brain. A physicist held up a slab of what appeared to be silicon, about the size of a large dictionary; in terms of raw processing power, he claimed, it was capable of outperforming all the computers in the Navcomms Headquarters building put together.

The ship was streamlined and strongly constructed, indicating that it was designed to fly through atmospheres and to land on a planet without collapsing under its own weight. Ganymean engineering appeared to have reached a level where the functions of a Vega and a deep-space interorbital transporter were combined in one vessel.

The propulsion system was revolutionary. There were no large exhaust apertures and no obvious reaction points to suggest that the ship had been kicked forward by any kind of thermodynamic or photonic external thrust. The main fuel-storages system fed a succession of convertors and generators designed to deliver enormous amounts of electrical and magnetic energy. This supplied a series of two-foot-square superconducting busbars and a maze of interleaved windings, fabricated from solid copper bars, that surrounded what appeared to be the main-drive engines. Nobody was sure precisely how this arrangement resulted in motion of the ship, although some of the theories were startling.

Could this have been a true starship? Had the Ganymeans left enmasses in an interstellar exodus? Had this particular ship foundered on its way out of the Solar System, shortly after leaving Minerva? These questions and a thousand more remained to be answered. One thing was certain, though: If the discovery of Charlie had given two years' work to a significant proportion of Navcomms, there was enough information here to keep half the scientific world occupied for decades, if not centuries.

The party spent some hours in the recently erected laboratory dome, inspecting items brought up from below the ice, including several Ganymean skeletons and a score of terrestrial animals. To Danchekker's disappointment, his particular favorite—the man–ape anthropoid he had shown to Hunt and Caldwell many months before on a viewscreen in Houston—was not among them. "Cyril" had been transferred to the laboratories of the Jupiter Four command ship for detailed examination. The name, graciously bestowed by the UNSA biologists, was in honor of the mission's chief scientist.

After lunch in the base canteen, they walked into the dome that covered one of the shaftheads. Fifteen minutes later they were standing deep below the surface of the ice field, gazing in awe at the ship itself.

It lay, fully uncovered, in the vast white floodlighted cavern, its underside still supported in its mold of ice. The hull cut a clean swath through the forest of massive steel jacks and ice pillars that carried the weight of the roof. Beneath the framework of ramps and scaffolding that clung to its side, whole sections of the hull had been removed to reveal the compartments inside. The floor all around was littered with pieces of machinery lifted out by overhead cranes. The scene reminded Hunt of the time he and Borlan had visited Boeing's huge plant near Seattle where they assembled the 1017 skyliners—but everything here was on a far vaster scale.

They toured the network of catwalks and ladders that had been laid throughout the ship, from the command deck with its fifteen-foot-wide display screen, through the control rooms, living quarters, and hospital, to the cargo holds and the tiers of cages that had contained the animals. The primary energy-convertor and generator section was as imposing and as complex as the inside of a thermonuclear power station. Beyond it, they passed through a bulkhead and found themselves dwarfed beneath the curves of the exposed portions of a pair of enormous toroids. The engineer leading them pointed up at the immense, sweeping surfaces of metal.

"The walls of those outer casings are sixteen feet thick," he informed them. "They're made from an alloy that would cut tungsten-carbide steel like cream cheese. The mass concentration inside them is phenomenal. We think they provided closed paths in which masses of highly concentrated matter were constrained in circulating or oscillating resonance, interacting with strong fields. It's possible that the high rates of change of gravity potential that this produced were somehow harnessed to induce a controlled distortion in the space around the ship. In other words, it moved by continuously falling into a hole that it created in front of itself—kind of like a four-dimensional tank track."

"You mean it trapped itself inside a space–time bubble, which propagated somehow through normal space?" somebody offered.

"Yes, if you like," the engineer affirmed. "I guess a bubble is as good an analogy as any. The interesting point is, if it did work that way, every particle of the ship and everything inside it would be subjected to exactly the same acceleration. Therefore there would be no *G* effect. You could stop the ship dead from, say, a million miles an hour to zero in a millisecond, and nobody inside would even know the difference."

"How about top speed?" someone else asked. "Would there have been a relativistic limit?"

"We don't know. The theory boys up in *Jupiter Four* have been losing a lot of sleep over that. Conventional mechanics wouldn't apply to any movement of the ship itself, since it wouldn't be actually moving in the local space inside the bubble. The question of how the bubble propagates through normal space is a different ball game altogether. A whole new theory of fields has to be worked out. Maybe completely new laws of physics apply—as I said before, we just don't know. But one thing seems clear: Those photon-drive starships they're designing in California might turn out to be obsolete before they're even built. If we can figure out enough about how this ship worked, the knowledge could put us forward a hundred years."

By the end of the day Hunt's mind was in a whirl. New information was coming in faster than he could digest it. The questions in his head were multiplying at a rate a thousand times faster than they could ever be answered. The riddle of the Ganymean spaceship grew more intriguing with every new revelation, but at the back of it there was still the Lunarian problem unresolved. He needed time to stand back and think, to put his mental house in order and sort the jumble into related thoughts that would slot into labeled boxes in his mind. Then he would be able to see better which question depended on what, and which needed to be tackled first. But the jumble was piling up faster than he could pick up the pieces.

The banter and laughter in the mess after the evening meal soon became intolerable. Alone in his room, he found the walls claustrophobic. For a while he walked the deserted corridors between the domes and buildings. They were oppressive; he had lived in metal cans for too long. Eventually he found himself in the control tower dome, staring out into the incandescent gray wall that was produced by the floodlights around the base soaking through the methane–ammonia fog of the Ganymedean night. After a while even the presence of the duty controller, his face etched out against the darkness by the glow from his console, became an intrusion. Hunt stopped by the console on his way to the stairwell.

"Check me out for surface access."

The duty controller looked across at him. "You're going outside?"

"I need some air."

The controller brought one of his screens to life. "You are who, please?"

"Hunt. Dr. V. Hunt."

"ID?"

"730289 C/EX4."

The controller logged the details, then checked the time and keyed it in.

"Report in by radio in one hour's time if you're not back. Keep a receiver channel open permanently on 24.328 megahertz."

"Will do," Hunt acknowledged. "Good night."

"Night."

The controller watched Hunt disappear towards the floor below, shrugged to himself, and automatically scanned the displays in front of him. It was going to be a quiet night.

In the surface access anteroom on the ground level, Hunt selected a suit from the row of lockers along the right hand wall. A few minutes later, suited up and with his helmet secured, he walked to the airlock, keyed his name and ID code into the terminal by the gate, and waited a couple of seconds for the inner door to slide open.

He emerged into the swirling silver mist and turned right to follow the line of the looming black metal cliff of the control building. The crunch of his boots in the powder ice sounded faint and far away, through the thin vapors. Where the wall ended he continued walking slowly in a straight line, out into the open area and toward the edge of the base. Phantom shapes of steel emerged and disappeared in the silent shadows around him. The gloom ahead grew darker as islands of diffuse light passed by on either side. The ice began sloping upward. Irregular patches of naked, upthrusting rock became more frequent. He walked on as if in a trance.

Pictures from the past rolled by before his mind's eye: a boy, reading books, shut away in the upstairs bedroom of a London slum . . . a youth, pedaling a bicycle each morning through the narrow streets of Cambridge. The people he had been were no more real than the people he would become. All through his life he had been moving on, never standing still, always in the process of changing from something he had been to something he would be. And beyond every new world, another beckoned. And always the faces around him were unfamiliar ones—they drifted into his life like the transient shadows of the rocks that now moved toward him from the mists ahead. Like the rocks, for a while the people seemed to exist and take on form and substance, before slipping by to dissolve into the shrouds of the past behind him, as if they had never been. Forsyth-

Scott, Felix Borlan, and Rob Gray had already ceased to exist. Would Caldwell, Danchekker, and the rest soon fade away to join them? And what new figures would materialize out of the unknown worlds lying hidden behind the veils of time ahead?

He realized with some surprise that the mists around him were getting brighter again; also, he could suddenly see farther. He was climbing upward across an immense ice field, now smooth and devoid of rocks. The light was an eerie glow, permeating evenly through mists on every side as if the fog itself were luminous. He climbed higher. With every step the horizon of his vision broadened further, and the luminosity drained from the surrounding mist to concentrate itself in a single patch that second by second grew brighter above his head. And then he was looking out over the top of the fog bank. It was just a pocket, trapped in the depression of the vast basin in which the base had been built; it had no doubt been sited there to shorten the length of the shaft needed to reach the Ganymean ship. The slope above him finished in a long, rounded ridge not fifty feet beyond where he stood. He changed direction slightly to take the steeper incline that led directly to the summit of the ridge. The last tenuous wisps of whiteness fell away.

At the top, the night was clear as crystal. He was standing on a beach of ice that shelved down from his feet into a lake of cotton wool. On the opposite shore of the lake rose the summits of the rock buttresses and ice cliffs that stood beyond the base. For miles around, ghostly white bergs of Ganymedean ice floated on an ocean of cloud, shining against the blackness of the night.

But there was no Sun.

He raised his eyes, and gasped involuntarily. Above him, five times larger than the Moon seen from Earth, was the full disk of Jupiter. No photograph he had ever seen, or any image reproduced on a display screen, could compare with the grandeur of that sight. It filled the sky with its radiance. All the colors of the rainbow were woven into its iridescent bands of light, stacked layer upon layer outwards from its equator. They faded as they approached its edge and merged into a hazy circle of pink that encircled the planet. The pink turned to violet and finally to purple, ending in a clear, sharp outline that traced an enormous circle against the sky. Immutable, immovable, eternal . . . mightiest of the gods—and tiny, puny, ephemeral man had crawled on a pilgrimage of five hundred million miles to pay homage.

Maybe only seconds passed, maybe hours. Hunt could not tell. For a fraction of eternity he stood unmoving, a speck lost among the silent towers of rock and ice. Charlie too had stood upon the surface of a barren waste and gazed up at a world wreathed in light and color—but the colors had been those of death.

At that moment, the scenes that Charlie had seen came to Hunt more vividly than at any time before. He saw cities consumed by fireballs ten miles high; he saw gaping chasms, seared and blackened ash that had once held oceans, and lakes of fire where mountains had stood. He saw continents buckle and break asunder, and drown beneath a fury of white heat that came exploding outward from below. As clearly as if it were really happening, he saw the huge globe above him swelling and bursting, grotesque with the deceptive slowness of mighty events seen from great distances. Day by day it would rush outward into space, consuming its moons one after the other in an insatiable orgy of gluttony until its force was spent. And then . . .

Hunt snapped back to reality with a jolt.

Suddenly the answer he had been seeking was there. It had come out of nowhere. He tried to trace its root by backtracking through his thoughts—but there was nothing. The pathways up from the deeper levels of his mind had opened for a second, but now were closed. The illusion was exposed. The paradox had gone. Of course nobody had seen it before. Who would think to question a truth that was self-evident, and older than the human race itself?

"Pithead Control calling Dr. V. Hunt. Dr. Hunt,

come in, please." The sudden voice in his helmet startled him. He pressed a button in the control panel on his chest.

"Hunt answering," he acknowledged. "I hear you."

"Routine check. You're five minutes overdue to report. Is everything okay?"

"Sorry, didn't notice the time. Yes, everything's okay . . . very okay. I'm coming back now."

"Thank you." The voice cut off with a click.

Had he been gone that long? He realized that he was cold. The icy fingers of the Ganymedean night were beginning to feel their way inside his suit. He wound his heating control up a turn and flexed his arms. Before he turned, he looked up once more for a final glimpse of the giant planet. For some strange reason it seemed to be smiling.

"Thanks, pal," he murmured with a wink. "Maybe I'll be able to do something for you someday."

With that he began moving down from the ridge, and rapidly faded into the sea of cloud.

chapter twenty-three

A group of about thirty people, mainly scientists, engineers, and UNSA executives, filed into the conference theater in the Navcomms Headquarters building. The room was arranged in ascending tiers of seats that faced a large blank screen at the far end from the double doors. Caldwell was standing on a raised platform in front of the screen, watching as the various groups and individuals found seats. Soon everybody was settled and an usher at the rear signaled that the corridor outside was empty. Caldwell nodded in acknowledgment, raised his hand for silence, and stepped a pace forward to the microphone in front of him.

"Your attention, please, ladies and gentlemen . . . Could we have quiet, please . . . " The baritone voice boomed out of the loudspeakers around the walls. The murmurs subsided.

"Thank you all for coming on such short notice," he resumed. "All of you have been engaged for some time now in some aspect or other of the Lunarian problem. Ever since this thing first started, there have been more than a few arguments and differences of opinion, as you all know. Taking all things into consideration, however, we haven't done too badly. We started out with a body and a few scraps of paper, and from them we reconstructed a whole world. But there are still some fundamental questions that have remained unanswered right up to this day. I'm sure there's no need for me to recap them for the benefit of anyone here." He paused. "At last, it appears, we may have answers to those questions. The new developments that cause me to say this are so unexpected that I feel it appropriate to call you all together to let you see for yourselves what I saw for the first time only a few hours ago." He waited again and allowed the mood of the gathering to move from one suited to preliminary remarks to something more in tune with the serious business about to begin.

"As you all know, a group of scientists left us many months ago with the Jupiter Five Mission to investigate the discoveries on Ganymede. Among that group was Vic Hunt. This morning we received his latest report on what's going on. We are about to replay the recording for you now. I think you will find it interesting."

Caldwell glanced toward the projection window at the back of the room and raised his hand. The lights began to fade. He stepped down from the platform and took his seat in the front row. Darkness reigned briefly. Then the screen illuminated to show a file header and reference frame in standard UNSA format. The header persisted for a few seconds, then disappeared to be replaced by the image of Hunt, facing the camera across a desktop.

"Navcomms Special Investigation to Ganymede, V. Hunt reporting, 20 November 2029, Earth Standard Time," he announced. "Subject of transmission: *A Hypothesis Concerning Lunarian Origins.* What follows is not claimed to be rigorously proven theory at this stage. The object is to present an account of a possible sequence of events which, for the first time, explains adequately the origins of the Lunarians, and is also consistent with *all* the facts currently in our possession." Hunt paused to consult some notes on the desk before him. In the conference theater the silence was absolute.

Hunt looked back up and out of the screen. "Up until now I've tended not to accent any particular one of the ideas in circulation in preference to the rest, primarily because I haven't been sufficiently convinced that any of them, as stated, accounted adequately for everything that we had reason to believe was true. That situation has changed. I have now come to believe that one explanation exists which is capable of supporting all the evidence. That explanation is as follows:

"The Solar System was formed originally with nine planets, which included Minerva and extended out as far as Neptune. Akin to the inner planets and located beyond Mars, Minerva resembled Earth in many ways. It was similar in size and density and was composed of a mix of similar elements. It cooled and developed an atmosphere, a hydrosphere, and a surface composition." Hunt paused for a second. "This has been one source of difficulty—reconciling surface conditions at this distance from the Sun with the existence of life as we know it. For proof that these factors can indeed be reconciled, refer to Professor Fuller's work at London University during the last few months." A caption appeared on the lower portion of the screen, giving details of the titles and access codes of Fuller's papers on the subject.

"Briefly, Fuller has produced a model of the equilibrium states of various atmospheric gases and volcanically introduced water vapor, that is consistent with known data. To sustain the levels of free atmospheric carbon dioxide and water vapor, and the existence of large amounts of water in a liquid state, the model requires a very high level of volcanic activity on the planet, at least in its earlier history. That this requirement was evidently met could suggest that relative to its size, the crust of Minerva was exceptionally thin, and the structure of this crust unstable. This is significant, as becomes clear later. Fuller's model also ties in with the latest information from the Asteroid surveys. The thin crust could be the result of relatively rapid surface cooling caused by the vast distance from the Sun, but with the internal molten condition being prolonged by heat sources below the surface. The Asteroid missions report many samples being tested that are rich in radioactive heat-producing substances.

"So, Minerva cooled to a mean surface temperature somewhat colder than Earth's but not as cold as you might think. With cooling came the formation of increasingly more complex molecules, and eventually life emerged. With life came diversification, followed by competition, followed by selection—in other words, evolution. After many millions of years, evolution culminated in a race of intelligent beings who became dominant on the planet. These were the beings we have christened the Ganymeans.

"The Ganymeans developed an advanced technological civilization. Then, approximately twenty-five million years ago, they had reached a stage which we estimate to be about a hundred years ahead of our own. This estimate is based on the design of the Ganymean ship we've been looking at here, and the equipment found inside it.

"Some time around this period, a major crisis developed on Minerva. Something upset the delicate mechanism controlling the balance between the amount of carbon dioxide locked up in the rocks and that in the free state; the amount in the atmosphere began to rise. The reasons for this are speculative. One possibility is that something triggered the tendency toward high volcanic activity inherent in Minerva's structure—maybe natural causes, maybe something the Ganymeans did. Another possibility is that the Ganymeans were attempting an ambitious program of climate control and the whole thing went wrong in a big way. At present we really don't have a good answer to this part. However, our investigations of the Ganymeans have hardly begun yet. There are still years of work to be done on the contents of the ship alone, and I'm pretty certain that there's a lot more waiting to be discovered down under the ice here.

"Anyhow, the main point for the present is that something happened. Chris Danchekker has shown . . ." Another file reference appeared on the bottom of the screen. ". . . that all the higher, air-breathing Minervan life forms would almost certainly have possessed a very low tolerance to increases in carbon-dioxide concentration. This derives from the fundamental system of microchemistry inherited from the earliest ancestors of the line. This implies, of course, that the changing surface conditions on Minerva posed a threat to the very existence of most forms of land life, including the Ganymeans. If we accept this situation, we also have a plausible reason for supposing that the Ganymeans went through a phase of importing on a vast scale a mixed balance of plant and animal life from Earth. Perhaps, stuck out where it was, Minerva had nothing to compare with the quantity and variety of life teeming on the much warmer planet Earth.

"Evidently, the experiment didn't work. Although the imported stock found conditions favorable enough to flourish in, they failed to produce the desired result. From various bits of information, we believe the Ganymeans gave the whole thing up as a bad job and moved out to find a new home somewhere outside the Solar System. Whether or not they succeeded we don't know; maybe further study of what's in the ship will throw more light on that question."

Hunt stopped to pick up a case from the desk and went through the motions of lighting a cigarette. The break seemed to be timed to give the viewers a chance to digest this part of his narrative. A subdued chorus of mutterings broke out around the room. Here and there a light flared as individuals succumbed to the suggestion from the screen. Hunt continued:

"The native Minervan land species left on the planet soon died out. But the immigrant types from Earth enjoyed a better adaptability and survived. Not only that, they were free to roam unchecked and unhindered across the length and breadth of Minerva, where any native competition rapidly ceased to exist. The new arrivals were thus free to continue the process of evolutionary development that had begun millions of years before in the oceans of Earth. But at the same time, of course, the same process was also continuing on Earth itself. Two groups of animal species, possessing the same genetic inheritance from common ancestors and equipped with the same evolutionary potential, were developing in isolation on two different worlds.

"Now, for those of you who have not yet had the pleasure, allow me to introduce Cyril." The picture of Hunt vanished and a view of the man–ape retrieved from the Ganymean ship appeared.

Hunt's voice carried on with the commentary: "Chris's team has made a thorough examination of this character in the Jupiter Four laboratories. Chris's own summary of their results was, quote: 'We consider this to be something nearer the direct line of descent toward modern man than anything previously studied. Many fossil finds have been made on Earth of creatures that represented various branches of development from the early progressive apes in the general direction of man. All finds to date, however, have been classed as belonging to offshoots from the main stream; a specimen of a direct link in the chain leading to *Homo sapiens* has always persistently eluded us. Here, we have such a link.' Unquote." The image of Hunt reappeared. "We can be fairly sure, therefore, that among the terrestrial life forms left to develop on Minerva were numbers of primates as far advanced in their evolution as anything back on Earth.

"The faster evolution characteristic of Minerva thus far, was repeated, possibly as a result of the harsher environment and climate. Millions of years passed. On Earth a succession of manlike beings came and went, some progressive, some degenerate. The Ice Age came and moved through into its final, glacial phase some fifty thousand years ago. By this time on Earth, primitive humanoids represented the apex of progress—crude cave dwellers, hunters, makers of simple weapons and tools chipped out of stone. But on Minerva, a new technological civilization already existed: the Lunarians—descended from the imported stock and from the same early ancestors as ourselves, human in every detail of anatomy.

"I won't dwell on the problems that confronted the developing Lunarian civilization—they're well-known by now. Their history was one long story of war and hardship enacted around a racial quest to escape from their dying world. Their difficulties were compounded by a chronic shortage of minerals, possibly because the planet was naturally deficient, or possibly because it had been thoroughly exploited by the Ganymeans. At any rate, the warring factions polarized into two superpowers, and in the showdown that followed they destroyed themselves and the planet."

Hunt paused again at this point to allow another period of consolidation for the audience. This time, however, there was complete silence. Nothing he had said so far was new, but he had formed a set selected from the thousand and one theories and speculations that had raged around Navcomms for as long as many could remember. The silent watchers in the theater sensed that the real news was still to come.

"Let's stop for a moment and examine how well this account fits in with the evidence we have. First, the original problem of Charlie's human form. Well, that's answered: He was human—descended from the same ancestors as the rest of us and requiring nothing as unlikely as a parallel line to explain him. Second, the absence of any signs of the Lunarians on Earth. Well, the reason is quite obvious: They never were on Earth. Third, all the attempts to reconcile the surface geography of Charlie's world with Earth become unnecessary, since by this account they were indeed two different planets.

"So far so good, then. This by itself, however, does not explain all the facts. There are some additional pieces of evidence which must be taken into account by any theory that claims to be comprehensive. They can be summarized in the following questions:

"One: How could Charlie's voyage from Minerva to our Moon have taken only two days?

"Two: How do we explain a weapons system, consistent with the Lunarian level of technology, that was capable of accurate registration over a range extending from our Moon to Minerva?

"Three: How could the loop feedback delay in the fire-control system have been sustantially less than the minimum of twenty-six minutes that could have applied over that distance?

"Four: How could Charlie distinguish surface features of Minerva when he was standing on our Moon?"

Hunt looked out from the screen and allowed plenty of time for the audience to reflect on these questions. He stubbed out his cigarette and leaned forward toward the camera, his elbows coming to rest on the desk.

"There is, in my submission, only one explanation which is capable of satisfying these apparently nonsensical requirements. And I put it to you now. The moon that orbited Minerva from time immemorial up until the time of these events fifty thousand years ago—and the Moon that shines in the sky above Earth today—are one and the same!"

Nothing happened for about three seconds.

Then gasps of incredulity erupted from around the darkened room. People gesticulated at their neighbors while some turned imploringly for comment from the row behind. Suddenly the whole theater was a turmoil of muttered exchanges.

"Can't be!"

"By God—he's right!"

"Of course . . . of course . . . !"

"Has to be . . ."

"Garbage!"

On the screen Hunt stared out impassively, as if he were watching the scene. His allowance for the probable reaction was well timed. He resumed speaking just as the confusion of voices was dying away.

"We *know* that the moon Charlie was on was our Moon—because we found him there, because we can identify the areas of terrain he described, because we have ample evidence of a large-scale Lunarian presence there, and because we have proved that it was the scene of a violent exchange of nucleonic and nuclear weapons. But that same place *must also have been* the satellite of Minerva. It was only a two-day flight from the planet—Charlie says so and we're confident we can interpret his time scale. Weapons were sited there which could pick off targets on Minerva, and observations of hits were almost instantaneous; and if all that is not enough, Charlie could stand not ten yards from where we found him and distinguish details of Minerva's surface. These things could *only* be true if the place in question was within, say, half a million miles of Minerva.

"Logically, the only explanation is that both moons were one and the same. We've been asking for a long time whether the Lunarian civilization developed on Earth or whether it developed on Minerva. Well, from the account I've given, it's obvious it was Minerva. We thought we had two contradictory sets of information, one telling us it was Earth and the other telling us it wasn't. But we had misinterpreted the data. It wasn't telling us anything to do with Earth or Minerva at all—it was telling us about Earth's or Minerva's *moon!* Some facts told us we were dealing with Earth's moon while others told us we were dealing with Minerva's moon. As long as we insisted on introducing, quite unconsciously, the notion that the two moons were different, the conflict between these sets of facts couldn't be resolved. But if, purely within the logical constraints of the situation, we introduce the postulate that both moons were the same, that conflict disappears before our eyes."

Shock seemed to have overtaken the audience. At the front somebody was muttering, "Of course . . . of course . . ." half to himself and half aloud.

"All that remains is to reconcile these propositions with the situation we observe around us today. Again, only one explanation is possible. Minerva exploded and dispersed to become the Asteroid Belt. The greater part of its mass, we're fairly sure, was thrown into the outer regions of the Solar System and became Pluto. Its moon, although somewhat shaken, was left intact. During the gravitational upheaval that occurred when its parent planet broke up, the satellite's orbital momentum around the Sun was reduced and it began to fall inward.

"We can't tell how long the orphaned moon plunged steadily nearer the Sun. Maybe the trip lasted months, maybe years. Next comes one of those million-to-one chances that sometimes happen in nature. The trajectory followed by the moon brought it close to Earth, which had been pursuing its own *solitary* path around the Sun ever since the beginning of time!" Hunt paused for a few seconds. "Yes, I repeat, *solitary* path! You see, if we are to accept what I believe to be the only satisfactory explanation open to us, we must accept also its consequence: that until this point in time, some fifty thousand years ago, planet Earth had *no moon!* The two bodies drew close enough for their gravitational fields to interact to the point of mutual capture; the new, common orbit turned out to be stable, and Earth adopted a foundling it has kept right up to this day.

"If we accept this account, many of the other things that have been causing problems suddenly make sense. Take, for example, the excess material that covers most of Lunar Farside and has been shown to be of recent origin, and coupled with that, the dating of all Farside craters and some Nearside ones to around the time we're talking about. Now we have a ready explanation. When Minerva blew up, what is now Luna was sitting there right in the way of all the debris. That's where the meteorite storm came from. That's how practically all evidence of the Lunarian presence on Luna was wiped out. There's probably no end to remains of their bases, installations, and vehicles still there waiting to be un- covered—a thousand feet below the Farside surface. We think that the Annihilator emplacement at Seltar was on Farside. That suggests that what is Farside to Earth today was Nearside to Minerva; hence it makes sense that most of the meteorite storm landed where it did.

"Charlie appears to have referred to compass direc- tions different from ours on the Lunar surface, implying a different north–south axis. Now we see why. Some peo- ple have asked why, if Luna suffered such an intense bombardment, there should be no signs of any compa- rable increase in meteorite activity on Earth at the time. This too now makes sense: When Minerva blew up, Luna was in its immediate vicinity but Earth wasn't. And a last point on Lunar physics— We've known for half a century that Luna is formed from a mix of rocky compounds different from those found on Earth, being low in volatiles and rich in refractories. Scientists have speculated for a long time that possibly the Moon was formed in another part of the Solar System. This indeed turns out to be true if what I've said is correct.

"Some explanations have suggested that the Lunari- ans set up advanced bridgeheads on Luna. This enabled their evident presence there to be reconciled with evo- lutionary origins on Minerva, but raised an equally problematical question: Why were they struggling to master interplanetary space-flight technology when they must have had it already? In the account I have de- scribed, this problem disappears. They had reached their own moon, but were still some ways from being able to move large populations to anyplace as remote as Earth. Also, there is now no need to introduce the un- supported notion of Lunarian colonies on either planet; either way, it would pose the same question.

"And finally, an unsolved riddle of oceanography

makes sense in this light, too. Research into tidal motions has shown that catastrophic upheavals on a planetary scale occurred on Earth at about this time, resulting in an abrupt increase in the length of the day and an increase in the rate at which the day is further being lengthened by tidal friction. Well, the arrival of Minerva's moon would certainly create enormous gravitational and tidal disturbances. Although the exact mechanics aren't too clear right now, it appears that the kinetic energy acquired by Minerva's moon as it fell toward the Sun, was absorbed in neutralizing part of the Earth's rotational energy, causing a longer day. Also, increased tidal friction since then is to be expected. Before the Moon appeared, Earth experienced only Solar tides, whereas from that time up until today, there have been both Solar and Lunar tides."

Hunt showed his empty hand in a gesture of finality and pushed himself back in his chair. He straightened the pile of notes on the desk before going on to conclude:

"That's it. As I said earlier, at this stage it represents no more than a hypothesis that accounts for all the facts. But there are some things we can do toward testing the truth of it.

"For a start, we have a large chunk of Minerva piled up all over Farside. The recent material is so like the original Lunar material that it was years before anybody realized it had been added only recently. That supports the idea that the Moon and the meteorites originated in the same part of the Solar System. I'd like to suggest that we perform detailed comparisons between data from Farside material and data from the Asteroid surveys. If the results indicate that they are both the same kind of stuff and appear to have come from the same place, the whole idea would be well supported.

"Another thing that needs further work is a mathematical model of the process of mutual capture between Earth and Luna. We know quite a lot about the initial conditions that must have existed before and, of course, a lot more about the conditions that exist now.

It would be reassuring to know that for the equations involved there exist solutions that allow one situation to transform into the other within the normal laws of physics. At least, it would be nice to prove that the whole idea isn't impossible.

"Finally, of course, there is the Ganymean ship here. Without doubt a lot of new information is waiting to be discovered—far more than we've had to work on so far. I'm hoping that somewhere in the ship there will be astronomic data to tell us something about the Solar System at the time of the Ganymeans. If, for example, we could determine whether or not the third planet from the Sun of their Solar System had a satellite, or if we could learn enough about their moon to identify it as Luna—perhaps by recognizing Nearside surface features—then the whole theory would be well on the way to being proved.

"This concludes the report.

"Personal addendum for Gregg Caldwell . . ." The view of Hunt was replaced by a landscape showing a wilderness of ice and rock. "This place you've sent us to, Gregg—the mail service isn't too regular, so I couldn't send a postcard. It's over a hundred Celsius degrees below zero; there's no atmosphere worth talking about and what there is, is poisonous; the only way back is by Vega, and the nearest Vega is seven hundred miles away. I wish you were here to enjoy all the fun with us, Gregg—I really do!

"V. Hunt from Ganymede Pithead Base. End of transmission."

chapter twenty-four

The long-awaited answers to where the Lunarians had come from and how they came to be where they had been found sent waves of excitement around the scientific world and prompted a new frenzy of activity in the news media. Hunt's explanation seemed complete and consistent. There were few objections or disagreements; the account didn't leave much to object to or disagree with.

Hunt had therefore met fully the demands of his brief. Although detailed interdisciplinary work would continue all over the world for a long time to come, UNSA's formal involvement in the affair was more or less over. So Project Charlie was run down. That left Project Ganymeans, which was just starting up. Although he had not yet received any formal directive from Earth to say so, Hunt had the feeling that Caldwell wouldn't waste the opportunity offered by Hunt's presence on Ganymede just when the focus of attention was shifting from the Lunarians to the Ganymeans. In other words, it would be some time yet before he would find himself walking aboard an Earth-bound cruiser.

A few weeks after the publication of UNSA's interim conclusions, the Navcomms scientists on Ganymede held a celebration dinner in the officers' mess at Pithead to mark the successful end of a major part of their task. The evening had reached the warm and mellow phase that comes with cigars and liqueurs when the last-course dishes have been cleared away. Talkative groups were standing and sitting in a variety of attitudes around the tables and by the bar, and beers, brandies, and vintage ports were beginning to flow freely. Hunt was with a group of physicists near the bar, discussing the latest news on the Ganymean field drive, while behind them another circle was debating the likelihood of a world government being established within twenty years. Danchekker seemed to have been unduly quiet and withdrawn for most of the evening.

"When you think about it, Vic, this could develop into the ultimate weapon in interplanetary warfare," one of the physicists was saying. "Based on the same principles as the ship's drive, but a lot more powerful and producing a far more intense and localized effect. It would generate a black hole that would persist, even after the generator that made it had fallen into it. Just think—an artificially produced black hole. All you'd have to do is mount the device in a suitable missile and fire it at any planet you took a dislike to. It would fall to the center and consume the whole planet—and there'd be no way to stop it."

Hunt looked intrigued. "You mean it could work?"

"The theory says so."

"Christ, how long would it take—to wipe out a planet?"

"We don't know yet; we're still working on that bit. But there's more to it than that. There's no reason why you shouldn't be able to put out a star using the same method. Think about that as a weapon—one black-hole bomb could destroy a whole solar system. It makes nucleonic weapons look like kiddie toys."

Hunt started to reply, but a voice from the center of the room cut him off, rising to make itself heard above the buzz of conversation. It belonged to the commander of Pithead Base, special guest at the dinner.

"Attention, please, everybody," he called. "Your attention for a moment, please." The noise died as all faces turned toward him. He looked around until satisfied that everyone was paying attention. "You have invited me here tonight to join you in celebrating the successful conclusion of what has probably been one of the most challenging, the most astounding, and the most rewarding endeavors that you are ever likely to be involved in. You have had difficulties, contradictions, and disagreements to contend with, but all that is now in the past. The task is done. My congratulations." He glanced toward the clock above the bar. "It is midnight—a suitable time, I think, to propose a toast to the being that started the whole thing off, wherever he may be." He raised his glass. "To Charlie."

"To Charlie," came back the chorus.

"*No!*"

A voice boomed from the back of the room. It sounded firm and decisive. Everybody turned to look at Danchekker in surprise.

"No," the professor repeated. "We can't drink to that just yet."

There was no suggestion of hesitation or apology in his manner. Clearly his action was reasoned and calculated.

"What's the problem, Chris?" Hunt asked, moving forward away from the bar.

"I'm afraid that's not the end of it."

"How do you mean?"

"The whole Charlie business— There is more to it— more than I have chosen to mention to anybody, because I have no proof. However, there is a further implication in all that has been deduced—one which is even more difficult to accept than even the revelations of the past few weeks."

The festive atmosphere had vanished. Suddenly they were in business again. Danchekker walked slowly toward the center of the room and stopped with his hands resting on the back of one of the chairs. He gazed at the table for a moment, then drew a deep breath and looked up.

"The problem with Charlie, and the rest of the Lunarians, that has not been touched upon is this: quite simply, they were *too* human."

Puzzled looks appeared here and there. Somebody turned to his neighbor and shrugged. They all looked back at Danchekker in silence.

"Let us recapitulate for a moment some of the fundamental principles of evolution," he said. "How do different animal species arise? Well, we know that variations of a given species arise from mutations caused by various agencies. It follows from elementary genetics that in a freely mixing and interbreeding population, any new characteristic will tend to be diluted, and will disappear within relatively few generations. However"—the professor's tone became deadly serious— "when sections of the population became reproductively isolated from one another—for example, by geographical separation, by segregation of behavior patterns, or by seasonal differences, say, in mating times—dilution through interbreeding will be prevented. When a new characteristic appears within an isolated group, it will be confined to and reinforced within that group; thus, generation by generation, the group will *diverge* from the other group or groups from which it has been isolated. Finally a new species will establish itself. This principle is fundamental to the whole idea of evolution: Given isolation, divergence *will* occur. The origins of all species on Earth can be traced back to the existence at some time of some mechanism or other of isolation between variations within a single species. The animal life peculiar to Australia and South America, for instance, demonstrates how rapidly divergence takes effect even when isolation has existed only for a short time.

"Now we seem to be satisfied that for the best part of twenty-five million years, two groups of terrestrial animals—one on Earth, the other on Minerva—were left to evolve in *complete* isolation. As a scientist who accepts fully the validity of the principle I have just outlined, I have no hesitation in saying that divergence between these two groups *must* have taken place. That, of course, applies equally to the primate lines that were represented on both planets."

He stopped and stood looking from one to the other of his colleagues, giving them time to think and waiting for a reaction. The reaction came from the far end of the room.

"Yes, now I see what you're saying," somebody said.

"But why speculate? What's the point in saying they should have diverged, when it's clear that they didn't?"

Danchekker beamed and showed his teeth. "What makes you say they didn't?" he challenged.

The questioner raised his arms in appeal. "What my two eyes tell me—I can see they didn't."

"What do you see?"

"I see humans. I see Lunarians. They're the same. So, they didn't diverge."

"Didn't they?" Danchekker's voice cut the air like a whiplash. "Or are you making the same unconscious assumption that everyone else has made? Let me go over the facts once again, purely from an objective point of view. I'll simply list the things we observe and make no assumptions, conscious or otherwise, about how they fit in with what we think we already know.

"First: The two populations were isolated. Fact.

"Second: Today, twenty-five million years later, we observe two sets of individuals, ourselves and the Lunarians. Fact.

"Third: We and the Lunarians are identical. Fact.

"Now, if we accept the principle that divergence must have occurred, what must we conclude? Ask yourselves— If confronted by those facts and nothing else, what would any scientist deduce?"

Danchekker stood facing them, pursing his lips and rocking back and forth on his heels. Silence enveloped the room, broken after a few seconds by his whistling quietly and tunelessly to himself.

"*Christ* . . . !" The exclamation came from Hunt. He stood gaping at the professor in undisguised disbelief. "They couldn't have been isolated from each other," he managed at last in a slow, halting voice. "They must both be from the same . . ." The words trailed away.

Danchekker nodded with evident satisfaction. "Vic's seen what I am saying," he informed the group. "You see, the only logical conclusion that can be drawn from the statements I have just enumerated is this: If two identical forms are observed today, they must both come from the *same* isolated group. In other words, if two lines were isolated and branched apart, both forms *must* lie on the *same branch!*"

"How can you say that, Chris?" someone insisted. "We know they came from different branches."

"What do you know?" Danchekker whispered.

"Well, I know that the Lunarians came from the branch that was isolated on Minerva . . ."

"Agreed."

". . . And I know that man comes from the branch that was isolated on Earth."

"How?"

The question echoed sharply around the walls like a pistol shot.

"Well . . . I . . ." The speaker made a gesture of helplessness. "How do I answer a question like that? It . . . it's obvious."

"Precisely!" Danchekker showed his teeth again. "You *assume* it—just as everybody else does! That's part of the conditioning you've grown up with. It has been assumed all through the history of the human race, and naturally so—there has never been any reason to suppose otherwise." Danchekker straightened up and regarded the room with an unblinking stare. "Now perhaps you see the point of all this. I am stating that, on the evidence we have just examined, the human race did not evolve on Earth at all. *It evolved on Minerva!*"

"Oh, Chris, really . . ."

"This is getting ridiculous . . ."

Danchekker hammered on relentlessly: "Because, if we accept that divergence must have occurred, then both we and the Lunarians must have evolved in the same place, and we already know that *they* evolved on *Minerva!*"

A murmur of excitement mixed with protest ran around the room.

"I am stating that Charlie is not just a distantly related cousin of man—*he is our direct ancestor!*" Danchekker did not wait for comment but pressed on in the same insistent tone: "And I believe that I can give you an explanation of our own origins which is fully consistent with these deductions." An abrupt silence fell upon the room. Danchekker regarded his colleagues for a few seconds. When he spoke again, his voice had fallen to a calmer and more objective note.

"From Charlie's account of his last days, we know that some Lunarians were left alive on the Moon after the fighting died down. Charlie himself was one of them. He did not survive for long, but we can guess that there were others—desperate groups such as the ones he described—scattered across that Lunar surface. Many would have perished in the meteorite storm on Farside, but some, like Charlie's group, were on Nearside when Minerva exploded and were spared the worst of the bombardment. Even a long time later, when the Moon finally stabilized in orbit around Earth, a handful of survivors remained who gazed up at the new world that hung in their sky. Presumably some of their ships were still usable—perhaps just one, or two, or a few. There was only one way out. Their world had ceased to exist, so they took the only path open to them and set off on a last, desperate attempt to reach the surface of Earth. There could be no way back—there was no place to go back to.

"So we must conclude that their attempt succeeded. Precisely what events followed their emergence out into the savagery of the Ice Age we will probably never know for sure. But we can guess that for generations they hung on the very edge of extinction. Their knowledge and skills would have been lost. Gradually they reverted to barbarism, and for forty thousand years were lost in the midst of the general struggle for survival. But survive they did. Not only did they survive, they consolidated, spread, and flourished. Today their descendants dominate the Earth just as they dominated Minerva— you, I, and the rest of the human race."

A long silence ensued before anybody spoke. When somebody did, the tone was solemn. "Chris, assuming for now that everything was like you've said, a point still bothers me: If we and the Lunarians both came from the Minervan line, what happened to the other line? Where did the branch that was developing on Earth go?"

"Good question." Danchekker nodded approval. "We know from the fossil record on Earth that during the period that came after the visits of the Ganymeans several developments in the general human direction took place. We can trace this record quite clearly right up to the time in question, fifty thousand years ago. By that time the most advanced stage reached on Earth was that represented by Neanderthal man. Now, the Neanderthals have always been something of a riddle. They were hardy, tough, and superior in intelligence to anything prior to them or coexisting with them. They seemed well adapted to survive the competition of the Ice Age and should, one would think, have attained a dominant position in the era that was to follow. But that did not happen. Strangely, almost mysteriously, they died out abruptly between forty and fifty thousand years ago. Apparently they were unable to compete effectively against a new and far more advanced type of man, whose sudden appearance, as if from nowhere, has always been another of the unsolved riddles of science: *Homo sapiens*—us!"

Danchekker read the expressions on the faces before him and nodded slowly to confirm their thoughts.

"Now, of course, we see why this was so. He did indeed appear out of nowhere. We see why there is no clear fossil record in the soil of Earth to link *Homo sapiens* back to the chain of earlier terrestrial man-apes: He did not evolve there. And we see what it was that so ruthlessly and so totally overwhelmed the Neanderthals. How could they hope to compete against an advanced race, weaned on the warrior cult of Minerva?"

Danchekker paused and allowed his gaze to sweep slowly around the circle of faces. Everybody seemed to be suffering from mental punch-drunkenness.

"As I have said, all this follows purely as a chain of reasoning from the observations with which I began. I can offer no evidence to support it. I am convinced, however, that such evidence does exist. Somewhere on Earth the remains of the Lunarian spacecraft that made that last journey from Luna must still exist, possibly buried beneath the mud of a seabed, possibly under the sands of one of the desert regions. There must exist, on Earth, pieces of equipment and artifacts brought by the tiny handful who represented the remnant of the Lunarian civilization. Where on Earth, is anyone's guess. Personally, I would suggest as the most likely areas the Middle East, the eastern Mediterranean, or the eastern regions of North Africa. But one day proof that what I have said is true will be forthcoming. This I predict with every confidence."

The professor walked around to the table and poured a glass of Coke. The silence of the room slowly dissolved into a rising tide of voices. One by one, the statues that had been listening returned to life. Danchekker took a long drink and stood in silence for a while, contemplating his glass. Then he turned to face the room again.

"Suddenly lots of things that we have always simply taken for granted start falling into place." Attention centralized on him once again. "Have you ever stopped to think what it is that makes man so different from all the other animals on Earth? I know that we have larger brains, more-versatile hands, and so forth; what I am referring to is something else. Most animals, when in a hopeless situation will resign themselves to fate and perish in ignominy. Man, on the other hand, does not know how to give in. He is capable of summoning up reserves of stubbornness and resilience that are without parallel on his planet. He is able to attack anything that threatens his survival, with an aggressiveness the like of which the Earth has never seen otherwise. It is this that has enabled him to sweep all before him, made him lord of all the beasts, helped him tame the winds, the rivers, the tides, and even the power of the Sun itself. This stubbornness has conquered the oceans, the skies, and the challenges of space, and at times has resulted in some of the most violent and bloodstained periods in his history.

But without this side to his nature, man would be as helpless as the cattle in the field."

Danchekker scanned the faces challengingly. "Well, where did it come from? It seems out of character with the sedate and easygoing pattern of evolution on Earth. Now we see where it came from: It appeared as a mutation among the evolving primates that were isolated on Minerva. It was transmitted through the population there until it became a racial characteristic. It proved to be such a devastating weapon in the survival struggle there that effective opposition ceased to exist. The inner driving force that it produced was such that the Lunarians were flying space ships while their contemporaries on Earth were still playing with pieces of stone.

"That same driving force we see in man today. Man has proved invincible in every challenge that the Universe has thrown at him. Perhaps this force has been diluted somewhat in the time that has elapsed since it first appeared on Minerva; we reached the brink of that same precipice of self-destruction but stepped back. The Lunarians hurled themselves in regardless. It could be that this was why they did not seek a solution by cooperation—their in-built tendency to violence made them simply incapable of conceiving such a formula.

"But this is typical of the way in which evolution works. The forces of natural selection will always operate in such a way as to bend and shape a new mutation, and to preserve a variation of it that offers the best prospects of survival for the species as a whole. The raw mutation that made the Lunarians what they were was too extreme and resulted in their downfall. Improvement has taken the form of a dilution, which results in a greater psychological stability of the race. Thus, we survive where they perished."

Danchekker paused to finish his drink. The statues remained statues.

"What an incredible race they must have been," he said. "Consider in particular the handful who were destined to become the forefathers of mankind. They had endured a holocaust unlike anything we can even begin to imagine. They had watched their world and everything that was familiar explode in the skies above their heads. After this, abandoned in an airless, waterless, lifeless, radioactive desert, they were slaughtered beneath the billions of tons of Minervan debris that crashed down from the skies to complete the ruin of all their hopes and the total destruction of all they had achieved.

"A few survived to emerge onto the surface after the bombardment. They knew that they could live only for as long as their supplies and their machines lasted. There was nowhere they could go, nothing they could plan for. They did not give in. They did not know how to give in. They must have existed for months before they realized that, by a quirk of fate, a slim chance of survival existed.

"Can you imagine the feelings of that last tiny band of Lunarians as they stood amid the Lunar desolation, gazing up at the new world that shone in the sky above their heads, with nothing else alive around them and, for all they knew, nothing else alive in the Universe? What did it take to attempt that one-way journey into the unknown? We can try to imagine, but we will never know. Whatever it took, they grasped at the straw that was offered and set off on that journey.

"Even this was only the beginning. When they stepped out of their ships onto the alien world, they found themselves in the midst of one of the most ruthless periods of competition and extinction in the history of the Earth. Nature ruled with an uncompromising hand. Savage beasts roamed the planet; the climate was in turmoil following the gravitational upheavals caused by the arrival of the Moon; possibly they were decimated by unknown diseases. It was an environment that none of their experience had prepared them for. Still they refused to yield. They learned the ways of the new world: They learned to feed by hunting and trapping, to fight with spear and club; they learned how to shelter from the elements, to read and interpret the language of the wild. And as they became proficient in these new arts they grew stronger and ventured farther afield. The spark that they had brought with them and which had carried them through on the very edge of extinction began to glow bright once again. Finally that glow erupted into the flame that had swept all before it on Minerva; they emerged as an adversary more fearsome and more formidable than anything the Earth had ever known. The Neanderthals never stood a chance—they were doomed the moment the first Lunarian foot made contact with the soil of Earth.

"The outcome you see all around you today. We stand undisputed masters of the Solar System and poised on the edge of interstellar space itself, just as they did fifty thousand years ago."

Danchekker placed his glass carefully on the table and moved slowly toward the center of the room. His sober gaze shifted from eye to eye. He concluded: "And so, gentlemen, we inherit the stars.

"Let us go out, then, and claim our inheritance. We belong to a tradition in which the concept of defeat has no meaning. Today the stars and tomorrow the galaxies. No force exists in the Universe that can stop us."

epilogue

Professor Hans Jacob Zeiblemann, of the Department of Paleontology of the University of Geneva, finished his entry for the day in his diary, closed the book with a grunt, and returned it to its place in the tin box underneath his bed. He hoisted his two-hundred-pound bulk to its feet and, drawing his pipe from the breast pocket of his bush shirt, moved a pace across the tent to knock out the ash on the metal pole by the door. As he stood packing a new fill of tobacco into the bowl, he gazed out over the arid landscape of northern Sudan.

The Sun had turned into a deep gash just above the horizon, oozing blood-red liquid rays that drenched the naked rock for miles around. The tent was one of three that stood crowded together on a narrow sandy shelf. The shelf was formed near the bottom of a steep-sided rocky valley, dotted with clumps of coarse bush and desert scrub that clustered together along the valley floor and petered out rapidly, without gaining the slopes on either side. On a wider shelf beneath stood the more numerous tents of the native laborers. Obscure odors wafting upward from this direction signaled that preparation of the evening meals had begun. From farther below came the perpetual sound of the stream, rushing and clattering and jostling on its way to join the waters of the distant Nile.

The crunch of boots on gravel sounded nearby. A few seconds later Zeiblemann's assistant, Jorg Hutfauer, appeared, his shirt dark and streaked with perspiration and grime.

"Phew!" The newcomer halted to mop his brow with something that had once been a handkerchief. "I'm whacked. A beer, a bath, dinner, then bed—that's my program for tonight."

Zeiblemann grinned. "Busy day?"

"Haven't stopped. We've extended sector five to the lower terrace. The subsoil isn't too bad there at all. We've made quite a bit of progress."

"Anything new?"

"I brought these up—thought you might be interested. There's more below, but it'll keep till you come down tomorrow." Hutfauer passed across the objects he had been carrying and continued on into the tent to retrieve a can of beer from the pile of boxes and cartons under the table.

"Mmm . . . " Zeiblemann turned the bone over in his hand. "Human femur . . . heavy." He studied the unusual curve and measured the proportions with his eye. "Neanderthal, I'd say . . . or very near related."

"That's what I thought."

The professor placed the fossil carefully in a tray, covered it with a cloth, and laid the tray on the chest standing just inside the tent doorway. He picked up a hand-sized blade of flint, simply but effectively worked by the removal of long, thin flakes.

"What did you make of this?" he asked.

Hutfauer moved forward out of the shadow and paused to take a prolonged and grateful drink from the can.

"Well, the bed seems to be late Pleistocene, so I'd expect upper Paleolithic indications—which fits in with the way it's been worked. Probably a scraper for skinning. There are areas of microliths on the handle and also around the end of the blade. Bearing in mind the location, I'd put it at something related fairly closely to the Capsian culture." He lowered the can and cocked an inquiring eye at Zeiblemann.

"Not bad," said the professor, nodding. He laid the flint in a tray beside the first and added the identification sheet that Hutfauer had written out. "We'll have a closer look tomorrow when the light's a little better."

Hutfauer joined him at the door. The sound of jabbering and shouting from the level below told them that another of the natives' endless minor domestic disputes had broken out over something.

"Tea's up if anyone's interested," a voice called out from behind the next tent.

Zeiblemann raised his eyebrows and licked his lips. "What a splendid idea," he said. "Come on, Jorg."

They walked around to the makeshift kitchen, where Ruddi Magendorf was sitting on a rock, shoveling spoonfuls of tea leaves out of a tin by his side and into a large bubbling pot of water.

"Hi, Prof—hi, Jorg," he greeted as the two joined him. "It'll be brewed in a minute or two."

Zeiblemann wiped his palms on the front of his shirt. "Good. Just what I could do with." He cast his eye about automatically and noted the trays, covered by cloths, laid out on the trestle table by the side of Magendorf's tent.

"Ah, I see you've been busy as well," he observed. "What do we have there?"

Magendorf followed his gaze.

"Jomatto brought them up about half an hour ago. They're from the upper terrace of sector two—east end. Take a look."

Zeiblemann walked over to the table and uncovered one of the trays to inspect the neatly arrayed collection, at the same time mumbling absently to himself.

"More flint scrapers, I see . . . Mmmm . . . That could be a hand ax. Yes, I believe it is . . . Bits of jawbone, human . . . looks as if they might well match up. Skull cap . . . Bone spearhead . . . Mmm . . ." He lifted the cloth from the second tray and began running his eye casually over the contents. Suddenly the movement of his head stopped abruptly as he stared hard at something at one end. His face contorted into a scowl of disbelief.

"What the hell is this supposed to be?" he bellowed. He straightened up and walked back toward the stove, holding the offending object out in front of him.

Magendorf shrugged and pulled a face.

"I thought you'd better see it," he offered, then added: "Jomatto says it was with the rest of that set."

"Jomatto says what?" Zeiblemann's voice rose in pitch as he glowered first at Magendorf and then back at the object in his hand. "Oh, for God's sake! The man's supposed to have a bit of sense. This is a serious scientific expedition . . . " He regarded the object again, his nostrils quivering with indignation. "Obviously one of the boys has been playing a silly joke or something."

It was about the size of a large cigarette pack, not including the wrist bracelet, and carried on its upper face four windows that could have been meant for miniature electronic displays. It suggested a chronometer or calculating aid, or maybe it was both and other things besides. The back and contents were missing, and all that was left was the metal casing, somewhat battered and dented, but still surprisingly unaffected very much by corrosion.

"There's a funny inscription on the bracelet," Magendorf said, rubbing his nose dubiously. "I've never seen characters like it before."

Zeiblemann sniffed and peered briefly at the lettering.

"*Pah!* Russian or something." His face had taken on a pinker shade than even that imparted by the Sudan sun. "Wasting valuable time with—with dime-store trinkets!" He drew back his arm and hurled the wrist set high out over the stream. It flashed momentarily in the sunlight before plummeting down into the mud by the water's edge. The professor stared after it for a few seconds and then turned back to Magendorf, his breathing once again normal. Magendorf extended a mug full of steaming brown liquid.

"Ah, splendid," Zeiblemann said in a suddenly agreeable voice. "Just the thing." He settled himself into a folding canvas chair and accepted the proffered mug eagerly. "I'll tell you one thing that does look interesting, Ruddi," he went on, nodding toward the table. "That piece of skull in the first tray—number nineteen. Have you noticed the formation of the brow ridges? Now, it could well be an example of . . . "

In the mud by the side of the stream below, the wrist unit rocked back and forth to the pulsing ripples that every few seconds rose to disturb the delicate equilibrium of the position into which it had fallen. After a while, a rib of sand beneath it was washed away and it tumbled over into a hollow, where it lodged among the swirling, muddy water. By nightfall, the lower half of the casing was already embedded in silt. By the following morning, the hollow had disappeared. Just one arm of the bracelet remained, standing up out of the sand below the rippling surface. The arm bore an inscription, which, if translated, would have read: KORIEL.